D1210090

TRUTH OR DARE
The final story in
The Curse of the Midnight Star series

By
Melanie Atkins

Triskelion Publishing
www.triskelionpublishing.com

Triskelion Publishing
15327 W. Becker Lane
Surprise, AZ 85379

First printing by Triskelion Publishing
First print on January 2007
ISBN: 1-933874-02-3
ISBN 13: 9781933874029

Cover design Triskelion Publishing.

"This story was jam-packed with action. From start to finish, Kaitlyn and Colin were battling for their lives. This reviewer had not read the earlier books in the series but was easily able to understand the ongoing plot and enjoy the conclusion. Perhaps, however, the feeling that the romance between Kaitlyn and Colin was not fully developed was due to not having read the entire series as the two characters had met previously and it is unclear if this was in another book.

Melanie Atkins has weaved together numerous paranormal elements in this book to create a riveting story that is hard to put down. She combines a curse, possession, zombies, ghosts, and witches together in such a way that the reader is sucked into her world. This is not a book to be picked up unless there is plenty of time to read it in its entirety as Atkins keeps the reader breathless with the action. After finishing this story, this reviewer was left wondering why she hadn't previously read anything by Atkins prior to this. Readers of paranormal romances will not be disappointed with this one." **Kwips & Kritiques**

"Kaitlyn Chambers is a witch to cleanse the Scarlet Oak hotel. As bodies of young women were recently found on their grounds, the owners wanted to make sure the hotel gets a good cleansing. Kaitlyn is surprised when she runs into handsome FBI deputy Colin Winter. They met a few years earlier, and she still cannot believe how attracted she is to him.

FBI deputy Detective Colin Winter is investigating the murders of the young women found on the grounds of Scarlet Oak. When he meets Kaitlyn Chambers is immediately attracted to her. However, Colin has an investigation to work on; and even though Kaitlyn is one hot lady, he could never imagine being with someone who thinks she is a witch.

As Colin investigates around the hotel, he lets Kaitlyn tag along at times, even though he does not believe in the hocus-pocus, he enjoys her company. However, as time goes on, Colin and Kaitlyn become closer, and now he is seeing things he cannot believe. When he realizes Kaitlyn is a target for murder, he is pressed harder to find the evil entity that is endangering her. While Colin struggles to understand what he is seeing with his own eyes, he also has to come to terms with the fact that Kaitlyn is a witch. When all is said and done, could Colin truly love a witch?

This is a fascinating paranormal that will give you goose bump chills and sexy thrills. From ghosts and zombies to witches and spells you are on the best haunted house ride of your life. Ms. Atkins does an amazing job of creating the setting with vivid descriptions and exceptional characters. Sizzling hot love scenes strategically placed in this book makes it a fabulous read. Paranormal romance lovers do not want to miss this one."
Coffeetime Reviews

PROLOGUE

Etienne Fabron took a deep breath and allowed his stunned senses to steep in the musky odor of the bayou, which melded with the coppery smell of fresh blood. He was alive only because his *gros bon ange*, his guardian angel, had invaded his body the day before, after Garner Reboulet had left him for dead. Recalling the vampire's vicious attack, Fabron sneered. Reboulet had wanted revenge. Etienne touched the healing wound on his neck. Too bad.

I own you.

The three words reverberated in Etienne's head. He gritted his teeth. Whoever would have thought his *gros bon ange* would be a ghost? Lyle Forrester, the former owner of Scarlet Oak Manor, was over a hundred years dead, yet he still wielded incredible power.

Etienne fisted his hands and concentrated on relegating Forrester to the darkest corner of his mind. No matter how hard he tried, he couldn't rid himself of this new entity, but as a *caplata*, a follower of the left hand, he had the power to override it thanks to black magic. He dipped his head as pain flared between his temples. A small price to pay for a moment of privacy so he could offer his sacrifice to his *loa*, his god.

He dipped his fingers into the shallow bowl and smeared warm blood across his bare chest. The dark red liquid glistened in the yellow moonlight. Across the bayou, a bullfrog croaked. Etienne fixed his eyes on the *poteau-mitan,* the sacred pole decorated with crimson and black ribbons, and asked his *loa* for strength.

Another visitor was to arrive soon at Scarlet Oak. Remy Terreau and his new wife, Gillian, were turning the old plantation just outside New Orleans into a picturesque resort. As concierge, Etienne was privy to such news. Usually he paid no attention, but this time was different. This new visitor was coming to *cleanse* the house.

The entity lurking in the back of Etienne's mind stirred to life at the thought.

I won't allow it. You have to stop her!

Etienne sucked the remaining blood from his fingertips. Its metallic tang honed his awareness and helped him shake off Forrester's fanatical influence. He had to focus on his *loa,* even though he and Forrester now had the same objective: To find the Midnight Star, the legendary sapphire that had led Forrester to kill and had thereby spawned a curse.

Imagining the enormous blue cut stone nestled in the palm of his hand, Etienne became aroused. He needed to find the sapphire and make his escape before the new visitor completed her mission. A genuine cleansing would rid Scarlet Oak of the eerie spirits roaming her corridors, including Forrester and his wife, Susannah, whom he had murdered after killing his mistress and stealing the Midnight Star from around her neck.

In a moment of remorse, Lyle had given the stone to Susannah. Legend had it that the Midnight Star had to be gifted in love—and he had broken that vital tenet by murdering Camille, the beautiful slave girl who had owned the sapphire.

Etienne battled a shiver and looked down at the nude girl splayed obscenely at his feet. His latest victim stared up unseeing at the heavens atop the *veve*, which he had drawn carefully upon the ground using fresh cornmeal.

In the distance, lightning flashed, a signal for him to begin. His nerves sharpened, and he dragged his gaze back to the *poteau-mitan*. He would find that damned sapphire, curse or no curse, and would have his vengeance. Finally.

Thunder rumbled, and the hairs stood up on his arms. Above him, the gnarled limbs of the oak rattled like ancient bones. He bent his head against the warm breeze, said a crude prayer, and offered up his sacrifice.

CHAPTER ONE

The sudden deluge of rain on the cab's roof jolted Kaitlyn Chambers awake. She sat up and blinked. Where was she? Thunder jarred the car. She clutched the jade pendant her mother had given her for protection and wisdom and peered out the window. A wall of tall trees slid by, and then they broke into an enormous clearing. A large house loomed before them.

"This is Scarlet Oak," the driver said, his heavy accent partially drowned out by the heavy rush of water. He halted the cab in the middle of a curving brick drive. "Make it fast. Okay, Lady?"

Kaitlyn aimed her sleepy gaze out the foggy window and drew in a sharp breath. The refurbished antebellum mansion was beautiful. With tall white columns, a neat brick portico that ran the length of the house, and forest green shutters. The sculpted lawn with its myriad flowers and shrubs stretched out before it like a canvas dotted with leftover paint. Beside the house, scattered shrubs hunkered beneath gnarled oaks dripping with Spanish moss. She spotted an old cemetery in the distance, and more trees marking what had to be the bayou.

A shudder slid though her. The place was supposed to be haunted—which was the reason for her visit. The hotel's new owners, Remy and Gillian Terreau, had asked Kaitlyn to cleanse the place of evil spirits. Thankful for her *grimoire*, the book of spells passed down from her mother that would help her do just that, she hugged herself. Cleansings weren't unusual for hereditary

witches of her caliber. She'd done many of them since she'd first accepted her destiny seven years ago. Just not in such a remote location with only a skeleton hotel staff for company.

The driver got out and scurried around the car, scattering rain as he opened her door. Kaitlyn opened her black umbrella and stepped onto the moist bricks. Humid, fish-scented air rose up to envelope her. She wrinkled her nose. *The bayou.* Creatures of every ilk lurked there, their slick bodies inured to the Deep South's stifling heat and thick dampness.

"Go on to the house. I'll get your bags." The driver dashed to the rear of the car like he couldn't get away fast enough, leaving Kaitlyn to start up the walk alone.

Just before she reached the covered portico, a dark-haired, suave man with flat black eyes stepped from the shadows.

Kaitlyn caught her breath. Where had he come from?

He looked her up and down with a disdainful eye. "You must be Ms. Chambers."

"Why, yes. I am." Kaitlyn eyed him with suspicion. He didn't look at all like the pictures she'd seen of handsome Remy Terreau. "And you are—?"

"Etienne Fabron." His lips curled back to reveal stubby off-white teeth. He extended his hand. "I am the hotel concierge. Mr. Terreau has been unavoidably detained on his trip out of the country. With him gone, I'm in charge."

Not a comforting thought. She gripped his fingers and was startled to find his hand ice cold. A shiver jolted up her arm. She caught the faint odor of something metallic and earthy.

He released her hand, but his gaze lingered on her face. "I have your room ready."

"Thank you." The man unnerved her, but she kept her expression carefully blank and focused on the manor's front door, which was behind him. "Just show me the way and I'm sure I can find it."

"No need for you to traverse the house alone. I'll show you up the stairs."

The driver walked up with her bags.

Etienne reached for them. "Thank you. I'll take it from here."

The man tossed them at his feet and snatched the bills Kaitlyn extended. Then he was gone. His hurried exit gave her pause. The rain pounded down even harder as he leapt into the cab and streaked away, the vehicle's windshield wipers beating out a frantic cadence.

Kaitlyn battled another shiver. Why was he in such a hurry to get away from this house? She turned to find Etienne watching her with those intense opaque eyes.

His mouth curved in a knowing smile. "Shall we go?"

"Of course." With reluctance, she closed her umbrella and followed him into the hotel. The interior was as gorgeous as the exterior, with a cozy library on her left and a large dining room to her right. Up ahead, a pair of sweeping staircases rose up from either side of the foyer. A glittering chandelier hung from the ceiling between them, and expensive silk draperies covered floor to ceiling windows straight ahead, through what appeared to be a ballroom. Terreau had done a magnificent job restoring the plantation to its former grandeur. Tara, Scarlet O'Hara's home in *Gone with the*

Wind, came to Kaitlyn's mind as the concierge halted at a desk outside the dining room.

Etienne put down her bags and retrieved a skeleton key from behind the counter. "Your room will be in the main part of the building on the second floor. We've almost finished repairing the east wing, but it's not quite ready for guests. We'll open it upon Remy's return."

"I was told I'd be staying in the room formerly occupied by Susannah and Lyle Forrester," Kaitlyn said, aware that they had occupied the master suite on the first floor. She'd been promised the room where Lyle had given the Midnight Star sapphire to Susannah.

Legend had it that the stone had to be gifted in love or all hell would break loose—and he had broken that vital tenet by murdering his mistress, Camille, for the stone. Out for revenge, her angry ghost invaded Susannah's body and smothered the Forrester children, sending Susannah reeling into madness. Distraught over the children's deaths, Lyle then killed his wife.

Kaitlyn had hoped to stay at the scene of the crime.

"I'm afraid that's not possible." Etienne's face turned blood red. "That's my room while the Remy and Gillian are away."

"Mr. Terreau promised it to *me*," Kaitlyn said sharply. "When will you speak with him again?" She hoped Terreau and his wife had changed their minds about putting off their return to Scarlet Oak.

"I don't know. He hasn't telephoned me since my move into the house," The concierge drew himself up to his full height, which made him several inches taller than Kaitlyn. "I had an electrical problem in my cottage yesterday, and immediately shifted my belongings here. I'm sure you understand."

Kaitlyn eyed the strange man suspiciously. "No, I don't understand. I had an agreement with Mr. Terreau to use his room. It's important that I stay in the correct place."

"In order to attract more errant spirits?" Fabron's thin lips twisted in that knowing smile.

She opened her mouth to deflect his sarcasm, but he put up his hand.

"Before you say anything, let me make it clear that I don't believe in the supernatural. You're free to do whatever you like inside the house. Conduct tests, hide cameras in the corners, even stay up all night. I don't give a damn. But I want you to stay away from my room. Is that clear?"

Taken aback, she stared at him. "Perfectly. But I warn you, I intend to discuss this issue with Mr. Terreau at my first opportunity."

"Go right ahead," he said brusquely, picking up her bags. "For now, I'll put you in Suite Two, which was formerly the nursery. You should feel very close to Susannah in that room."

Kaitlyn frowned. That might work, but she'd rather be in the bedroom the woman had shared with her husband. Their spirits were bound to be stronger there.

She followed Etienne up the left stairs and into a tiny hallway, where the air was distinctly cooler and carried the scent of herbs. Her senses went on red alert as they passed an extremely icy area. Excitement tingled along her skin. She fought the urge to glance behind her, to see what or whom she had passed.

The concierge stopped beside an ornately carved door and inserted the key into the door. The lock popped open. He led her inside.

She halted just inside the door and looked around. The room had been redone to look much as it had when the Forrester's children had resided there, with two cribs and one small bed along one wall and chest of drawers and matching four-poster twin bed on the other. The sight of the tiny beds took Kaitlyn's breath away. According to legend, the children had been murdered in this very room.

Etienne set down her bags. "You should be comfortable here." He indicated a small door off to the right. "Remy added baths to all the rooms. You should find plenty of towels and other amenities, along with all the modern conveniences."

"Thank you."

He turned to leave, but halted at the door. "Oh, and by the way. Since we're not officially open, dinner is served in the dining room at six for only one hour each evening. So you must be prompt."

"That won't be a problem." She bared her teeth in a brilliant smile, irked at his condescending tone.

He let his gaze roam over her one last time, and disappeared into the hall. The room immediately felt warmer. Relieved that he was gone, Kaitlyn closed the door and locked it. He irritated her. She considered casting a spell to keep him out, but decided he wasn't a genuine threat. Better to use her powers to rid the house of the Forresters.

She rubbed her arms and examined the room. It was quiet. *Too quiet.* Kaitlyn reached for her suitcase, which contained a radio. She would turn that on and listen to the news as she unpacked.

But before she could lay her bag on the bed, the cribs came alive with movement. Tiny eyes blinked up at her.

Two small children held out their arms. She heard their frightened cries.

Mommy! Mommy, help me, don't hurt me. Save us!! Save us, please!

Kaitlyn dropped the suitcase and stumbled backwards. Her eyes flew wide. Ghosts, already. Her precious *grimoire* and her tools were tucked away inside her bag. She needed to get them out. She had been a witch since the day she was born, yet it never hurt to be prepared.

The children's voices echoed through the room as she snatched up the suitcase and threw it on the bed. The *grimoire* sat beneath her clothes in the middle of the bag, along with her bag of supplies. She took out the book, sat down, and carefully opened its cracked red cover.

She thumbed through its ancient pages to the section on the spirit world and quickly reread it. The spells for freeing spirits were just as she remembered, although none of them specified what to do differently if the ghosts were children.

Feeling great empathy for them, Kaitlyn rose and pressed both arms over her breasts to symbolize their mother's love. Their young spirits longed for her to find and nurture them.

The crying stopped immediately, and she became aware of the children's gentle breathing.

"Go now," she urged them, her soul touched by the depth of their need. "You will find her."

The pitter-patter of small running feet filled the room, and then grew quiet.

Suddenly more bone weary than she'd ever been, Kaitlyn lowered her arms and sank down on the bed next to the book of spells. Her trip from New York to

Louisiana had been long and tiring, and casting spells took work.

Her hand strayed to the necklace her mother had given her. Wearing it made her feel enshrouded in love and safety, and she valued it. With luck, it would help her complete her task here in Louisiana. Yet it didn't protect her from weariness.

She let it go and checked her watch. Still two hours until dinner. Etienne had made it clear that she must be prompt, but she should have time for a warm bath and a quick nap. Maybe that would revitalize her.

She hoped to begin a cleansing after she ate. To this end she got out her sage wand and a variety of stones. Smoky quartz for cleansing, tourmaline for grounding and deflecting evil spirits, hematite, for dispelling negativity, red jasper for strength, and lapis lazuli for wisdom. The sooner she made contact with Susannah and Lyle Forrester and dealt with them, the quicker she could get back home to her fiancé.

Her cheeks grew warm as she corrected her faulty thinking. Jason McDonald, a hereditary witch who also fancied himself a television writer, was no longer her intended. She'd cast a spell to remove the obstacles in their relationship, namely, her former best friend, Cathy Sullivan, before she'd left New York. But she wouldn't know if he'd countered it until she returned home. She wanted him. Yet he seemed determined to make a new life without her.

Kaitlyn shook her head. If he was determined to leave her behind, so be it. She would forget him and go on with her life. Yet it had been five years since she'd been on a first date, and she didn't relish the idea of starting at square one. Provided she could even find a proper date.

Her requirements in a mate were stringent. She preferred a man like Jason who was also a witch. But those were hard to come by these days. With her luck, he was the last straight, sane male witch in America.

She dug out fresh underwear, a pair of faded blue jeans, and a comfortable white Henley T-shirt. No point in dressing up for dinner with that sinister concierge and his pals. The more barriers she kept around herself, the better. Etienne Fabron gave off strange dark vibes she'd rather not disturb.

Gathering her bag of toiletries, she tucked her clothes beneath her arm and headed for the bathroom. The spirits could wait until she was clean and rested.

*****

Colin Winter, FBI Assistant Deputy Director of Criminal Investigations, leaned back in his chair, adjusted his reading glasses, and reread Special Agent Jack Navarre's resignation for what had to be the tenth time. He couldn't believe his top two agents were leaving the Bureau. Navarre and Special Agent Lynsee Frost had eloped after their last assignment with the New Orleans Violent Crimes Major Offender squad, and had just mailed in paperwork outlining their plan to walk away from their jobs immediately upon their return to Washington D.C. Colin turned the paper over, and smiled wryly at himself. He was looking for an explanation, but of course there wasn't one. He simply didn't understand Navarre's reasoning. Why would anyone leave the Bureau for love?

He tossed Navarre's letter on top of Lynsee's. The two of them had been thrown together at that beautiful antebellum plantation outside New Orleans. *Scarlet Oak*. Colin took off his glasses and rubbed a hand down his face. They never had gotten to the bottom of that string of murders. Three teenage girls, all strangled. Two of them had been raped and all three bodies had been dumped on the grounds of the resort owned by Forrester heir Remy Terreau.

Now Michael Burrell, their main suspect, had disappeared and was thought to have left the country. Terreau was on his honeymoon. And Garner Reboulet, Remy's cousin, whom the local police had questioned in the case, had been cleared of any wrongdoing.

Colin tossed the glasses on his desk, bolted from his chair, and began to pace. He had plenty of room, since his office was neat as a pin. He looked around. *Everything is in its proper place.* That was his motto. He despised disorganization almost as much as he hated loose ends. And this case had too damned many of them. The Deputy Director was on his back because of it, and his nerves were shot. To top it off, Scarlet Oak was supposed to be haunted.

He laughed out loud. Odd paranormal happenings? Unhappy spirits roaming the hotel's freshly renovated halls? Ghosts on parade? That idea was simply too bizarre for his sensibilities. But someone had to find the answer to those murders. And his boss was convinced that with Navarre and Frost gone and their other agents tied up with the Joint Terrorism Task Force, he had no choice but to send Colin to the old house outside New Orleans. Fighting off his distaste, Colin halted beside his desk and picked up the telephone.

Ten minutes later, he had an e-Ticket tucked safely in his suit pocket and was on his way home to pack. It wouldn't take him long, since he lived alone and was highly organized — which was precisely why his marriage to high maintenance model Maria Townsend had failed. She was his polar opposite, all glitz and no brains.

Yeah, he was lonely. But better to be lonely and in control than to live with someone who lived on the edge and never planned a damned thing.

His flight landed safely at Louis Armstrong International Airport in New Orleans late that afternoon, and he wasted no time renting a car.

The upscale Chrysler 300 got him to Scarlet Oak in a little over an hour. The day was hot and steamy, with evidence of the previous day's rain in large puddles on the ground. The soggy moss hanging from the trees reminded Colin of his dead grandfather's wet beard. He tightened his lips as he pulled into the wide brick drive.

The giant house seemed to beckon him. Still, he took his time examining the place. According to his notes, the dead girls had been discovered in back of the house near the old family cemetery. He made a mental note to check that out first thing.

He took his bag from the car and marched up to the wide veranda. The air was still and damp. The muggy heat seemed to seep into his skin and warm him from the inside out. He slapped at a pair of buzzing mosquitoes and nailed both with one hand. Wiping his fingers, he opened the door.

Cool air enveloped him. He inhaled a combination of fresh paint and something delicious from the kitchen. His stomach growled, reminding him he'd skipped both lunch and the paltry snack on the airplane. His mind had been too busy going over Navarre's detailed notes on the case.

Pushing the door shut behind him, he turned to see a small library on one side and a dining area on the other. Straight ahead down the wide hallway, two ornate stairways arced up to the second floor. The place had been artfully redone, and was pleasing to the eye. Too bad he was too tense to enjoy it.

He approached the desk outside the dining room just as a tall, dark-haired man stepped from the office behind it. His icy black eyes zeroed in on Colin.

"I'm sorry, sir." He folded his arms. "We're not open for guests just yet."

"I'm not a guest."

The man's eyebrows flew up. "You certainly don't work here."

"No." Colin reached inside his coat and pulled out his FBI shield. "I work for the federal government."

"FBI." A cloud passed over the man's angular face. "I should've known. Especially after the other two agents left Scarlet Oak empty handed a week or two ago."

Colin tucked his shield away. "You must be the concierge Agent Navarre told me about."

"That's right. I'm Etienne Fabron." He pulled out a book and set it on the counter. "I need you to sign right here, sir. And I'll need your credit card."

"Of course." Colin pulled out his wallet.

"You have ten minutes if you want dinner."

"Excuse me?" He hiked his eyebrows.

Fabron made an odd noise. "Since we're not open to the public yet, our dining room is open for only one hour in the evenings. Closing time is seven o'clock."

"I see." Colin retrieved his credit card and the key Fabron gave him. "I'll go eat."

"Your room is on the second floor in the center section of the house." The concierge pointed at the ceiling. "Suite Five. Take the right set of stairs and you'll be at your door."

With a brisk nod, Colin picked up his bag and stepped into the dining room. He hadn't eaten all day, and waiting until breakfast wasn't an option.

To his surprise, he was the only person at the small buffet set out on a trio of linen-covered tables against the wall. He set his bag beside his chair and helped himself to the delicious home cooked New Orleans fare and ate quickly. Fabron was not at the desk when he came out.

He headed up the stairs the concierge had mentioned. The short upstairs corridor was cool and filled with deep shadows. He paused at his door and pulled out his key.

A flash on the other side of the landing caught his eye. He turned. What the hell?

The light seemed to dim.

He blinked and stared into the growing darkness.

An eerie silence enveloped him.

Shaking off an unsettling tingling sensation, he jerked his gaze back to the ornate door. Someone must have opened a door or a window nearby.

He stuck the key into the lock and twisted the knob. The door opened with a loud squeak. He winced and caught a movement out of the corner of his vision. Was someone in the room? The maid maybe, finishing up?

He slid his hand beneath his coat to grip the Glock .40 that sat snuggly in his shoulder holster. Pulling it from his coat, he stepped across the threshold. The room was large, with a tall four-poster bed, a matching oak chifferobe, and an antique dresser topped by a beveled oval mirror. A green striped chair sat below a window facing the bayou.

A clock on the dresser ticked softly. He heard the steady drip of a bathroom faucet and the rapid piston beat of his own heart. *Nothing else.* The room was empty as a tomb.

Colin shut the door and released a breath he hadn't realized he was holding. He was too tired, he thought as he loosened his hold on the pistol's textured grip. He needed sleep. Lots and lots of deep sleep. Then he would get to work on the case.

He re-holstered the Glock, opened his suitcase, and pulled out his black leather shaving kit. A dim white glow in the corner of the room caught his attention. He watched as the ball of light slowly became brighter and moved eerily across the floor. He blinked. *What the hell was that?*

An icy coldness rolled over him. Goosebumps prickled his arms.

The light grew brighter.

Colin tossed down the bag and grabbed the Glock. His cell phone bleated.

Shit! He struggled to keep his eyes on the drifting light.

The longer the phone rang, the dimmer the gleam of light became, until it disappeared. He lowered the pistol and yanked out his phone. "Hello?"

Silence.

"Hello?" He scowled. "Is anyone there?"

No answer. Must be a wrong number, because he didn't recognize it on the display.

Irritated, he dialed it back. A child answered.

He mouthed an expletive and hung up. His nerves frayed to the breaking point, he sat down heavily on the edge of the bed. Once his heartbeat finally slowed, he studied his surroundings more carefully. The room looked just like it had when he'd first opened the door. Where in heaven's name had that strange ball of light come from?

He checked the lamps and the overhead fixture. No way could any of them have provided the moving glow he'd seen. He glanced out the window. The moon was partially covered by a cloud, its pale white light casting eerie shadows across the front lawn. *Moonlight.* It must have been the moon. Those clouds were moving fast.

He yawned and wiped his face. Damn, he was tired. He didn't want to be here. The place was already playing hell with his rational thinking. Still, he wanted answers. His eyes strayed to the sleek white telephone on the nightstand, which was totally incongruous with the rest of the room.

He walked around the bed, put on his glasses, and dialed the front desk.

No answer there, either. He cursed the gruesome concierge. No guests, no Fabron. What a prick. Colin re-holstered the Glock, rose, and quickly unpacked. He tucked his backup weapon in the drawer of the nightstand.

Then he strode to the door. He made sure he had his key, then left the room and made a beeline for the stairs. Someone in this damned hotel had to have an answer for what he'd just seen. If not—

Loud pounding echoed from the other side of the stairs.

He halted and peered into the shadows. Etienne Fabron stood beside one of two doors facing the front of the house, his hand poised to knock again.

Anger flared in Colin's gut. He started toward the concierge. "Mr. Fabron! I want a word with you."

Etienne turned just as the door in front of him opened, and a pretty blonde woman in a white terrycloth robe stuck out her head.

Colin strode up to the concierge. "I've just seen something really odd in my room—"

"Colin?" The inquisitive female voice curled around him like smoke.

He turned to see the statuesque blonde staring up at him with startled green eyes. She held her robe together with one beautifully manicured hand. "Colin Winter?"

Recognition flashed through him with the force of a freight train. He suddenly felt weightless. "Kaitlyn? What are you doing here?"

"Working." Her mouth curved in a welcoming smile. It transformed her face from pretty to radiant. "What about you?"

"The same." He cleared his throat and tried to remember just exactly why he'd come over here after Fabron. Right now, it escaped him. He took off his glasses.

She raised her perfectly shaped eyebrows. "Here?"

"Yes."

"May I help you, Assistant Deputy Director Winter?" Fabron asked, his words cold.

Colin turned. "What is it?"

"You said something happened in your room."

"Oh, yes. I did." Crap. Anything he said would sound ridiculous, and he didn't want to look like a fool in front of Kaitlyn. So, feeling a bit sheepish, he shook his head. "Never mind."

Fabron shrugged his shoulders and turned to Kaitlyn. "I came by to let you know breakfast will be served promptly at eight a.m. Don't be late."

"Thank you," she said. "I won't."

"You either, Winter." With a sneer, Fabron started off. "Sleep tight."

Kaitlyn rubbed her arms as he stalked away. "He gives me the creeps."

"He's one cold bastard. But he seems to have a handle on the routine around here."

"I don't care." She shivered. "I shook his hand and he gave me chills. His fingers are like ice cubes."

"Fancy that."

"You know, if you think you saw something odd in this old house, you probably did."

His senses went on red alert. "Why do you say that?"

"Because it's haunted, silly." She lowered her voice to a conspiratorial whisper. "That's why I'm here."

"You said you were working."

"I am." A gentle smile bloomed across her face. "I'm here to cleanse the house."

*****

Etienne halted on the landing and peered through the shadows at the two of them. Fury rose within him as his gaze landed on the woman's animated face. She claimed she was a witch. That she could rid the house of the frenzied spirits that had roamed Scarlet Oak's halls for over a century.

Well, he'd show her. His *loa* was all powerful. The god had made Etienne a *caplata*, a master of the left hand. So he would fight fire with fire. His spells were more potent than the witch's could possibly be, and he would counter her until he had that enormous sapphire in his hands. It belonged in his family. He would have his revenge. After that, he didn't care what she did with Lyle and Susannah Forrester. But for now, they had to stay in the house.

That's not good enough.

The entity in his head stirred to life.

Kill them.

"No." He ground his teeth against the pain suddenly spreading through his head. "Go away!"

You're alive only because of me. You must do what I say, or I will leave you. And you know what that means. The entity laughed.

Etienne's brain began to throb. He pressed both hands to his aching temples.

Kill them, and throw their bodies in the bayou.

Etienne scowled. There had to be an easier way. It was true that once the witch and the FBI agent were out of the way, he would have an easier time searching the house and grounds for the Midnight Star. But he still might not have time to find it. Remy and Gillian Terreau would return to Scarlet Oak in only six days.

Don't make excuses. You know the power I have over you.

The hot pain of Reboulet's slash arced through Etienne's neck, just like it had on that fateful night. He tried to scream, but only managed a gurgle as cool air funneled through the ragged tear in his throat. Red lights dotted his vision. He dropped to his knees and smelled blood, thick and rich and filled with death. His blood.

You're only alive because of me. Confess it!

Etienne's hands grew slick with crimson liquid as he tried in vain to cover the weeping wound. Blood rushed between his fingers and he felt his life force draining away. Desperate, Etienne dropped to his knees and called on his *loa* for help.

The entity cackled like a crone. *Even your loa can't help you now.*

The pain in Etienne's head increased. His own *gros bon ange* wanted him dead.

His vision dimmed. Suddenly he was falling, sailing face down into a deep black hole.

The cackling ceased. *Obey me, and live.*

With a loud groan, he capitulated. A loud buzzing filled his head. And immediately, the blackness clouding his vision began to fade.

"Fabron?" A booming male voice rattled his skull. "Are you all right?"

He blinked and discovered he could see, although the light hurt his eyes. He was sitting on the colorful carpet covering the landing, his head between his knees. He looked up. Colin Winter stood over him like a skulking giant.

"I-I'm fine," he rasped, happy he'd found his voice. He pressed a shaking hand to his neck. No blood, no slash. Only the scar from where Reboulet had attacked him. Thank God. Hoping his legs would support him, he pushed himself off the floor and propped his shoulder against the wall. His head swam like he'd just gotten off a roller coaster.

"What the hell happened to you?" Winter adjusted his glasses and frowned down at him. "Did you have a seizure? Lose your balance?"

"No. I-I'm just light headed. From low blood sugar." *Yes, that was it.* Etienne pushed away from the wall. "It often happens to me this time of day."

"You just had supper."

"I ate early." He pasted a smile on his quivering lips. "It's time for my evening snack."

"Well, then. You'd better go get it."

"Yes, sir." Etienne swallowed. "Thanks for your concern."

Winter nodded.

Ignoring the entity chuckling in his head, Etienne started for the stairs. He had a mission now; one he had to accomplish before he could find the sapphire. He had to kill Ms. Chambers and the FBI agent to get them out of the way. It would not be easy. Contemplating it, he shuddered.

You have no choice.

"Damn it, I know," he muttered. Ideas swirled in his brain as he gripped the banister and stumbled downstairs to the foyer. He could grab the woman in her sleep, subdue her, and haul her out of the house without much trouble. Winter, however, would be another story. He was trained to kill.

A bright flash startled Etienne as he stepped into the library. He hurried across the room, ducked into the hotel's tiny office, and shut the door. It wouldn't keep them out, but it would at least keep other people from seeing him talk to ghosts. He held his breath and waited.

Moments later, the entire Forrester family materialized in front of him. He forced himself to stand his ground as the children milled around their mother, pulling on her skirts. Susannah cowered away from Lyle, who glared menacingly at Etienne.

"Don't worry." Etienne's nerves danced. With trembling hands, he fingered the scar on his neck. "I'll take care of them just like you said."

"You'd damned well better," Lyle growled, his mouth twisting into a cruel sneer. "Vodun is useless against the angel of death."

CHAPTER TWO

Kaitlyn woke the next morning with a feeling of excitement. Not only had she already made contact with the spirit world, thanks to the ghosts of the Forrester children, but also Colin Winter was staying in a room just across the landing. She'd met him early last year, and had run into him again about three months ago at her cousin's wedding. They'd shared a few slow dances, one of which had left her breathless. Sure, he was uptight and hopelessly anal. But he was also one of the kindest men she'd ever met—and beneath that stuffy exterior, he was . . . well, *hot*.

She looked at the alarm clock. Seven-fifteen a.m. Good. She threw off the covers. She had plenty of time to bathe and dress before breakfast. Last night, she'd found the Jacuzzi tub to be a delight, and she wanted another luxurious dip before she got to work.

She turned on the water and adjusted the jets. In the warm tub, her mind again drifted to Colin. To his long, powerful limbs and that scrumptious chest. She'd never seen him in anything other than a stuffy suit, but he certainly filled out his coat quite nicely, and his pants. She grinned. He'd been surprised to see her. She liked that in a man.

With a giggle, she picked up the soap. This week could prove interesting, what with the spirits roaming loose in Scarlet Oak's shadowy halls and Agent Winter's priggish attitude. He obviously didn't believe in ghosts. Kaitlyn absently scrubbed her arms and legs. She would have to change that, somehow. Too bad she'd wasted that perfectly good love spell on Jason. She was allowed to cast only one of those spells at a time. *Drat.* She'd have to fall back on her feminine wiles to capture Colin Winter's attention.

She arrived downstairs just as a staff member set out a pitcher of fresh milk for the continental buffet. Cereal, muffins, orange juice, fresh apples, orange slices, cubed melon, milk, and coffee. Not bad for a closed hotel.

Kaitlyn chose a muffin, fruit, and coffee, and sat down. Just as she picked up her muffin, Colin walked in wearing faded blue jeans and a brick red polo shirt. His wire-rimmed glasses perched on his nose. Oh, my. Her mouth went dry. Unable to take her eyes off him, she dropped the muffin and it bounced across the floor like a lopsided ball.

He bent and scooped it up. With a disapproving look, he held up the stray muffin. "Is this yours?"

"Yes. Thank you, but I'll get another one." Her cheeks burned as she rose.

He tossed the discarded pastry into the trash.

She followed him to the buffet and nabbed a fresh muffin. "Would you like to join me?"

"Sure, why not?" He loaded his plate with fruit, muffins, and a box of cereal. "As long as you don't turn me into a frog or something even worse."

"I keep the really important spells under wraps."

He raised his eyebrows. "Promise?"

She dragged her hand across her chest in a crisscross pattern. "Cross my heart and hope to die."

"Stick a needle in my eye," he said with a wry wink.

She laughed.

He poured himself a glass of juice and followed her back to the table.

Kaitlyn sipped her coffee. "Are you working on a case?"

"Yes."

She widened her eyes. "Here, at Scarlet Oak?"

"I can't say."

"Oh, you are." She put down her mug and leaned closer to him. "I bet it concerns those girls that went missing a few weeks ago."

"What do you know about that?" He popped a hunk of melon in his mouth.

Her eyes followed his sexy lips as he chewed. The temperature in the room went up a notch. "Only what Maggie told me."

"By Maggie, you mean Garner Reboulet's wife."

"Yes. I spoke with her before Remy and Gillian asked me to come here. As a matter of fact, I think my visit to Louisiana was her idea." Kaitlyn tore off a piece of muffin. Blueberry. It was delicious. Wiping her mouth, she met Colin's friendly chocolate eyes. "Maggie had attempted to cleanse the house herself, but she had to leave before she completed the process. It seems her life was in danger."

"From the spirits?" Colin frowned.

"No. Garner, her husband, apparently had strayed from their marriage, but he came back to Maggie. His former mistress was stalking her. Or so I was told."

"I see." He poured milk and sugar on his bran flakes. "No real intrigue there."

"Nothing involving spirits. Just plain, old fashioned jealousy."

"A normal human emotion." He picked up his spoon and dug in.

She ate another piece of muffin. "You still don't believe."

"In what? Ghosts?" He scoffed at her. "No. There are no such beings."

"Then what did you see in your room last night?"

"Certainly not ghosts. I was just tired and stressed out."

"You were upset enough by whatever it was to search out Mr. Fabron."

"I overreacted." Colin put down his spoon and picked up his orange juice. "Do you find anything strange about him?"

"Who? Fabron?"

"Yes." His throat moved in a sexy rhythm as he drank down the juice. He licked his lips. "I found him in the hall on his knees after I left your door. He seemed to have had some sort of seizure."

Thinking about the skulking concierge, Kaitlyn shivered. There was definitely something eerie about him. His eyes were practically opaque, and his hands were ice cold. Yet she hadn't witnessed any collapse. "I don't know about that, but he really gives me the creeps."

"I'm going to do a little digging into his background."

"You and the mighty FBI." She grinned wickedly. "Is there anything you can't get into?"

"The supernatural world." Colin's lips turned up in a wicked smile as he set down his glass and got up.

We'll just see about that, Kaitlyn thought. She rose beside him. "Will I see you later today?"

"I hope so." He reached out and curled a lock of hair around his finger. "I find you fascinating."

A slow burn began inside her. He was pretty damned fascinating himself. "I thought you didn't believe in the supernatural."

"I don't. But that doesn't mean I can't fraternize with someone who does, does it?"

She shook her head, brushing her cheek against his fingertips.

He dropped his hand. "I'm going to check out the cemetery."

"Ooh." She wanted to see that place herself, in hopes she might run into Lyle Forrester, the former master of the house. Maggie had reported tangling with him the same night she'd endured a face-off with Garner's angry mistress. Kaitlyn gave Colin her most winsome smile. "I'd like to go with you, if you don't mind. For research purposes only, of course."

"Research." He cocked his head. "What are you doing? Trying to resurrect the dead?"

"Not exactly." No way was she going into detail with him about her work. Not at this stage of the game. But she needed to scout the entire property before trying to rid the house of the Forresters. "I just need to know the lay of the land. Certainly you understand that."

He laughed. "You sound like a pioneer."

"In a way, I am." She winked at him. "So, may I come along?"

"I don't see why not," he said. "I need to run up to my room first, though. Then we'll go."

She nodded.

While he was gone, she wandered through the foyer
and library looking for Fabron. The concierge was an odd
duck, and he gave off strange vibes. Colin's story made
her even more wary of him. Still, she was intrigued. The
man was like the walking dead.

"Ms. Chambers." Fabron's obsequious tone broke
into her thoughts, startling her.

She spun around and spotted him standing next to a
shelf filled with ancient tomes. "Oh, Mr. Fabron. Hello."

"May I help you with something?"

"Not right now." She smiled cautiously. "I just
wanted to tell you how much I'm enjoying my visit. The
house is beautiful."

"Thank you." His flat eyes fixed her with a
disconcerting stare. "The former nursery must be to your
liking after all."

"It's perfect." Well, almost. She felt close to
Susannah and the children, but she had yet to meet up
with Lyle Forrester. Until she saw him face to face, her
imagination would continue to run wild.

Fabron inched closer to her, allowing her to draw in
his odd, earthy smell. "I'm glad. Will you do me the
honor of joining me for dinner tonight?"

"I appreciate your invitation, but I have other plans."
Just as when she'd first arrived, she wrinkled her nose at
the odor coming from his skin. She edged back a step. "I
hope you understand. I've already agreed to have dinner
with Director Winter."

"I see." Fabron's tone was clipped. His black eyes
narrowed to slits. "You two must be very close."

"Actually, we have met before. It's good to see him
again."

"I'll bet." Fabron's mouth curled into a sneer. His disturbing gaze dropped to her chest. "Any contact with the spirit world yet?"

"I'd rather not say." She crossed her arms, hoping to ward him off. "Talking about a task before it's completed can jinx it."

"You can talk to me. I'm no jinx." He reached for her hand.

The stunning iciness of his fingers repelled her. She jerked away. "No, I have to go. I'm meeting Colin."

"Oh, so it's *Colin* now, is it?" Anger flashed across Fabron's pale face. "What happened to *Assistant Deputy Director Winter*?"

"Nothing. I'm right here." Colin materialized beside Kaitlyn as if she'd conjured him up. He'd put on a tan jacket, but he still looked good enough to lap up with a spoon.

She breathed a huge sigh of relief. "What took you so long?"

"I was only gone five minutes." He looked at Fabron. "And as you can see, I'm just fine. We're going to explore the property."

"Be careful out there." Fabron's tone ominous. His lips turned up menacingly at the corners. "The place can be, shall we say, *hazardous*, even in the daytime."

"And just why is that?" Colin asked, placing his hand protectively in the small of Kaitlyn's back. She liked the feel of it there.

Fabron's expression hardened. "Because the place is haunted, of course."

"Let's go, Colin," Kaitlyn said, eager to get away from the man who was giving her the creeps, which said a

lot considering some of her contacts in the spirit world.
"Clouds are moving in. We need to beat the rain."

"Yes, you two certainly don't want to get wet."
Fabron stared at Kaitlyn.

His sinister tone crawled across her nerves as she
imagined pitching headfirst into the murky bayou. A
shudder slid through her.

She left her comfortable spot beside Colin to lead the
way out the door. Once outside, she felt like she could
finally breathe. The air was humid but alive, a welcome
change after being so close to Etienne Fabron.

Colin turned to her and slid his glasses higher on his
nose.

"There's something suspicious about that guy."

"I agree." She frowned. "I'd cast a spell on him, but
I don't know which one would fit."

"Give it up, Kaitlyn." Colin shook his head. "We
both know that hocus pocus mumbo jumbo you keep
spouting is nothing but a crock."

"Excuse me?" She tamped down the urge to slap
him. He'd always been a stuffed shirt, but that comment
was just plain rude. "I've been learning that *hocus pocus
mumbo jumbo* all my life and have seriously studied it for
the past seventeen years. Does that mean *I'm* a crock?"

"Of course not."

"Come on, Colin. You diss witchcraft, you diss me."

"Diss?" His mask of superiority cracked, if only
slightly. "What the hell does that mean?"

"To put down. Talk bad about something or
someone."

"Then I'm not *dissing* you. I just don't believe in the
supernatural."

"You will." She sent him a challenging glare.

His chiseled chin lifted. "You think so?"

"Yes." She loved getting a rise out of him. Baiting him was fun. But she had a job to do. "Hey—are we going to the cemetery, or not?"

"Oh. Sure." Obviously flustered, he laughed and tore his intense chocolate gaze away from her face. He scanned the lawn beyond the veranda. "We'd better go before the rain sets in."

He guided her off the porch and led her through the tall grass flanking the house.

Kaitlyn felt dwarfed by Colin's height and hard muscles. Even with his jacket on, he seemed more masculine than he did in a suit. He was sexy as hell, with clipped dark hair, elegant cheekbones, and a full, well-shaped mouth. He looked ready to take on the world. Her mouth watered with wanting to kiss him. *Oh, dear.* Her face flamed. Her thoughts were in the gutter.

He didn't believe in witchcraft and the supernatural—which meant that before she could entertain any ideas of getting closer to him, much less trying to kiss him—she had to set him straight about the paranormal realm. Thunder rumbled in the distance.

"Uh oh." He scowled up at the low hanging clouds. "We'd better hurry."

Kaitlyn struggled to keep up with him. Colin had long legs, and he was clearly on a mission. She sucked in a deep breath. "You don't have to run."

"Sorry." He slowed down and waited for her to catch up. "I'm used to walking alone."

"Obviously."

"What does that mean?" He turned suddenly and leveled her with his dark eyes.

She ran into him.   The delicious scent of his spicy aftershave washed over her as she grabbed his arms for balance. She let go and backed away. "N-nothing. It's kind of like the witchcraft thing. I'm not really *dissing* you, but—"

"*Touché.*" His mouth quirked in a smile.

She wanted to melt right there on the ground, but figured that would totally wreck her credibility. So she stayed whole and tried to focus on her surroundings, which were becoming more ominous by the second. It was morning, but the sky had grown increasingly dark. Thunder grumbled again, and the wind slithered through the trees.

She caught his hand and tugged him along. "Let's go. The rain is getting closer."

"Will you melt if you get wet?"

Talk about reading her mind. She laughed. "You must've been watching *The Wizard of Oz*." Her body hummed with need. "No, a little rain won't melt me." *But overloaded hormones just might.*

Colin nodded. He enjoyed the feel of her small hand in his. He knew he should release it, but he couldn't make himself let go. The humid breeze whipped at his hair. Just a few more minutes, he told himself. The cemetery was just ahead, covered by a light layer of fog. That was odd, because he didn't see low clouds anywhere else.

Kaitlyn's green eyes lit on the cemetery's ancient wrought iron gate. "This place is filled with spirits, you know. That's why it's so sinister."

His heart hardened. He released her hand. "There are no such things."

She just smiled and kept walking.

Colin halted at the spot where the bodies of the three teenaged girls had been found. The dirt was still piled up and their shallow graves left open for all to see.

Kaitlyn paused beside him. "Hope you find out who killed them."

"Me, too," he said, anger filling him at the idea of some monster preying on defenseless young girls in the area. He had to solve these crimes before another young woman died.

Thunder rolled, low and deep. The hairs on Colin's arms stood up. He looked at the sky, expecting to see a streak of lightning, but instead he spotted an eerie dark blur. It was a large black bird, circling over them like a buzzard hovering over the dead. He started toward the fence.

"It's a raven," Kaitlyn said, following him. "They symbolize death."

"I see you've read Edgar Allen Poe."

"Of course I have." Her voice carried a note of exasperation. "But literary interpretation aside, the symbolization is correct. Ravens are intermediaries between earth and the after life."

"We're at a cemetery." He reached for the gate. "What did you expect?"

The ancient metal was icy to the touch. He jerked back his hand. That was strange. The weather was warm. He scowled and gripped the gate anyway, pushing it open. His palm ached from its contact with the cold iron.

"They're not native to Louisiana."

"You mean the ravens?" He held the gate open for her as lightning split the sky. He began to regret being so quick to invite Kaitlyn to join this party. "Birds can go anywhere."

"None have ever been counted in this part of the country."

Colin pointed up at the circling fowl. "One."

"Go ahead. Make jokes." She glared at him. "You'll live to regret it."

"What are you gonna do?" He asked, growing more irked at her strong defense of the supernatural. "Cast a spell on me?"

"I might if you don't quit acting like such an ass."

He released the gate, and it swung shut with a spine-chilling groan. He wiped his freezing hand on his jeans and eyed the lush grass crowding the stained marble headstones. Some sat at odd angles, signaling that the ground had shifted, and others had been sheared off by neglect and maybe even vandalism. The entire cemetery was in serious need of attention.

"This place hasn't been touched in years." The fog around them thickened as Colin ran his hand over the top of a leaning grave marker. The marble was rough and pitted from weather and time. He backed up to read the name, but it had none. He frowned. How odd.

The wind increased, whipping the reedy grass against his legs. Kaitlyn disappeared around a bend in the path, under the enormous limbs of a spreading oak dripping with Spanish moss.

"Oh my God!" Her wind-carried words startled him.

His heart pounding, he hurried after her. "What is it?"

"Look!" She stood in the middle of the grass-filled path, her arm outstretched. It was shaking.

He gaped at a cluster of old-fashioned stick figures and stars dangling by pieces of faded string from one of the limbs. The figures clicked together like primitive

wind chimes. He swallowed around the growing lump in his throat. "What the hell are those?"

"Symbols of Vodun," she said. "You probably know it as Voodoo. It's popular in New Orleans."

"Holy shit." He edged closer. "Why are they in the cemetery?"

"I don't know." She turned toward the bayou, which snaked along the edge of the property like a waiting serpent. He followed her rapt gaze.

The murky brown water, now visible through the thick trees, looked even darker with the encroaching bad weather. Thunder crashed overhead. Another of the raven's eerie calls split the air, and Colin nearly leapt out of his skin.

"That bird is trying to tell us something," Kaitlyn said, watching the raven circle around them. It flapped its wings and landed on a broken marble marker lying in the grass.

"I don't give a damn what it's doing," Colin said, marching over to it and waving his arms. It made his skin crawl. He wanted it gone. "Go 'way!"

The bird focused its beady black eyes on him, and he felt a heavy jolt inside his chest. He reeled backwards. *Shit.*

"Leave it alone, Colin," Kaitlyn said quietly. "Please."

The raven squawked, cocked its head and continued to stare.

Colin lowered his arms. His lungs ached. He couldn't breathe. What the hell was happening to him? He pressed both hands to his chest. Was he having a heart attack?

Kaitlyn stepped up beside him, raised her right hand and said, "From north, south, east and west, guardians please rise, come forth and give us protection."

Colin gaped as a cool circle of mist seemed to gather from the fog and swirl around them. The raven gave one last loud squawk and ruffled its feathers, and then flew away to circle overhead. The pain in Colin's chest immediately disappeared. He stumbled backwards. What the hell?

I'm watching you.

The softly spoken words floated on the wind along with the bird. Finally, the raven circled up, up into the clouds and disappeared.

Lightning flashed, raising goose bumps on Colin's arms despite the jacket he wore. Kaitlyn closed her eyes, put her hand out again, and the mist circle dissolved. Thunder crashed around them as he stared after the bird. What in hell had he just witnessed?

Kaitlyn crept over to him. "Are you okay?"

"I guess so." Shaken, he glanced down at the tombstone lying partially concealed in the high grass, and he did a double take. It read, *Lyle Forrester, d. 1862.*

Colin's blood ran cold. Forrester and his wife were responsible for the deadly curse that supposedly embraced the house. How was that for coincidence?

The raven cried out once more from somewhere high above them.

Kaitlyn put her hand on his arm. "Now, do you believe?"

"In what?" He struggled to understand what she was getting at.

"The supernatural. You just watched me call up a circle of protection, which chased off the raven that was going to kill you."

Colin laughed. "That bird wasn't gonna kill me. It was a black bird, for crying out loud."

"You grabbed your chest."

"I was startled." He walked past the headstone toward the bayou, which was now obscured by fog. He reached the fence and realized the fog ended there— meaning it hovered over the cemetery and nowhere else. He cursed under his breath.

"How do you explain the circle of mist?"

"In case you haven't noticed, it's foggy." He halted.

Kaitlyn walked up beside him. "I know it's hard for you to comprehend."

"Don't go there, Kaitlyn." He didn't want to hear her defense for the strange activities in this place. He was the FBI Assistant Deputy Director of Criminal Investigations, and he dealt in solid facts. Not a bunch of supernatural mumbo jumbo.

He glanced once more at the bayou. A white object on the ground near the water caught his eye. He narrowed his gaze. What was that?

The fence was ice cold and topped with tall iron spikes, but he gripped two of the bars and stepped on a fallen headstone, so he could safely climb over the barrier without puncturing anything vital. Once slip, though, and he'd be singing soprano. He gritted his teeth.

"What are you doing?" Kaitlyn lifted her eyebrows. "Running away from me?"

"No." He gauged the distance from the headstone to the top of the fence. "I see something in that clearing near the bayou. Give me a second."

"What do you see?" She peered over the fence.

He levered himself neatly over the spikes and landed on the other side of the wrought iron barrier with a soft grunt. Piece of cake. He wiped his hands. "I'll tell you when I know."

"Be careful."

"Don't worry, I will." He wiped his fogged up glasses on his shirt and started toward the bayou, carefully negotiated the dense underbrush. Vines tore at his jeans and low-hanging limbs slapped his face. He scowled at the annoying buzz of mosquitoes. Just as he reached the area where he'd seen the white object, a soft rain began to fall. Another roll of thunder told him the storm was just beginning.

He sidestepped a large cypress, and abruptly halted. What he'd thought were mosquitoes were actually blowflies, doing what they were meant to do—laying their eggs on a dead body. The odor of putrefying flesh made the contents of his stomach swirl.

"What is it, Colin?" Kaitlyn called, her voice caught up in the falling rain.

"Go call the sheriff."

"Oh my God." Her eyes wide, she peered at him through the fence. "What did you find?"

"A body."

She went still. "Who is it?"

"I don't know. It's a blonde female. Young." He released a string of expletives. "Just like the other three victims. Damn it."

"The ones found in the graves near the house?"

"Yes." He rubbed the back of his neck, and then squatted beside the nude girl. Dried blood covered her chest. Her throat was slit from ear to ear. No need to go into detail with Kaitlyn, though. He turned his head and met her uneasy gaze. "Go back to the house and call the parish sheriff."

"Okay, I'm going."

He heard her crash back through the high grass. The cemetery gate squawked like the raven had when she opened it. He shook off the urge to jump up and follow her.

The rain continued to pepper down, washing away any footprints or trace evidence that might have remained on the corpse. He fumed. Lack of evidence was why Lynsee and Jack hadn't been able to solve their case. Figured he'd have the same awful luck.

He rose to his feet, took off his damp glasses, and peered down at the dead girl staring up at him with wide, unseeing blue eyes and he couldn't help but wonder about her last moments on earth. She'd died a horrible death, frightened out of her wits. Poor kid. A chill slid over him. And standing here between the fog-filled cemetery and the teeming bayou, he couldn't help but notice the irony.

Cold, unfeeling death vs. the vitality of life. He'd choose life every time. Even his staid, lonely existence was better than the alternative. He aimed his gaze at the house and pictured Kaitlyn in his mind's eye. She was beautiful, witty, and outgoing to the point of being flamboyant—the exact opposite of his uptight personality, and too much like Maria to be good for him. He shook his head and stuck his glasses in his pocket. Then why did he suddenly feel more alive than he had in years?

Too bad they had to meet here, under these odd circumstances. Soon, the case would be solved and they would go their separate ways. She would go about her

business thinking she was a witch. And he would return
to Washington D. C. to push paper and help the agents
under his command solve unexplainable crimes. He
shook his head. The thought of leaving Kaitlyn behind
hurt, and he barely even knew her.

Yet he was glad she hadn't returned to the scene.
Nobody needed to see the awful sight lying at his feet. He
studied the area around the girl more closely, but saw
nothing of value. The stick figures and stars hanging in
the cemetery clattered in the rain.

His skin crawled.

A few minutes later, he watched two sheriff's
department vehicles, a white crime scene van, and an
unmarked black car wind their way up the long brick
drive toward the house. A morbid parade.

Careful not to dislodge any possible evidence, he
trudged toward them through the woods and met the
officers at the cemetery gate.

*****

Kaitlyn peeked out her bedroom window as the
sheriff's department cruisers arrived, and again when
they left the property. Thinking about the young dead
girl lying alone in the rain beneath the canopy of trees, she
wrapped her hand around her necklace. What horrors
had that poor girl suffered before she'd died? And why
had she died here, at Scarlet Oak?

She died so I could live.

The softly whispered words brushed over Kaitlyn's
skin like a physical touch. She released the pendant and
spun to see a tall, mustached man in an out-dated suit

lurking like an ogre beside the bed. His dark green eyes were blank—much like Etienne's.

She caught her breath.

"You're here to kill me," he said matter-of-factly. "Just like the evil being who murdered those unfortunate young girls killed them. Only you won't get the chance."

"Wh-who are you?" There was a quiver in her voice.

His mouth curved in a sly grin. "Don't be coy. You know who I am."

He was right. His ancient suit and prim conduct gave him away. It was the ghost of Lyle Forrester—and he frightened the hell out of her. She forced herself not to react.

He toyed with the ends of his mustache. "You won't succeed in what you're trying to do, you know. It's not possible."

"Is that right?" She looked into his flat, dead eyes and squared her shoulders. "Why do you say that?"

"Your form of witchcraft is no match for me."

"I didn't realize greed was such a strong motivator."

His eyes turned fiery, and he stepped toward her. The musky odor of death filled the room. "You're walking a fine line, *Miss Chambers*."

She stifled a gasp. How did he know her name? The only person at Scarlet Oak besides Colin who knew her identity was that disturbing concierge, Etienne Fabron.

"That's right. I know everything about you." He crept closer. "You inherited your powers from your mother. Now you believe you're infallible."

Surprise at his arrogance ambushed her, but she didn't move except to raise her right hand and cast a circle. A blue bubble rose quickly to surround her, and she murmured, "As above, so below and all around. The circle is sealed."

"Very impressive." Fabron smirked and clapped his hands. "You may be far from a novice, but you have never encountered Vodun in its purest form. Have you?"

"I know enough about it to defeat you." Secure in her circle of protection, she lifted her chin.

He laughed bitterly, the sound cutting her like a knife. "No, you don't. I'm going to stay right here in this house and find that missing sapphire. The Midnight Star will be my salvation." He halted only inches away from Kaitlyn.

She didn't so much as flinch. Instead, she ignored the sickening smells suddenly flowing into the circle and flicked her hand at him, as though he were nothing more than an annoying bug.

A startled look flashed across his face as Forrester dissolved in a crackling white cloud that swirled around her like a tornado, icing her skin and making her stomach churn. Kaitlyn blinked.

She had done it. He was gone.

"Kaitlyn?"

Numb with disbelief that she had rid herself of him so easily, she bid the circle go and stared at the door. "Yes?"

"Kaitlyn!" Colin's deep baritone echoed through the closed panel. "Are you in there?"

"Oh, Colin, it's you," she said, the recognition of his voice snapping her back to reality. She rushed to the door and yanked it open. "Yes. I'm here."

He stood in the hallway, soaking wet, his usual stiff demeanor soggy and disheveled. His glasses were in his shirt pocket, and water droplets glistened on his forehead.

She clamped a hand over her mouth and stifled a giggle.

"Are you all right?" His brow furrowed and he looked her up and down. "I heard strange noises in there."

"I-I'm fine," she said, unwilling to share what she had just seen. Not with Colin. Not yet. Even though in her heart she was shaken. Lyle Forrester, even dead, was an imposing figure. She could only imagine what hell poor Susannah had endured living with him all those years and bearing his two children.

Colin dried his face with the sleeve of his jacket. "I didn't see you downstairs and wanted to make sure you'd returned safely to the house. After finding that body —"

"Yes. I was . . . resting," she lied, her hungry gaze eating him up. His jacket and shirt were plastered to his broad torso. He was over one hundred seventy pounds of soaking wet male, with muscle and sinew in all the right places. Her body hummed with leftover energy.

"You should put on some dry clothes."

"I intend to." He wiped his hand on his blue jeans. "But I wanted to warn you first."

"About what?" A fresh wave of uneasiness washed over her.

His expression grew dark. "You know about the latest body. Just remember you shouldn't go out alone, especially at night. Not until we catch whoever is killing women and leaving them on the property."

"I'm not some flighty teenage girl."

"I realize that. But you're blonde and pretty, and someone might very well mistake you for —"

"A teenager?" She laughed. Her insides warmed, and her weakness fled as quickly as it had come. She smiled up at him. "Not likely. But thank you for the compliment."

"You're welcome." Water dripped down his cheek. He wiped it away and lingered on the threshold. "Are you still having dinner with me tonight?"

"Of course I am." She smiled. She'd like nothing better than to get to know him better.

His razor-sharp expression softened. "Good. I thought you might bail on me after some of the things I said outside. You know, about the raven and all.

"Let me guess," she said. "Your skittishness is because I'm a witch, and you're not."

"Well, yeah." He looked terribly uncomfortable. "But there's more to it than that."

"Like what?" She folded her arms. She enjoyed seeing Mister Uptight flustered like an embarrassed schoolboy. A smile nibbled at her lips. She managed to suppress it.

He shrugged. "It's just that…well…you're so, well— I don't know. *Out there.*"

Her smile escaped. She started laughing. If he discovered she'd spent the past ten minutes conversing with Lyle Forrester's ghost, he'd think she was more than just *out there*. He'd think she was totally nuts. She eyed the *grimoire* on the nightstand. What he needed was a good spell.

She bit her lip, and began to scheme.

"Well?" He stuck his hands in his pockets. "Do you think we can get along?'

"Yes." She lifted her chin. "As long as you accept me as I am."

"Spells and all?" He eyed her warily.

"Yes." She bit her lip. "And you let me explain the complete history of the house — including the part about ghosts."

"That's a total waste of time." He shook his head. "Ghosts don't exist."

She met his disbelieving gaze with a searing one of her own. "Ghosts are all around us. Just because you can't see them, doesn't mean they're not there. Can you see the wind?"

"No, but I—" He furrowed his brow. "Damn it, Kaitlyn. Okay—I'm willing to try. Just don't get too pushy with the paranormal mumbo jumbo."

"Oh, trust me. I won't." Her lips curved, and she murmured a spell of hope.

CHAPTER THREE

Colin adjusted his shoulder holster and pulled on his still-damp coat. He didn't want to think about why he was suddenly so obsessed with his appearance. Asking Kaitlyn to dinner had been a spur of the moment thing this morning, one he hoped he wouldn't regret. She made him want to scream with all that witchcraft nonsense she spouted.

He put on his glasses, made sure he had his wallet in his pocket, and started for the door. His cell phone rang. He halted and pulled it out. "Winter."

"Colin, this is Burl Johnson. We met at Scarlet Oak yesterday. I'm a lab tech working out of the New Orleans field office."

Surprise filtered through Colin. He hadn't expected to hear from the lab people so soon. "Hey, Burl. Got something for me already?"

"No. We haven't gotten the body yet. That's why I'm calling."

"Are you serious?" Colin frowned. "The sheriff promised me the morgue would have it ready for you no later than four o'clock."

"I know," Burl said. "We got there on time. The place was dark."

"That's odd." Colin raked a hand through his hair. Orleans Parish was one of the busiest in Louisiana, meaning their morgue should be open 24/7. No way would they close by mid-afternoon.

"I called the sheriff and he didn't know what had happened. He's supposed to check it out and give me a call back ASAP."

"Thanks. Keep me posted." Still puzzled, Colin ended the call and glanced at his watch. Five after six. He cursed. Dinner had already started.

He flung open the door and hurried toward the stairs.

Kaitlyn met him at the entrance to the dining room. She smiled that brilliant smile, and a pleasant warmth blossomed inside his chest.

"I was giving you five more minutes, and then I was eating without you." She crossed her arms. "You know what Mr. Fabron said. The food will be out for only a short time.

"Sorry." Damn, but she made him feel good, even when she was fussing. And that worried the hell out of him. "I had a call on my cell."

"About the case?"

"Yes. I'll explain while we eat." He led her to the buffet. "We'd better get to it, or Fabron will kick us out of here."

They loaded their plates with delicious-looking food, and Colin chose a table by a window overlooking the side lawn. With the hotel empty they had their choice of seats, and he deliberately picked one with a view of the cemetery. There was something strange about that place. The rain had finally stopped, and the remaining moisture lent the foliage a curious gleam.

Kaitlyn sat down in the chair across from him, and he got a whiff of her sexy herbal scent. It wasn't exactly perfume, but it fit.

"You smell good," he said, wanting to drink her in. He slid into the seat across from her and smiled.

She seemed surprised by his comment. "It must be the sage. After you left my room, I did a cleansing in most of the —"

"Whoa." He held up his fork. "None of that witch talk. Not while we're eating."

She lifted her chin. "You must enjoy insulting me."

"I don't mean any offense." He looked around to make sure no one was listening. He was on a case, and he wanted to appear professional. "It's just that you know how I feel about the supernatural."

"Yes, I do." Fire flashed in her pretty green eyes as she picked up a baked chicken leg. "And I intend to change your mind."

"That's not going to happen."

"We'll see about that," she said, her eyes glittering with determination. She pulled off a piece of chicken and popped it into her mouth.

Colin was mesmerized with the play of her lips as she chewed, and he found himself becoming aroused. He squirmed. How in hell could just watching the woman chew make him want her so bad? No one had ever affected him like this.

"Aren't you going to eat?" she asked, raising her eyebrows.

He narrowed his gaze. She knew exactly what she was doing to him. Damn her. He looked at his plate, which was piled high with chicken and vegetables. Food no longer held any appeal. But he smiled anyway and dug in. "Sure I am."

"You were going to tell me about the case."

He put down his fork. "My lab people are working with the local VCMO squad—the Violent Crimes Major Case Unit—and they tried to pick up the girl's body this afternoon. The morgue was closed."

"Is that unusual?"

"It is in a city as big as New Orleans." Irritation rose within him. "I just don't understand it."

"Maybe the medical examiner was on a break or something."

"I'm sure he has a staff."

Kaitlyn scooped up a carrot. "What are you going to do?"

"Wait for my forensics team to call me back. We need that body."

She nodded, and grew solemn. "Do you have a theory about the murders?"

"Nothing concrete." He scooped up a bite of mashed potatoes. "It's damned confusing."

"Ghost murders."

"What?" He halted with the fork halfway to his mouth.

She toyed with her tea glass. "Ghosts killed them. Or should I say—one ghost. Lyle Forrester."

"Don't tell me you believe that theory." Colin gaped at her.

"You bet I do." Her eyes held his with rapt intensity. "He's the reason I'm here."

"He used to own the house."

"That's right." She moved her plate aside and leaned forward, sending her beautiful jade pendant swinging between her breasts. "Legend has it that he had an affair with a beautiful slave girl named Camille, much to the chagrin of his wife."

"What does that have to do with these murders?'

"Hear me out." Kaitlyn grew animated. "Camille owned a beautiful sapphire known as the Midnight Star."

"Which had been passed down to her from her mother. I've heard the story."

"I see."

"Well, maybe only bits and pieces." He didn't want to rain on her parade. "Go on."

"Okay." Her eyes glimmered with excitement. "Lyle wanted the necklace, so he killed Camille and took it off her body while it was still warm."

"Talk about greed."

"Exactly." She shifted her glass over by her plate. "Problem was, the sapphire was only supposed to be gifted in love. Once Lyle killed Camille and stole the necklace, he broke that important rule."

"And?" Intrigued, Colin cocked his head.

Kaitlyn smiled. "Camille came back to haunt him."

"I should have known." His expression hardened, and he stabbed at a piece of chicken. "You really had me going there for a minute."

"Wait." She put her hand on his arm. "Let me finish."

"You know I don't like ghost stories."

"Please, Colin." She smiled at him with a twinkle in those beautiful jade eyes he just couldn't resist.

He put down his fork. "Okay, I'll listen. But don't get too far out there."

She laughed and released his arm. "I wasn't entirely correct with that last statement."

"About Camille?"

"Yes." She lowered her voice to a conspiratorial whisper. "Lyle gave the Midnight Star to his wife—"

"Susannah."

"Yes." Kaitlyn nodded. "And Camille—or rather, her ghost—was furious. She took over Susannah's body and murdered the two Forrester children."

Colin sent her a skeptical look.

She held up her hand. "Let me finish."

He grinned. This show was too good to stop. A beautiful woman, excellent fiction, and maybe even a chance for a good night kiss. He went still, and dropped his gaze to Kaitlyn's mouth. She stirred him in a way he never would have expected.

"Are you listening to me?" She furrowed her brow.

He jerked his gaze up to her eyes. His face burned with sexual heat. "Yeah, sure I am. What did you say?"

She laughed. "That after her children died, Susannah descended into madness."

"In other words, she went nuts."

"If you want to be crude about it." Kaitlyn cocked her head. "Lyle was a cruel man. Many people speculate he killed Susannah to put an end to her misery. I think he got tired of her hounding him about Camille."

"What happened to the sapphire?"

"No one knows." Her eyes sparkled. "That's why Lyle still roams these halls. He's desperate to find it. He truly believes it will bring him salvation."

"Have you seen him in the house?" Colin couldn't keep the sarcasm from his voice.

"Yes." Her expression soured. "As a matter of fact, I have."

"I'm sure he introduced himself."

"He didn't have to. I knew exactly who he was. We had a conversation."

Colin made a choking sound. She had really gone around the bend on this one. Ghosts didn't exist, much less talk back. Unbelievable.

She glanced out the window and sat back in her chair with a startled look on her face. "Oh my goodness. Will you look—it's Etienne Fabron. How odd."

Colin followed her gaze. Sure enough, Fabron glided across the side lawn toward the cemetery, his gait much too smooth to be natural. It was almost like he was floating. He was dressed all in black, and carried a small white bundle in the crook of his arm.

"He's a strange bird." Kaitlyn frowned. "What's that he's got?"

"I have no idea." Colin eyed the pillow-shaped package tucked beneath Fabron's left arm with concern. He didn't trust the man as far as he could throw him. The concierge paused briefly at the cemetery gate, opened it, and disappeared into the fog. Colin put his napkin on the table. "But I'm damned well going to find out."

"I'm coming with you." Kaitlyn rose.

Colin opened his mouth to protest, but she cut him off with a wave of her hand.

"Don't you dare try to stop me from going with you. If he's into the supernatural, you may need my help."

"Why do you think he might be?"

She shrugged. "You saw how he was walking."

"I wasn't gonna mention it." Colin's chest grew tight. All this ghost talk was making him nervous, and he wasn't the jittery type. Kaitlyn warped his sense of reason.

She motioned toward the foyer. "Let's go. I won't let them get you."

"Very funny." He made a face at her.

Kaitlyn couldn't help grinning. Talking about the paranormal with Colin was a real treat. She loved getting under his skin. Too bad right now all she could think about was getting under him—literally. Her body hummed with sexual energy, which had nothing at all to do with ghosts, psychic phenomenon, or even witchcraft, and everything to do with her growing attraction for Assistant Deputy Director Winter.

Her cheeks burned as she accompanied him across the side yard to the cemetery gate. The fog inside had thickened, obscuring the headstones. She shivered in the chilly evening air. The temperature must have fallen ten degrees since early this morning—around the graveyard, anyway. The rest of the property felt normal.

"Where did he go?" She rubbed her arms to keep warm. Mr. Fabron had vanished, courtesy of the ominous blanket of fog.

Colin reached around her and opened the gate. "I don't know. I'm going to look for him."

"Be careful." Kaitlyn hugged herself. "I don't want you to disappear, too. That would just be too weird."

He laughed and vanished into the fog.

Watching him go, her heart pounded. He needed her protection. Rather than just standing here, she stepped through the gate, raised her right hand, and formed a large circle of mist around the cemetery to protect them both. Her feeling of security immediately increased and her skin warmed.

She opened her eyes to find a thick fog wall swirling around the perimeter of the cemetery. The wind had kicked up, and raindrops dripped off the trees into her face. She wiped her cheek with her sleeve. Minutes ticked by. The steady click-clack of the stick figures across the way unnerved her, yet she didn't feel at all threatened. She clutched her necklace and searched the mist for Colin.

When he didn't readily reappear, she turned and wandered among the headstones. She couldn't see but a few feet in front of her, but thanks to the late summer twilight it was enough to allow her to read the names engraved on the ancient granite. Nearly every one of them was a Forrester. Not surprising, but seeing the names etched in stone made her skin crawl, especially after her eye-opening conversation with Lyle's evil ghost.

"Hello, Ms. Chambers." Fabron's obsequious voice raised the hairs on the back of her neck. She spun, but didn't see him. Where was he?

All at once he materialized in front of her, his ill-fitting black suit hanging off his thin form like a drape. "I didn't expect to see you here."

Jolted by his gaunt appearance, she stared into his vacant eyes. How had he gotten inside the circle? "Where's Colin?"

"Mr. FBI?" Fabron's mouth curved. "I wouldn't know."

"He came out here looking for you." She frowned down at the concierge's hands. They were as empty as his eyes. "What did you do with your parcel?"

"What are you talking about?"

"You were carrying a package when you walked out here."

He gave her a patronizing smile. "You must be imagining things."

"I know what I saw."

"Excuse me." He held out his hands. "Empty."

She bit back a sharp retort. "What did you do with Colin?"

"Like I told you, I haven't seen him." He reached for her hand.

She sidestepped him. "Don't touch me." If he was up to what obviously looked like black magic, she didn't want to be within ten feet of him.

"Now, now, Ms. Chambers. Is that any way for a good witch to act?"

Anger funneled through her. "I want to know what you did with him."

"Look around." He swung his arms in a large arc. "Do you see him?"

Kaitlyn took a wide path around the infuriating man and scurried to the far end of the cemetery. Fog shrouded the headstones and the thick grass swayed in the growing breeze. Her breathing quickened. There was no sign of Colin, or any evidence that anyone had visited that part of the cemetery in years. If he had been outside the circle she had made, anything could have happened to him. She looped around the crowded grave markers and headed back to the worn part of the path. Fabron had disappeared.

"Colin?" Kaitlyn's nerve endings tingled. She checked the other side of the graveyard. *Nothing.* She was alone in the fog. Drawing to a halt, she drew in a deep breath and fingered her mother's necklace.

`The piercing cry of a raven startled her, and she broke off. The omen of death circled overhead, its shiny wings scattering the fog and sending a fresh chill tumbling through her. Kaitlyn backed toward the fence.

The raven landed on a headstone near the gate, its keen eyes studying her as if she were its next meal. She froze. The bird cocked its head.

"Go away," she said, her insides churning. She waved her arms. "Shoo!" With a loud squawk, it flapped its wings and took off.

Her stomach threatened to heave up her supper. She pushed open the gate and stumbled from the cemetery. Maybe Colin had climbed the fence like yesterday, and he was exploring the area near the bayou.

"Colin?" she called. Her eyes scanned the sky for the raven's return as she skirted the fence and entered the woods. The trees were thick here. Dense underbrush scratched at her legs. The fog was lighter here, and between the trees she got a glimpse of murky brown water.

There was no sign of him, or the bird.

"Colin!" she shouted again. She batted a low-hanging tendril of moss away from her face. "Where are you?"

Her words echoed off the trees. She drew in the musty odor of the bayou and the earthy aroma of dead leaves. Then a startling metallic smell reached her nose. *Blood.*

Her heart thumped harder. "If you're playing a trick on me, I swear—"

She slipped past an enormous cypress and entered a small clearing. At its center stood a tall wooden pole strung with fluffy black feathers. On the ground around it was an odd white powdery substance, laid out in an unfamiliar pattern. A fresh crimson pool marked the design's center. Kaitlyn clapped a shaky hand over her mouth.

Something—or someone—had died here, probably as some sort of ritual offering. *Vodun.* Kaitlyn gulped back her terror and let her gaze roam over the small clearing. A neat pile of tiny bones sat next to a bloodstained bowl, and a plethora of footprints marred the neat edges of the white powder. Other than that, the place was empty. She continued on to the edge of the bayou, calling for Colin to answer her. It would be dark soon. She should quit looking and simply divine his location.

She halted, closed her eyes, and conjured up a vision of his chiseled face. Mesmerized by his dark features, she shook off her attraction to him and forced herself to concentrate on his surroundings. He was indoors, next to a big four-poster bed. She saw an antique chifferobe and shiny new plumbing fixtures. *The house.*

He was back at Scarlet Oak? Her eyes flew open. Why had he left her alone at the cemetery with Mr. Fabron? Making a fist, she turned and looked through the trees. There was only one way to find out. She would find him and confront him.

Her heart pounded with fury as she made her way back to the house. The front door creaked as she entered the foyer. She was surprised to see Mr. Fabron standing rigidly behind the desk. Gone were his saggy clothes, disheveled hair, and gaunt appearance. He looked refreshed and ready to take on the world—except for his dead eyes.

"Ms. Chambers," he said, watching her every move exactly like the raven had. "How are you? I hope you're having a good stay at our hotel."

"Cut the crap." She stalked over to the desk. "How did you and Colin get back here so fast?"

"Are you referring to Assistant Deputy Director Winter?"

"Of course I am. The two of you left me at the cemetery."

"You must be delusional. I've been here the entire evening, and Mr. FBI is upstairs in his room. I'm quite sure of it."

"Why are you lying?" Her face flushed with anger. "I saw you."

"Believe what you want." Fabron's mouth curved in a sinister smile. "But Deputy Winter and I have both been inside since dinner. He just requested more towels."

She snapped her mouth shut.

"Why don't you ask him about it if you don't believe me?" He nodded toward the stairs. "That is, if you aren't afraid of what lurks in the bowels of the house. Winter is in room five, which is directly across the parlor from your room."

"I'm not afraid of anything." She lifted her chin. *She was a witch, after all.*

Fabron narrowed his eyes. "Maybe you should be. Spirits are running rampant in these halls."

A flare of embarrassment made her cheeks burn. He was right. She hadn't taken time to do her job. She'd been too caught up in her attraction to Colin to consider the Forresters.

Totally irritated with herself and Fabron, Kaitlyn hurried toward the stairs. Her heartbeat skittered with nerves as she climbed the curving steps to the second floor. The air on the landing was warm and clammy. She turned right and approached Colin's door.

She put her ear against it and listened for any sound telling her he was inside—but she heard nothing. He had to be in there. She'd seen him.

She raised her hand and knocked. "Colin?"

"Just a minute."

Kaitlyn sucked in her breath. He *was* inside, and he sounded perfectly normal. She stared at the ornate wooden door. How—and, more importantly, *why*—had he slipped past her in the cemetery only to come back to the house?

The door swung open and Colin stood in front of her bare-chested, a yellow towel looped around his neck. His pectorals were magnificent, strong and muscled, with a light dusting of dark hair. She struggled to speak, but only managed to sputter.

"Why—um—I didn't—you just—"

He furrowed his brow. "What's the matter with you?"

"Nothing. Wh-where did you go?" she finally managed. "You left me in the cemetery."

"No, I didn't." He gripped both ends of the towel, and his pectorals tightened. "You came back to the house with me this morning. Tonight, we had dinner and—"

"Yes." Trying to keep her eyes off his tempting six-pack abs, she clung to the remnants of her sanity. "And after that, we followed Mr. Fabron to the cemetery. Don't you remember?"

Colin gave her an odd look. "I came up here after dinner and took a shower."

Kaitlyn pressed her fingers to her temples. She was losing her mind.

He gripped her hand and tugged her into the room. "Why don't you have a seat and relax?"

"I don't understand," she muttered, startled to hear a wicked chuckle echoing down the hall. She pulled her hand free and peered into the shadowed corridor, only to see Mr. Fabron's thin face locked in a condescending sneer.

I told you so, he mouthed.

She caught the door with both hands as Colin tried to close it. "Wait! Fabron's out there telling me that you and he—"

"Don't you worry about him," Colin said, pulling her hands off the door and shutting it with a soft click. He ushered her to one of two chairs beside the room's only table and pulled the towel from around his neck. He tossed it on the bed. The look in his eyes told her he would brook no argument. She reluctantly sat down.

He took the other chair and recaptured her hand, rubbing it briskly between both of his. "Your fingers are ice cold."

"I-I know." She couldn't stop shaking. The picture of that small pool of blood slowly soaking into the sandy ground had ingrained itself in her mind.

He dropped that hand and reached for the other one. She felt dwarfed by his sheer size and overwhelming masculinity. The sight of her smaller hand trapped between his large ones sent a jolt of warmth flooding through her. This evening was becoming more and more bizarre.

His gaze flicked to her face. "Why were you in the cemetery?"

"You and I were following Mr. Fabron. He carried some sort of package in the crook of his arm and walked like he was floating."

Colin gave her a skeptical look.

Her stomach knotted. "You really don't remember?"

"No." He shook his head. "I'm sorry."

"He disappeared into the fog, and you went after him. I waited for you in the cemetery." She swallowed, hard. "I looked all over for you, but only found Mr. Fabron instead. He'd ditched his package, and he looked all skinny and gaunt. Scary."

"You must have been dreaming."

"No. And it wasn't my imagination, nor was I in a trance." Still, she was flummoxed by Colin's odd disappearance. Anxiety wrapped a tight fist around her heart and wouldn't let go. She frowned at him. "This is just too bizarre. Between your vanishing, Fabron entering my circle of protection, and the blood I saw on the ground—"

"What blood?" He scowled. "Where?"

"In a clearing at what looked like the site of a Vodun ritual." She chewed her lip. "I don't know too much about black magic, but I'm guessing someone around here is well versed in it. It might be Mr. Fabron. That might explain how he broke into the circle."

"Forget that. You're sure you saw blood?"

"Yes. A pool of it soaking into the dirt. It might have been from an animal. I don't know." She crossed her arms. "But after not being able to find you—"

"I'm right here." Colin rose and knelt beside her, so close she drew in the soothing scents of soap and man. "I don't know what happened to you tonight, but I do know you're perfectly sane."

She tapped her foot.

"Look at me." He cupped her chin.

She raised her head and met his searching gaze. His eyes were twin mocha pools, waiting for her to dive in headfirst. Her throat closed up.

"It's this house," he said. "Strange things are happening here. It doesn't mean you're crazy. I'd bet my next paycheck that Fabron is in on it—hell, I'd bet a year's pay he's behind what happened to you tonight. He's trying to scare you off the property."

"I wouldn't doubt it, the way he was laughing at me. He wants me to leave Scarlet Oak and take my *grimoire* with me."

"Don't go." Colin dropped his hand. "Not until we have more time to get to know each other."

His words rocked her. She stared at him.

"Kaitlyn, if you leave now—"

"Oh, Colin," she whispered, a startling wave of longing washing away her dismay. She touched his stubbled cheek. "I don't want to leave. I want to get to know you better, too."

His lips parted and an electric current seemed to flow between them, charging her heart and making her insides melt. *He was going to kiss her.*

Kaitlyn couldn't move. Mesmerized by the ravenous look in his eyes, she sat in stunned silence as he slowly leaned forward and brushed his parted lips over hers, his touch feather light and so seductive she lost her breath.

He wanted her. The idea shocked her. None of her beaus had ever looked at her with this kind of carnal longing. Certainly not Jason, the opinionated male witch who had begged her to marry him then cast her aside.

Her nerve endings burned as she put a trembling hand on Colin's shoulder. The clean scent of soap on his bare skin made her body flame with desire. She wanted to feel the pulse of his heartbeat beneath her hands and taste his delicious mouth, tossing herself into the terrifying abyss opening like a giant maw beneath her feet.

"Come here, beautiful," he said softly, slipping his arms around her and pulling her close. His warm breath bathed her cheek

Reveling in his tempting heat, she stared at his enticing mouth. Her lips opened. She closed her eyes. Just one teensy weensy taste—

"Ms. Chambers?" A loud banging on the door made her eyes fly open.

Colin let her go and sat down hard on the floor, a stunned look on his face. The knocking echoed again. With a frustrated growl, Colin pushed himself up.

Kaitlyn's eyes locked on his bulging fly, and heat flamed through her. He was every bit as aroused as she was.

"Ten bucks says it's Fabron." He scowled.

"Ms. Chambers?" Fabron's reedy voice carried through the door. "I need to speak with you. It's urgent."

"Of course it is," Colin snapped, marching over to the door. He yanked it open and glowered at the disturbing concierge. "What do you want, Fabron?"

"Colin." Kaitlyn came to her feet. "He asked for me."

"Thank you for being so gracious, Ms. Chambers." Fabron's mouth curved in a wicked smile. He held out a small brown envelope. "I have a message for you. It came in today's mail, but unfortunately it was misplaced. I apologize for the delay."

Colin reached for it, but Fabron jerked it away.

"It's not yours."

He held it out to Kaitlyn. "At least *you're* being civilized about the interruption."

Intrigued, she took it from him and peered at the return address. She turned to Colin. "It's from Remy and Gillian."

"Open it." He furrowed his brow.

She clutched the missive to her chest and edged toward the door. "I believe I'll wait until I get to my room."

He caught her arm. "Kaitlyn—don't leave."

Surprised by his obvious show of affection, she shook him off and shot a warning glance at Fabron, who was watching them closely. "This was a mistake. I'll see you tomorrow."

She pushed past the concierge and hurried from the room.

Etienne's chest tightened as he watched her disappear across the landing. She was beautiful, yet she had the power to destroy him. Only now, thanks to him, she had begun to doubt her strength. He absently touched the scar at his neck. Soon, she would have her own nasty wounds to nurse.

"Leave her alone, Fabron," Colin growled.

Etienne jumped. He'd forgotten the director was standing there.

Colin stepped closer. "Make one wrong move, and you'll answer to me."

The entity inside Etienne's head began to pound on the lining of his skull, screeching, Stop *wasting time! Kill him!* He shook his head in an effort to get him to shut up.

Colin put his hand on the doorknob. "I mean it, Fabron. If Kaitlyn reports any more strange behavior—"

"She won't get the chance." Etienne plastered a fake smile on his face.

"What does that mean?"

"Anything you want it to." Etienne spun on his heel and walked away. His head throbbed. He began to perspire. *Yellow-bellied snake!* The entity growled like a pit bull. *He has to die.*

Etienne clutched his temples and slithered around the corner to the top of the stairs. Halting there, he addressed the being in his brain. "Stop railing at me! I've got to take care of the woman first," he muttered aloud. "*She's* a witch, which makes her ten times more dangerous than he is."

Not more dangerous than me!

Pain suddenly knifed through Etienne's neck. Panic seized him, and he clawed at the scar beneath his collar, which began to burn like it was on fire. His vision blurred.

You have two days to kill them and find the sapphire, or you will feel my wrath!

Etienne tried to focus on the words ricocheting around inside his head. The stairs in front of him seemed to pitch and roll. He grabbed the railing to keep from tumbling down the steps headfirst. Sweat trickled down his spine.

Two more days, or I finish what Garner Reboulet started. The entity cackled. *Is that understood?*

"Y-yes," Etienne hissed through his tightly clenched teeth. "Please—stop the pain!"

The pounding continued inside his head. A red haze formed behind his eyes. He couldn't see a damned thing. He clung to the stair railing and waited to die.

Until a door slammed down the hall. His stomach clenched around what was left of his supper. He blinked. And finally, the scar's fiery sting began to ease. The pounding inside his skull lessened, and his heart stopped bouncing around inside his chest.

"Son of a bitch," he said, sucking in a shaky breath. His hands ached from being wrapped around the railing like a drowning man holding a rope. He gradually loosened his grip on the polished wood. His shirt was soaked clean through. The haze behind his eyes lifted, and all at once he could see. Terrified, he looked around. He saw no one. *Thank God.*

Relief anchored him to the floor. He was so glad the hotel was mostly empty and no one lurked in the shadows watching his strangle torture.

Two days. The words were seared into his brain matter. He released the railing and stepped back on trembling noodle legs. He had no choice but to go ahead with his plan.

Either he killed Kaitlyn Chambers and Colin Winters, or he would die.

CHAPTER FOUR

Colin sat down on the edge of the bed and raked his hand through his hair. What the hell was wrong with Kaitlyn? All that crazy witch mumbo jumbo was going to her head. Now in addition to her spells, circles of protection, and strange herbs, she was imagining things. She claimed he'd met her at the cemetery tonight, while he'd been right here in this room the entire time, talking to the sheriff about why the morgue had been closed when the FBI team came to get the dead girl's body. Then he'd taken a shower.

Had the weird concierge fed her some sort of hallucinogen? Fury burned inside Colin's chest at the thought. Fabron had better stay away from her unless he wanted to pay, and pay big.

Colin felt a fierce protective urge every time he was around her. Despite her self-confident attitude, he sensed a sweet vulnerability inside her that called out to him. Damn it, he wanted her. And that was wrong. He'd just put his failed marriage behind him, and he had no business getting involved with anyone else so soon. Not to mention the fact that he was at Scarlet Oak to work a case. Falling in love was *so* not on his agenda. He rubbed his bare chest. Maybe he was so damned hot for her because he was lonely. He hadn't been with a woman since his marriage had ended over six months ago. It was time he got laid, yet he didn't need to involve his emotions. That would only get messy and cause more loose ends—his greatest pet peeve. He'd finally found closure with Maria once the divorce had become final.

Now he just needed find a way to keep Kaitlyn at arm's length.

He twisted his lips. Yeah, right. She was beautiful and flamboyant, just the answer for his boring life. All he needed was his body betraying him at every turn.

No. He could not get involved with her. Not now, maybe not ever. Still, he ached for her. Staying away from her wasn't going to be easy. If he could only focus on the fact that she believed she was a witch. There was no place in his orderly life for a flighty woman who practiced witchery. That alone should be enough to douse his flaming libido.

Colin rose and reached for the file folder beside the bed. Enough mind play. Time for him to get back to work. He put on his glasses and opened the manila cover. The papers inside outlined the discovery of the first three bodies, their subsequent autopsies, and contained case notes written by Navarre and Frost. His stomach churned as he studied the autopsy reports for what had to be the hundredth time. The throats of all three girls had been slit from ear to ear, just like the one he and Kaitlyn had found yesterday. All three had cornmeal embedded in their skin.

Cornmeal.

His senses went on high alert. Scattered white grains had also been found beneath the last girl. He didn't have forensics back on them yet, but he was willing to bet they were ground corn, too. And hadn't Kaitlyn mentioned seeing a granular substance on the ground in the clearing tonight?

He picked up his cell phone and dialed Burl's number. The forensic specialist had grown up in New Orleans, and he knew a lot about Voodoo—a religion from the Caribbean islands that floated under society's radar. He frowned. Kaitlyn called it *Vodun*.

"Johnson."

Burl's gruffness made Colin smile. "Bad day?"

"Hell yeah, Winter." He sighed heavily. "I was just about to call you."

"You pick up the girl's body yet?"

"Nope. According to the ME, it's disappeared."

"What do you mean? They can't find it?" Colin's mouth dropped open. He'd talked to the sheriff about an hour ago, and the man had assured him the corpse would be turned over to Burl as soon as he and a VCMO squad agent returned to the morgue.

"That's what he said."

"Damn it." A flood of frustration rolled through Colin. He cursed. "Hasn't Sheriff Townsend heard that evidence tampering is a crime?"

"Doesn't seem like it, although he did seem as surprised as I was when I called him five minutes ago and he went looking for the body, just to make sure."

"Something fishy is going on here."

"You can say that again. The morgue seems to be well run. Someone must have stolen the remains, if the sheriff or any of the medical examiner's staff don't know anything about it being gone."

"Fabron."

"Who's that?"

"A weird guy who works here at the Scarlet Oak. Long story." Colin rubbed his thumb across his eyebrow in an effort to quell the fierce headache budding behind it. "Look—do you know anything about Voodoo?"

Burl paused. "You mean *Vodun*?"

"Yeah." Colin dropped his hand. "Vodun."

"I know a few facts." Burl hesitated again. "But you know that already. Why are you asking?"

"Just curious." Colin stared down at the floor. "Is cornmeal used in some of their rituals?"

"Yeah, sometimes. To draw a *veve*."

"A *veve*." It was Colin's turn to pause. "What the hell is that?"

"A symmetrical pattern on the ground around the *poteau-mitan*, a sacred pole decorated with red and black ribbons, or maybe even feathers. All of it's done to please the worshipper's *loa*. Their god. It can be the earth, fire, wind, maybe even water—"

"I get the picture." Colin frowned. Sounded a lot like witchcraft—which, of course, made him think of Kaitlyn. Sweet heaven.

Burl cleared his throat. "There are some who practice black magic. You might want to check into that."

"Black magic really exists?"

"In the minds of its practitioners. They're called *caplatas*—followers of the left hand."

"As in evil."

"Yep." Burl yawned. "Wish I knew more about it, but that's pretty much the extent of my knowledge."

"One more question before you go to sleep on me."

"Okay, okay." Burl chuckled. "I can manage one more, if you promise to find that girl's body for me."

"I'll do my best," Colin said, making a fist. *He'd find that girl if he had to turn this parish upside down to do it.* And if he found out Etienne Fabron was responsible—

"You wanted to ask me something else, boss?" Burl asked.

"Oh. Yeah, I do—and it's a big one."

"No problem. Shoot."

"Here goes." Colin took a deep breath and plunged ahead. "Do Vodun believers dabbling in black magic— *caplatas*—ever practice human sacrifice?"

Silence.

"Burl?"

"I'm here." The lab tech cleared his throat. "Shit. You don't ask easy questions, do you?"

"Guess not. But please give me an answer, if you can. It's important."

"Well then, yes. Once upon a time, human sacrifice was fairly common—especially in the islands. But in the last few hundred years or so, no. Although most *caplatas* fly under the radar and don't make themselves known. What happens in the dark remains in the dark—know what I mean?"

"Sure I do." That's what frightened Colin the most about this case—the fact that *caplatas* did whatever they damned well pleased. They were sociopaths who didn't care who they hurt in their quest to please their *loas.*

*****

Etienne lifted the slender black-handled boning knife from the case in the hotel's state-of-the-art kitchen, and stared down at its shiny silver blade. It was razor sharp and very effective for use in his rituals. He'd borrowed it four times already, always cleaning the blood off afterwards and putting it back. Remy's wife, Gillian, the hotel chef, had put a crimp in his plans for a while. But now that she was out of the country —

He caressed the delicate blade. His *loa* was becoming more and more demanding, as was the frightening entity that kept flaring to life inside his head. He had to get rid of the witch. So Kaitlyn Chambers would be his final sacrifice — allowing him to kill two birds with one stone, so to speak. He laughed. Assistant Deputy Director Winter was merely a stumbling block in his path.

In the meantime, he had to continue his search for the sapphire.

Etienne tucked the knife into the sheath he carried in his pocket and left the kitchen. His pulse rang in his ears as he picked up a large metal spoon and slipped out the back door. The damp night breeze was redolent with the musky scent of the bayou.

No one was about.

He struck out across the yard for the Keep, a rear appendage of the house used years ago for storing foodstuffs and weaponry. Past it were cottages used by the hotel staff. The wet grass slapped at his shoes, and the warm wind ruffled his hair. The rain had stopped, and eerie tendrils of fog floated beneath the trees. He shivered.

Despite the strangeness of the night, he focused on the picture of the Midnight Star burned into his mind's eye. It had once belonged to his family, and he wanted it back. He'd searched every inch of Scarlet Oak already, and he was about to begin again. He had to find that necklace.

The Keep was draped in dark shadows. Soggy beards of scraggly gray moss scraped its arched roof, and moonlight bounced off the brick exterior. Etienne battled a chill and called on his *loa* for strength.

The entity in his mind roared to life. *You should be calling on* me!

"No!" Etienne cried, as his skull began to throb. Not now, he begged. Panic seized him. He dropped the spoon and clutched at his head. He couldn't let that *thing* take over his body.

The roaring inside Etienne's skull increased, and a thick red haze formed behind his eyes.

I am not a thing. *I am the living, breathing being keeping you alive — and don't you forget it!*

"Yes sir." Etienne sank to his knees on the wet ground. Fog curled around him like a greedy snake, chilling him to the bone.

Bow to me.

"No!" He deliberately shook his head. His refusal would only bring more pain, yet he was compelled to defy the creature within him. It was the only way he'd ever regain control of his faculties and be his own man.

As if on cue, the scar on his neck began to burn. Etienne's eyes rolled back in his head and he clutched wildly at his collar. His fingers came away soaked with blood.

"No!" he cried, his high-pitched wail carried off by the damp wind. "Stop hurting me — please!"

Kiss the ground in homage to me, and your pain will leave you.

Etienne's stomach swirled with nausea. He lay down on the wet grass and sucked in the pungent odors of earth and old leaves. Trying his best to remain motionless, he gave up when his body began to tremble like that of a sick old man.

Cold, calculated laughter filled the night. *Good*, the entity said. *Now, get up! Find the sapphire, and enjoy your freedom.*

Etienne's pain began to ease. Blinking the crimson haze from his eyes, he sat back and tried to get himself under control. But he couldn't stop shaking. His legs wobbled as he picked up the spoon and gingerly levered himself to his feet. The world around him spun. He couldn't pinpoint the reason since it seemed the entity had finally quieted down.

Sweat trickled down Etienne's spine. Ignoring it, he crept over to the Keep door and pulled it open. A loud creak sent a shiver through him. He peered inside, but saw no one. Tension made his body rigid. There was a door from the Keep leading into the kitchen, but he preferred to enter this way. It was much less conspicuous.

He entered the dank circular room and pulled the cord to turn on the single light, which had been added as an afterthought sometime during the last century. Boxes and a couple of broken chairs sat to his left, and a rickety wooden cabinet stood near the door to the kitchen. The crude bricks beneath his feet were uneven and smelled of dirt. His heartbeat quickened as he walked around the room and began to explore, as if he'd never been inside the place.

According to legend, this storage facility had once been the site of a series of secret trysts between Lyle Forrester and his slave mistress, Camille. Until the day he'd demanded she give him the sapphire, and she had refused. That night, he'd killed her and claimed the stone as his own.

Etienne's skin grew clammy as he peered down at the rough floor. Perhaps Forrester had hidden the Midnight Star beneath the ancient bricks. Anything was possible. Etienne sank to his knees and wedged the spoon's slim handle into a narrow crevice. Pushing down on it, he grunted. If he could pry up one of the handmade building blocks, he would reveal what was beneath it. And with any luck—

The brick sprang free and he sat down hard on his ass.

A shiny gold speck in the dirt caught his eye. He scrambled to his knees. His breath caught. The speck looked like metal, maybe gold. He started digging.

******

Kaitlyn hurried back to her room and tore open the note from Remy and Gillian. Maybe they had changed their mind about having her cleanse the house—which wouldn't be a problem, since she hadn't yet started. In a way, she hoped—

No. Her eyes roamed down the page to an international cell phone number. They merely wanted her to give them regular updates on her progress. A knot formed in the pit of her stomach. She needed to get to work right now.

Kaitlyn put down the note and opened the *grimoire* with trembling hands. That breathtaking brush of Colin's lips against her mouth had shaken her to her core. She wouldn't call it a kiss, exactly. But that brief contact had been more powerful than any kiss she'd ever experienced.

She paused to light a pair of purple rune candles on the nightstand, then sat down against the ancient headboard and pulled the heavy book onto her lap. What had she been thinking? Colin Winter was the most rigid man she'd ever met—and he didn't believe in the paranormal, much less in the art of witchcraft. That fact alone should send her running in the opposite direction. Still, she wanted him. And that had to stop. She had to focus on her work.

She had come to Scarlet Oak to cleanse the house of evil spirits, and that's exactly what she intended to do. Yet it was apparent that Lyle and Susannah Forrester were deeply entrenched making them virtually impossible to banish with a traditional cleansing spell. What she needed was a trigger to put them in an uproar and break the bonds holding them to this place.

She flipped a page and ran her finger down the ancient paper. *Religious symbols* were a possibility. Except she didn't know just how religious the Forresters had been. If their faith wasn't strong, they wouldn't react with enough distress. Better to stay with something tried and true.

Like *salt.*

She sat back and let her mouth curve in a knowing smile. She would use a triangle to draw them out, and use the salt to get them in an uproar. Banishment would be easy after that. For the salt triangle to work its magic, she needed to lay it out where the spirits originated. In this case, that would be inside Lyle and Susannah's bedroom—where Mr. Fabron was staying. He'd already forbidden her from entering his room, so she would have to sneak in while he was out. That shouldn't be too difficult. Fabron would be furious if he caught her, but she simply would have to overcome his black magic.

Setting the book aside, she rose and pulled her box of supplies from her suitcase. Her hands were sure as she took out three pieces of glistening quartz and the bag of salt.

Go now, and get it over with. Her mind centered on the ritual she was about to perform. She gripped the minerals and salt tightly, and opened the door. Fabron's room was down the stairs to the right.

To her relief, the parlor was empty. The battling odors of lemon furniture polish and fresh paint drifted on the cool air. She moved silently down the stairs and halted when she reached the foyer. Luckily, no one was about. She turned right and spotted Fabron's closed door. She checked again to ensure she wasn't being watched, and then edged up to it and listened.

Silence.

She smiled and stared hard at the ornate brass doorknob. Telekinesis wasn't her specialty, but she'd dabbled in it from time to time. If only she could concentrate hard enough—

She stared at it until her head ached. Then slowly, ever so slowly, the knob began to turn. Heat roared up inside her and her lungs burned from holding her breath. She ordered the lock to break.

And after a few more tense moments, it gave with a soft creak. A wave of elation washed over her. She'd opened it, lock and all. Her powers of telekinesis were growing stronger.

Kaitlyn released her pent up breath and wiped tears of happiness from her eyes. Excited that her faculties were in working order, she pushed the door open wide and wrinkled her nose at the strong earthy smell that enveloped her. Cold air chilled her limbs.

At first glance, the room seemed perfectly normal. It had been redone in the style favored by Susannah and Lyle Forrester, with a big four-poster bed, a sturdy chest of drawers, and a chifferobe wide enough to hold a closet full of clothes. The bed sported a green velvet duvet that matched the thick curtains and reminded Kaitlyn of Scarlet O'Hara's dress in *Gone with the Wind*. A small table sat next to the chifferobe. She took one step over the threshold, and was immediately bombarded by a flushed, nervous sensation. What in the world?

She stepped back into the hall. The rush of nerves ceased. Damn that Fabron.

She scowled. He had used a ward to guard the room. She wouldn't be able to go inside without overcoming it, or she might have a full-blown anxiety attack. That had happened to her once before. She raised her arms and cast a circle of protection around her body, murmuring, "As above, so below and all around. The circle is sealed."

Then, surrounded by a soft blue glow, she stepped into the room and focused on finding the source of her anxiety. Her eyes almost immediately zeroed in on a small leather bag on the dresser. She hurried over to it and picked it up. It contained dirt, which had to have come from his *gris gris*, and what looked like crushed bone, and gave off an odd, fetid odor. She wrinkled her nose. Damp earth, death and…blood? A cold chill ran over her. She dropped the bag on the dresser and shook off the frightening idea forming in her mind.

No point in speculating. She would worry about Fabron later. Right now, she needed to concentrate on

conjuring up Lyle and Susannah Forrester. The blue bubble enlarged and moved with her as she centered herself in the middle of room and arranged the three pieces of quartz in the form of a giant triangle on the polished wooden floor. Then she knelt beside it, opened the bag of salt, and poured a circle around her for extra protection.

She put down the bag and took a moment to free her mind.

When she was finally ready, she called out, "Susannah?"

Silence.

Kaitlyn closed her eyes and focused. "Susannah, are you there?

The room grew so quiet it was downright eerie. She remained motionless, hoping to convince the ghost she wasn't a threat — even though in reality she was.

"Lyle?" She didn't want to see him, but she had to banish him, too. Remy and Gillian wanted them both out of the house. "Hello?"

Nothing moved. There was no sound.

"Are you in here?" Kaitlyn asked, beginning to wonder if she was going to make contact. *"Please don't let him hurt me."*

The softly spoken words whispered across Kaitlyn's skin like a puff of air. She jerked.

"He'll kill me if he discovers I have talked to you."

"Are you talking about Lyle?" Kaitlyn opened her eyes and stared at the triangle. A light mist had formed over it. "Come on, Susannah. Sit down and talk to me. You know I won't tell him."

"All he wants is my necklace. Never my love."

Susannah Forrester suddenly materialized within the triangle, holding out a magnificent blue stone that hung from her neck on a gold chain. Kaitlyn recognized it immediately as the Midnight Star, the infamous sapphire that Lyle had been after when he'd murdered Camille.

Kaitlyn swallowed. "You need to leave this place before he hurts you."

"*I can't do that.*" Susannah's eyes filled with tears. "*My babies –* "

Kaitlyn bit her lip. "I'm afraid you don't have a choice."

The ghost's skittish gaze landed on the bag of salt, and a panicked look crossed her face. She shook her head and began to back away. "*No! Please!*"

"If you go now, you'll be free of Lyle forever." Kaitlyn rose. She didn't know whether or not that was true, but she hoped Susannah would take the bait. "Wouldn't you like that?"

"*You know I would. But I can't leave Scarlet Oak without my children.*"

The haunted expression on Susannah's thin face tugged at Kaitlyn's heartstrings. After a brief hesitation, she gave in. "Okay. But hurry. We're running out of time."

Susannah whirled around in a swish of dark blue and called out, "*Children, come!*"

"*Mama, mama! Here we are!*" Three pairs of small feet pattered across the polished wooden floor, and the children latched on to her skirts.

Susannah turned to Kaitlyn and sent her a bleak smile. "*Now, I am ready.*"

Kaitlyn raised her arms and closed her eyes.

A strong wind began to blow through the room. She heard the swish of the curtains and the startling whir of the ceiling fan. Her hair blew into her eyes.

A soft feminine cry billowed on the breeze. The doorknob rattled. Kaitlyn waited another tense beat, and then opened her eyes. *Susannah and the children were gone.*

Relief soared through her. The wind ceased its blowing. She clutched her mother's necklace and drew in a deep, thankful breath. The wind had scattered the salt across the room. She smiled. That should bug the hell out of Fabron. Kaitlyn eased her hold on the jade pendant and watched the curtains settle back against the windows. Overhead, the ceiling fan gradually slowed its revolutions, and finally stopped.

She had done it. Susannah Forrester and her children were free of their torment. Warm satisfaction mixed with the anxiety filling her breast. They were gone, but Lyle Forrester still lurked nearby. Once he discovered his wife and little ones had been ripped free of his hold—

Kaitlyn shivered. He would become enraged. He was a man who thrived on being in control. It wasn't love that had made him steal the sapphire from Camille; it was greed. He'd wanted her body, so he'd taken it. The same with the Midnight Star. He considered his wife and children his property as well. What he wanted, he took; and what he had, he intended to keep. Forever. That's why he was so intent on reclaiming Camille's sapphire.

The doorknob rattled again, and Kaitlyn spun around. That was no spirit. Someone was inserting a key into the lock. She snapped up the pieces of quartz, lifted her chin, and planted her feet. Her hair stood on end.

The door opened. A man entered.

Etienne Fabron. Covered in dirt, walking stiffly, his hair and clothes in disarray. He looked like he hadn't slept in weeks.

He shut the door and raised his head. His weary gaze locked on Kaitlyn, who narrowed her eyes and stood staunchly in the center of the blue bubble of protection. His face darkened, and his flat black eyes suddenly snapped to life. He fisted his hands at his sides. His jaw tight, he stepped toward her. "What the hell are you doing in my room?"

"Just doing my job. What Remy and Gillian asked me to do here at Scarlet Oak."

His expression soured further. The smell of decaying flesh radiated from his body. He growled, "Get out."

With a brisk nod, she started for the door.

He blocked her path. "There won't be any more witchcraft in this house. Do you understand?"

"I have a job to do, Mr. Fabron," she snapped. "And I'm going to do it. *Understand*?" She couldn't keep the sarcasm from her tone as she took a wide berth around him and angled for the door. At the last minute, she realized she'd just made a grave error and stepped out of the circle.

He grabbed her arm, his bony fingers biting into her tender flesh. His rancid breath washed over her. "What have you done with Susannah?"

"Nothing she didn't want to do."

His eyes took on a demonic glint, and he gave an evil hiss. Fog swirled around them both. Kaitlyn tried to yank free of his hold, but he held her fast. She smelled death and dirt and the rank odor of formaldehyde. Concentrating all her powers on his hand, she broke his grip. He snarled.

All at once, the fog cleared.

And she found herself face to face with Lyle Forrester.

CHAPTER FIVE

Lyle's thin face flamed with fury. *"Get them back."*

"No," Kaitlyn leveled her gaze at him, raised her right hand, and drew another, stronger circle tight around her. Let him try to touch her now. "They left to get away from you."

"You have to do this," he growled. *"Susannah is my wife!"*

"She's scared of you."

"As she well should be," he boomed. His flat dark eyes narrowed to slits. *"And so should you. No woman is going to prevent me from finding that sapphire. It's my destiny."*

"Is that all you want? To find that stupid necklace?" Kaitlyn tempted fate and scoffed at him. "Greed is one of the seven deadly sins, you know."

"The sins of man don't concern me. I'm already condemned to hell."

"You should be concerned." His horrid breath made her gag. She gripped her necklace and murmured a curse. "Your sin put you where you are today."

"Bah. I demand that you to give me back my wife!"

"What about your children? Do you want them back as well?"

"Whiny brats." His face contorted with disgust. *"Yes. I know Susannah. She won't return to the house without them."*

"I'll do what I can." When hell froze over.

"You'll get them back or you'll go to your grave," he snarled. His glassy eyes radiated fury. *"And stay the hell out of my room."*

"This is Etienne Fabron's room."

"No, it is not. It's mine." Lyle's thin lips curled ominously. *"And so is he."*

"What do you mean?" Intrigued, she stood her ground.

He laughed and stroked his pencil thin mustache. *"Can't you tell with your supposed powers? Fabron and I are one and the same."*

Nausea swirled in the pit of her stomach. That was it—what had struck her as so odd about Fabron and his ward. His amazing transformation and Lyle's words confirmed it. Etienne Fabron was a Zombie. The walking dead.

Lyle continued to laugh. *"Scared of me now, witch?"*

"No." She raised her chin a notch. "Winning over a dead man takes no power."

"You know that is not the case. Fabron's black magic is all powerful. He's proving very useful for my purposes." His mocking tone halted and his face grew solemn. *"I want my wife back. By tomorrow, understand?"*

No way was she bringing Susannah and those poor children back into this dreadful house. They deserved a peaceful afterlife. She nodded and met his flat, dead eyes, as if she were going along with his crazy plan. She'd been in his room long enough. "Fine. Tomorrow."

"We'll be waiting." Lyle's mouth curved again with that sinister smile. *"Be gone, witch."*

Without another word, she put out her hand and visualized her circle closing into a purple ball of energy, and then it was gone. She turned and sailed out the door. Fury rose in her breast. She halted in the parlor and struggled to even out her breathing. How dare he challenge her powers with Fabron's impotent black magic?

The air near the stairs was cool and carried a pleasant lemon scent, but it wasn't enough to calm her racing nerves. She gripped the bag of salt and headed for her room.

Her fingers ached as she reached into her pocket and drew out the key. Kaitlyn unlocked the door and hurried inside. To keep out Fabron or anyone else who dared try to enter, she formed a circle around the perimeter of the room. Now she could relax.

The book of spells lay open on the bed, just as she'd left it. Her case was on the dresser. She put away the quartz and the salt and closed the book. As she moved about the room, her anger began to seep away bit by bit, leaving only a soul-deep weariness and physical fatigue. She needed sleep.

After consulting the alarm clock on the nightstand, she decided to call it a night. A yawn stretched her mouth as she undressed and donned her favorite cotton sleep shirt. It had a feminine cut and fell to the bottom of her hips. She felt more at home in it than in any fancy gown. As splashy as some of her clothes were, she preferred comfort.

The sheets on the bed were cool and welcoming. She stretched out and luxuriated in the fact that she had accomplished at least one of her goals tonight. Susannah and the children were finally out of the house. That left Lyle and Camille. Fabron was a complication she hadn't planned on; yet she was certain she could defeat him. She only had to find the right tools.

Her hand drifted to the jade pendant around her neck. The gold was cool against her skin. She never took off the necklace, and for good reason. Her mother had used it as a medium for gifting Kaitlyn not only with her powers, but also with her insight into using them. *As it harm none, do as ye will*, she had seared into Kaitlyn's mind. She smiled. She didn't plan to harm anyone, but she must defeat Lyle Forrester, who was inherently evil. Fabron was merely his puppet, a pawn in Forrester's sick game to reclaim the sapphire.

She closed her eyes. And unwittingly, her thoughts turned to Colin. She felt safe enough inside the circle, yet somehow she knew she would feel even more secure within the circle of his strong arms. He was smart and brave and innately, a good man. She pictured his taut, chiseled features and his sexy bare chest. She had to wonder what the rest of his muscular body looked like.

Heat suffused her body as she imagined strong thighs, a tight butt, and—

No. She would *not* go there. Not if she wanted to sleep tonight. She rolled over, and kept a picture of him prominent in her mind. She would never try to manipulate his free will. To do so would be go against everything in which she believed. But she would consider a quick spell to remove the obstacles keeping him from embracing the existence of her powers—if it became necessary. Right now, she would wait and see what developed. *For the good of all.*

*****

Colin woke up the next morning feeling rested, but cranky. He was angry with himself for letting Kaitlyn get so deep under his skin. He didn't even feel like humming in the shower, a habit he'd picked up during the months he'd lived with Maria. She'd found it fascinating. Now, even with her out of his life, he couldn't seem to quit. Until now.

He drew his brows together and yanked the towel off the rack. As he dried off, he thought about what else was bothering him. He'd never had heard back from Burl or the VCMO squad about the missing body. That, and Kaitlyn's insistence that he'd accompanied her to the cemetery last night, when he knew he hadn't. That was just a little too weird.

He wondered what had been in the note Kaitlyn had received from Scarlet Oak's owners. He'd been tempted to follow her to her room last night and demand she open it in front of him, but he hadn't had the guts. He didn't believe for a minute she was a real witch. Yet he could just imagine her embarrassing herself by trying to turn him into a toad, or worse, if he made her angry—and that would be downright humiliating.

Once he had dressed and shrugged into his shoulder holster, he put on his glasses and reached for his cell phone. Flexing his fingers, he punched in Burl's number. The lab tech didn't answer. With a sharp curse, Colin shrugged into his jacket and headed downstairs to breakfast.

Kaitlyn wasn't in the dining room. After last night's fiasco, he was glad. He checked his watch. It was almost eight-thirty. She still might show. He grabbed a plate and filled it quickly.

He'd just sat down when she walked in, her beautiful blonde hair still damp from the shower. Her face was fresh and clean and that fascinating jade pendant that dangled between her generous breasts made her eyes look as green as bottle glass.

Colin's body reacted instantly.

She spotted him, and strolled over to his table. "I thought you'd be finished with breakfast by now."

"Meaning, you hoped I would be."

"Well, to be honest—yes." A light blush stole over her cheeks.

He leaned back in his chair and studied the dark circles underscoring her eyes. She looked tired. He furrowed his brow. "Did you get any sleep last night?"

"Some." She looked uncomfortable. "I had a rather late night."

"Because of the note Fabron brought you?"

"No. Because I—" She broke off and shook her head. "Never mind. It's not important."

"If you say so."

"It's also none of your business." She shot him a withering look, and turned to eye the dwindling buffet. "I'd better grab some food while I can."

"You're welcome to join me if you like," he said, secretly hoping she wouldn't sit down. Her claim to witch fame irked him. Yet to his consternation, he was attracted to her. And he wanted to find out what she was hiding.

She backed away. "Thank you, but I don't think that would be a good idea."

"Come on, Kaitlyn. You know I don't bite."

"Do I really?" Her perfectly shaped eyebrows arched upwards and without another word, she spun on her heel and headed for the buffet.

His eyes immediately locked on her swaying backside. He shifted in his chair to offset the growing tumescence behind his fly. This was not good. Witch or no witch, Kaitlyn Chambers turned him on. To avoid watching her every move, he took a long swallow of orange juice and forced himself to concentrate on its sharp, fruity tang.

She filled her plate and sat down at a table across the room.

Both relieved and disappointed, Colin put down his glass and broke open a biscuit. He had to think about the case and forget his raging libido. It would be tough. But still—

His cell phone bleated, the sound startling him.

He jerked it from his pocket and checked the display. It was Burl. Finally.

Colin lifted the device to his ear. "Winter."

"Colin—good morning. How are you?"

"Fine, Burl. I tried to call you earlier, but you didn't answer. What news do you have for me?"

"Nothing you're gonna like." Burl sighed. "We still don't have the girl's body. And the sheriff's balking at our investigation, big time. Agent Samuels was about to phone you, but he was sent out on a bank robbery call that turned into a murder investigation. Totally fucked up my day."

Anger fired through Colin at the mention of the sheriff's lack of cooperation. He put down the biscuit and made a fist. "Boudreaux can't do that. This became a federal case the minute he suspected one or all of the first three dead girls was brought across state lines."

"That's what I told him. But hell, we don't have a clue where to start looking for the body. He's not being very forthcoming with any information."

"Start here."

"What do you mean?"

"Bring anyone the lab and VCMO can spare out to Scarlet Oak. There are some things in this house I want checked out." *Mainly, Mr. Etienne Fabron.* Colin eyed the door leading to the foyer, where the concierge usually lurked behind the desk. He saw no one, but knew the creep had to be around the house somewhere. "I have some prints I want you to lift. It's important."

"Okay, sure. I'll see you soon as I finish logging in evidence here. Should take me another half hour, tops."

"Thanks a lot, Burl." Colin ended the call, feeling like he was at least getting something done. Fabron had been printed when he'd been arrested, but something about this guy struck him as odd. He wanted to make sure he was who he claimed to be.

"Was that phone call about the case you're working?"

He looked up to see Kaitlyn standing beside him holding an empty coffee mug. She shifted nervously from foot to foot.

"Yes," he said with a frown. "What's the matter?"

"I need to talk to you about Mr. Fabron."

"Why?" Worry lanced through Colin. "Did something happen?"

"Well, I wasn't going to tell you this. But he accosted me last night when I—"

Colin came to his feet. "Did he hurt you?"

"No." She bit her lip. "It wasn't like that."

His cell phone rang again. Aggravated at the interruption, he cursed.

She stepped toward the buffet. "Go ahead. Take your call. I'll fill you in after I finish eating."

"All right." He snatched out the shrilling device. The display showed a number he didn't recognize. He met Kaitlyn's eyes. "Meet me in the foyer when you're done. I need to talk to Fabron myself."

She nodded and turned away.

He took the call. It was a wrong number. Frustration frayed his already thinly-stretched nerves as he watched Kaitlyn fill her coffee cup and return to her table. He shoved the phone back into his pocket. Damn it. Try as he might, he just couldn't get away from her. Not that he really wanted to—but he could never buy into that witchcraft mumbo jumbo, which meant their relationship could never go anywhere. He could never marry a witch.

Whoa. That idea brought him up short.

Who'd said anything about marriage? He shook his head to clear it, and glanced back at Kaitlyn. Yeah, he could see spending the rest of his life with her—*if* she didn't believe she was a witch. Which, of course, made any discussion of wedlock moot.

His brain raced with ways to torture himself as he stepped into the foyer.

Still no sign of Fabron. Colin drew his brows together, and suddenly noticed weak light spilling from a partially open door inside the library. Lucky for him, the room was empty.

He slipped across the ancient rug and peeked through the crack into a small office. Etienne Fabron sat in a brown leather chair behind a wide cherry desk, his head lolling on his scarred neck and his eyes rolled back like a pair of white marbles.

Alarm filtered through Colin. He knocked on the door. "Mr. Fabron?"

No answer.

Colin scowled. To hell with pleasantries. The concierge looked dead. He pushed the door open with a creak and said loudly, "Hey, Fabron—are you okay?"

The man's head jerked up and he snapped to attention. His flat black eyes zeroed in on Colin. He blinked and spread his hands on the desk as if bracing himself for an attack.

"Director Winter. May I—" He cleared his throat. "Excuse me. May I help you?"

"I saw you in here and became concerned. You looked…well…*strange.*"

"I was napping."

"I see. Okay. Long night?"

"You could say that." The concierge's thin lips curled up in the semblance of a smile. "I had a visitor in my room."

Colin's silence seemed to irk Fabron. He rose. "It was your old friend, Ms. Kaitlyn Chambers."

"In *your* room?" Now at least Colin knew why she looked so tired. She'd been with this ghoul. Fury churned in Colin's gut. "What the hell for?"

"What do you think?" The concierge cocked his dark head, reminding Colin of the raven that had stalked him and Kaitlyn at the cemetery. A fresh chill slid through him.

"Colin?" Kaitlyn's lilting voice broke into his ominous thoughts.

He spun to see her standing behind him in the middle of the library.

She looked from him to Fabron. "Are you two about finished?"

"Yes, we are," Fabron said, rounding the desk and hurrying toward the door. He pushed past Colin, leaving an odd, earthy odor in his wake. He walked over to Kaitlyn. "Are you here about what happened in my room last night?"

"No," she hissed. Her face turned red, and she eyed Colin. "I'm here to meet Director Winter."

"Yes, ma'am." Fabron bowed from the waist. "Whatever you say."

Colin stalked across the rug and took Kaitlyn's arm. "Let's go outside. We need to talk."

She went along, but he could tell she wasn't keen on the idea. Like she knew this conversation wasn't going to be pretty.

Warm, humid air washed over them the moment they stepped out the door onto the veranda. Thick gray clouds layered the morning sky.

Colin released her arm and glared down into her wary green eyes. "Okay. Spill. What the hell happened between you and Fabron last night? Tell me the truth."

"Nothing."

"Nothing, my ass." Despite his vow to keep his distance from her, he put his hands on his hips and got in her face. Her cheeks were candy apple red. "You and that weird little concierge have a nasty little secret, and I want to know what it is."

Her eyes widened to the size of saucers. "You're jealous of Etienne Fabron?"

"What happened in his room last night, Kaitlyn?"

"I conjured up a ghost."

"Excuse me?" Flummoxed, he stepped back. "What in the world for?"

"I talked to Susannah Forrester. She agreed to leave the house and take her children with her."

Colin blinked. She'd mentioned casting a spell before, but he hadn't imagined it would have been in the concierge's room, and that she would actually talk to a ghost. Or rather, *believe* she had talked to one. The manure was getting deeper by the minute. "I see."

"No, you don't," she blurted out, "I had go to his room, because it was once Lyle and Susannah's bedroom. I'd hoped to see all of them. But she and the children were the only ones I conjured up."

"That's the only reason you were in there?"

"Of course it was." She frowned. "Surely you don't believe I was in there *with him*." A visible shiver passed over her body. "Ewww! Gross."

"No. Still—" He shook his head. "I don't know you that well."

"You should know me better than that." She shot him a hot glare. "I've told you before that just being around Fabron makes my skin crawl. He's a Zombie, and they—"

"A what?"

"A Zombie. You know—the walking dead. Like in the movies."

"Let me get this straight. You're saying that Etienne Fabron is...not alive?" Colin's mind slid back to earlier, when he'd walked into the concierge's office and found him sprawled in his chair like he was dead. *No.* It couldn't be. He'd sat up and talked, even going so far as to badmouth Kaitlyn. And when he'd left the room, he'd bumped into Colin. Literally. Unnerved, Colin reached down and touched his forearm where Fabron had brushed it. "You and I both just saw him. He ran into me."

"Believe what you want." She shrugged. "But Lyle Forrester is living inside his body. That's how he's walking around and breathing."

"You actually expect me to believe that?"

"Not really." She lifted her chin. "But I would like you to help me."

"How?" He eyed her warily. What could she possibly want him to do?

Her lips curled in a wicked smile. "Well, last night I had a little trouble breaking into Fabron's room. So I thought that next time you might agree to—"

"You broke in?" Colin raised his eyebrows. "That's a crime."

"I didn't jimmy the lock, if that's what you mean. I used telekinesis."

Colin wagged his head. "This is all too bizarre. First you swear you're a witch, conjuring up ghosts. And now, you claim Fabron is a Zombie. I can't just accept this. I deal in facts, not myth."

"This is no myth. I *am* a witch, and he's dead."

"Yeah, right. And now you want me to believe you use telekinesis."

"It's one of my tools, like casting spells." She bit her lip. "I can't freeze time or see into the future, though. All witches are limited to some extent."

Especially if one only *thought* she was a witch. A very sweet, very beautiful and very smart witch. Colin crooked his lips. Despite Kaitlyn's claim to paranormal fame, he couldn't tear his eyes from her gorgeous mouth. His body tightened to the point of pain.

"Colin?"

"Huh?' He jerked his gaze up to her eyes.

She crossed her arms. "Do you believe me?"

"Kaitlyn—"

"You don't, do you?" She dropped her arms and began to pace along the edge of the veranda. The wind kicked up, enveloping them both in warm, moist air. "I knew it. I'm going to have to do something to convince you."

"You don't have to prove yourself to me."

She stopped pacing. "Don't I?"

"No."

She made a face at him and stepped off the veranda.

"Where are you going?" He started after her.

She whipped around. "For a long walk to clear my head. Alone, if you don't mind."

"Fine." He halted. "I get the picture."

"I'll just bet you do," she said. And then she was gone.

Colin frowned at her swaying backside until she disappeared around the corner of the house. She was fiery-tempered and beautiful. Not to mention delusional. Why in hell couldn't he stop thinking about her? He dragged a frustrated hand through his hair.

The door behind him opened, and Etienne Fabron stepped outside.

Colin scowled at him. "What do you want?"

"I'm going for a walk." The concierge gave him a wicked smile. "Through the cemetery."

"What's your fascination with that place?"

Fabron leered at him. "Let's just say I feel a certain . . . *connection* with the people there."

Colin stared at him with increasing trepidation. His skin had a deathly pallor, and his eyes looked...well, dead. And that strange, earthy smell that surrounded him—it couldn't be normal. Could it? Yet it had to be. Zombies didn't exist, except as the brainchild of those lunatic moviemakers in Hollywood. He frowned. "I'd like to ask you a few questions before you go, if you don't mind."

"Questions about what?" The concierge gave him a wary look.

"Your whereabouts the night I arrived."

Fabron drew himself up to his full height and still the top of his head only reached Colin's nose. "I was here working. Not that it's any of your business."

"It is my business." Reassured by the weight of the Glock in his shoulder holster, Colin stepped closer to the cocky little man. Again that strange, earthy odor swept over him. He fought the urge to gag. "I'm conducting an active investigation into the murder of four teenage girls. Do you know anything about their deaths?"

"You know I don't. I was arrested before, by your people—and then cleared. Why bring that up now?"

Colin adjusted his glasses and studied Fabron's sallow complexion more closely. The man's face was thin to the point of gauntness. Every bone was visible. His flat black eyes had no soul, and Colin could tell evil lurked there. Not death, as Kaitlyn claimed. The man was a psycho. "Do you like young girls, Fabron?"

"No. Not in *that* way. I'm no pervert."

"Do you enjoy torturing them and watching them die?"

"I've had enough of this conversation, Director Winter." Fabron backed away.

Colin smelled fear, so he moved in for the kill. "What'd you do with the last girl's body? It never made it to the morgue."

"I don't know what you're talking about."

"Do you practice Voodoo in the cemetery? I believe you refer to it as *Vodun*."

"Why are you asking me that?" Fabron nervously dampened his lips.

Bingo. Colin kept probing. "Those weird stick figures dangling from the trees, the cornmeal *veve* on the ground in the clearing. The *poteau-mitan* with all those black feathers. Someone's been performing rituals out there."

The concierge tried to show no reaction, but alarm flickered in his eyes.

Colin twisted his mouth. "That's right. I did my research."

"Then you know *Vodun* is extremely popular in New Orleans. Those rituals could have been performed by anyone looking for privacy."

"Here at Scarlet Oak?"

"Why not?" Fabron lifted a shoulder. "It's isolated, away from the city. Sinister, even."

"True enough." The thrill of the hunt stirred in Colin's gut. Eager to badger the man into yet another reaction, he tried another tactic. "But tell me—do you know the meaning of the word *caplata*? I believe they're called *masters of the left hand*—dabblers in black magic."

Colin was rewarded with the slight tensing of the concierge's face.

He leaned forward. "Are *you* a caplata, Mr. Fabron?"

The concierge didn't answer.

"*Caplatas* sometimes practice human sacrifice. Am I right?"

"I wouldn't know."

"Of course you wouldn't."

"I'm afraid I must be going now." Fabron backed away, toward the corner of the house nearest the cemetery. "I'm running late."

"Oh?" Colin lifted his eyebrows. "Do you have another date with the dead?"

Fabron blew out a disgusted breath. "You're insane, Winter."

"We'll talk later. For now, just make sure you leave Kaitlyn the hell alone. I mean it."

The concierge's dead eyes flickered to life. "Only if she stops bothering *me,* and interfering with my work. That could be hazardous to her health."

"That sounds like a threat."

"No threat. I just want her to be careful. That's all." The entity in Fabron's head screeched, making his skull feel like it was about to split wide open. He whirled around and headed for the Keep. It was broad daylight. Yet still he heard that familiar mantra echoing through his mind.

Find the sapphire. Kill the witch.

His legs wobbled as he stumbled over the uneven ground, drawn to the chilly brick room as if it was a magnet and he was a nail. The low gray clouds pressed down upon him. Drawing in another smothering dose of humid air, he began to sweat. After his chance encounter with Kaitlyn Chambers last night, he'd spent the next few hours digging beneath the bricks in the Keep, only to find a few old coins, a bent silver spoon and a weathered gold locket, none of which had any real value.

Find the sapphire. Kill the witch.

"Damn it," he snarled, shaking his head hard from side to side. "I'm trying to find the stone!"

He yanked open the outer Keep door and plunged into the musty darkness. His hand shook as he reached for the light cord and gave it a tug. With a loud *pop*, the light blew out.

Fabron hit the ground. The edge of a brick bit into his cheek, and his breath came out in ragged pants. What was that?"

Get up, fool. It was nothing.

Dust entered Fabron's nose. He sneezed. With trembling hands, he pushed himself onto his knees. The cord above his head swayed back and forth like a pendulum. The bulb above his head was out. Damn it. He was a fool.

His flashlight lay on the floor near where he'd finally stopped digging in the wee hours of the morning. Turned up bricks lay scattered about, dirt heaped haphazardly on top of them like he had done a piss-poor job of hiding them. He had dug into the soft loam without rhyme or reason. His fingers ached now with the memory.

Find the sapphire. Kill the witch.

He snatched up the flashlight and flipped it on. Its weak white beam illuminated an arc of dirt surrounding him. He drew in the substance's rich, ripe scent and felt a sudden jolt of energy.

He picked up his spoon and began to dig. The bricks came up more easily now, after the difficulty he'd had with the first one last night. Flip a brick, dig beneath it. If the sapphire was buried in the soft dirt, it wouldn't be too deep even after all these years. The floor had protected it.

He worked faster and faster, until his arm muscles ached and his legs went numb from kneeling on the rough bricks. He ripped one of his fingernails to the quick, and pain flared in his hand. He cursed. Then he sucked away the blood. Refreshing.

The entity in his head laughed. *Keep digging.*

A flame of desperation burned within Fabron and he dug like a man possessed—which, of course, he was. Sweat rimmed his brow. He had to keep the entity in his head happy, or he would die a horrible death.

"What on earth are you doing?"

The shrill female voice disturbed his fevered reverie. He dropped the spoon and bolted up.

"Mr. Fabron?" Kaitlyn Chambers stood just inside the open Keep door, her eyes wide. "Are you all right?"

He longed to dig a hole and bury himself in the freshly turned earth.

She dropped to her haunches beside him and touched his sweaty arm. The heat of her fingers seared him. "Mr. Fabron?"

"I'm fine," he rasped, hoping she'd just go away. He shrugged off her hand and reached for the spoon. But before he could restart his digging, the entity in his mind rose up and shrieked.

Kill her!

Etienne turned his head slowly and peered into her wary green eyes. A wave of strength infused him. His lips curled into a sneer.

She frowned, the motion darkening her pretty face. "Why are you acting like this?"

He put his hand on the back of her neck, and the odor of dirt rolled over her. His cold fingers bit into her flesh and she felt her energy seeping out. Slowly, like blood being sucked through a tube. With a shriek of disgust, she jerked free of his hold and quickly formed a circle of protection around herself. He lunged after her, and was deflected by it.

Kaitlyn leapt to her feet and, encircled by her bubble of safety, dashed outside into the dreary light. Fabron's frustrated growl followed her as she sprinted through the overgrown grass toward the corner of the house. She paused in the shadows of a spreading oak to make sure he wasn't on her heels. The yard was empty.

She stood there for moment to catch her breath. Wind whispered through the leaves overhead as she gulped in the heated air and ordered her racing heart to slow. Perspiration dripped down her back. The clouds overhead seemed lower than before, making her feel boxed in. She wiped her face with trembling hands and started to turn away, when Fabron opened the Keep door.

Wary of him despite her armor of protection, she backed deeper into the shadows. The jade necklace around her neck gave her comfort.

He didn't come after her. Didn't say a word. Instead, he merely halted on the threshold, his eerie black eyes sparking with the need for blood.

She turned and dashed for the front door, hoping it was still unlocked. Her sweaty hand slipped off the doorknob. She gripped it with both hands, and it turned. Kaitlyn stepped inside and locked the door behind her. Her heart banged against her ribs. Finally catching her breath, she leaned against the wall and bid her circle go. It vaporized in the palm of her hand.

She murmured a curse. She should have known better than to approach Fabron, but she was looking for some way to convince Colin that the concierge really was a Zombie. Bad idea.

She walked through the foyer to the back of the house and pulled back the curtain on one of the ballroom windows. Her pulse settled back into its normal rhythm as she peeked across the yard toward the Keep door. Fabron had disappeared. Low gray clouds bunched on the horizon, and thunder rumbled in the distance.

She knew she was safe, yet an icy chill ran down her spine.

Colin. Just thinking about him conjured up an image of warmth and safety. She imagined burrowing into that hard chest and feeling his steely arms wrap around her. No one could touch her then. Not Etienne Fabron and certainly not the hooligans in her hometown wanting to banish her because she dared cast a spell for the protection of area school children. Her cheeks flamed, and she struggled to contain the desire that suddenly swept over her. Knowledge of how Colin felt about her craft warred with the passion she felt for him inside her heart.

If only he could get past the fact that she was a witch. Once he gave her his trust, she could turn to him and ask for his help, should she need it. Now, she didn't dare. He would only scoff at her.

She let the curtain fall and wiped a trickle of sweat from her temple. The house was cool, but the oppressive heat outside and her dash away from the Keep made her swelter inside. And for the first time, she glanced at her surroundings and discovered she was alone in a room that crawled with vibrant spirits. The curtains were made of rich copper-colored velvet and the original oak floor, an intricate pieced design, gleamed like it was brand new. An enormous portrait of a stoic couple graced the wall above a beautiful grand piano. Her breath caught. The man and woman had to be Lyle and Susannah Forrester. She recognized Susannah from meeting her spirit in Fabron's room last night.

She stepped back. Lyle's eyes seemed to follow her.

Unease rose inside her chest. She was ready to go to her room to retrieve her sage wand and lighter. This room needed to be smudged as well.

A clanging to her right told her that the door on that wall led to the kitchen. She drew in the delicious odors of frying catfish and sliced lemons. Another pot clanged. The low murmur of voices accompanied the sound of bubbling grease and the occasional *whump* of a knife.

Eager to stay clear of Fabron, she reentered the hallway and tiptoed up the stairs. She'd only taken a few steps when a loud thud from the foyer drew her attention. She edged back down the stairs and peered toward the front door. Colin and another man stood just inside while a third man holding a small black case sauntered past them on his way to the desk. Colin closed the door and followed him.

"Any particular surface?" the man asked him, setting the case on the tall desk. The third man opened it.

"All of them, including those inside the office." Colin motioned toward the library. "It's through there. Fabron works in this entire area."

"And you really suspect him in the murders?"

"You know how it works, Burl." Colin twisted his lips. "Right now, everyone's a suspect. Including Fabron.

He was cleared in the earlier murders, but he gives me bad vibes."

Kaitlyn gasped. Her hand quivered as she pressed her fingertips to the spot on her neck where Fabron had touched her. It burned like she held a match to it. She jerked her hand away.

A shiver roamed over her skin. Good thing she had evoked a circle.

Colin turned and met her eyes, almost as if he'd expected to see her standing there. His gaze turned hot, and her nerve endings tingled in response.

"Kaitlyn," he called. His deep voice was suddenly gruff. "Why don't you join us?"

Her face heated, and she considered continuing on to her room. But then she thought better of it and descended the last step.

Colin introduced her to his associates. She watched intrigued as, under Colin's direction, the two crime scene technicians lifted fingerprints from every available surface in Etienne Fabron's workspace. They printed the doorknobs, the front desk and several surfaces in the library before disappearing into the tiny office. Kaitlyn folded her arms and stepped over to Colin.

"You really believe Mr. Fabron might have killed those girls?"

"It's a possibility, even though he was cleared earlier in the case. We had a nice little chat on the veranda after you left for your walk. I called the U.S. Attorney, and he gave us a warrant."

"I see. Your conversation with Fabron must not have taken very long." Debating whether or not to tell him about her latest encounter with the creepy concierge, she swallowed. The movement made her throat hurt.

He cocked his head. "Why do you say that?"

"I just saw him inside the Keep a few moments ago."

Colin looked confused. "Where's that?"

"It's a small round brick room off the kitchen with both an inside and outside entrance. Remy told me that long ago it was used to store ammunition, food and other supplies."

"I see. Go on."

"Fabron was in there just now. Digging."

"*Inside* the house?" Colin frowned.

She nodded. "He was pulling up bricks and digging beneath them with a big spoon. Frantically, like he was possessed. Which, of course, he is."

"Did he see you?"

"Yes. He—he touched my neck before I thought to call up a circle of protection." Her hand flew to the spot where Fabron had squeezed her tender skin. Her worried eyes locked with Colin's intense brown gaze. "Then he lunged at me, like he was going to grab me. I called up a circle which kept him away, and I ran like hell."

"That son of a bitch."

"He didn't hurt me."

"Maybe not, but I bet he wanted to." Colin's expression turned fierce, and he gripped her elbow. "I'm just glad you didn't give him the chance. Did he follow you?"

"I don't think so. I haven't seen him since I reentered the house."

"He must be looking for that damned sapphire." He murmured a curse and released her arm.

She edged closer to him. "Legend has it that the Keep is where Lyle and Camille used to meet for their illicit trysts. It might even be where he killed her."

"Fabron must know that."

"Yes." Kaitlyn nodded. "And he would realize that Lyle probably hid the Midnight Star there. So it's a safe bet to assume I interrupted Fabron's search for the stone."

"Yes. Or there could be a more ominous reason why he tried to grab you." Colin drew his brows together. "Have you ever seen him practicing Voodoo?"

A frisson of dismay slid through her. "Do you mean *Vodun*?

"Vodun. Voodoo." He shrugged. "I'm referring to all those strange items near the cemetery. The weird wind chimes, the blood in the bowl, the *poteau-mitan*. The *veve*, those four dead girls —"

Kaitlyn's dismay turned into alarm. "You think he sacrificed them to his *loa*?"

"His what?"

"His god."

"Yes." Colin bobbed his head. "We're looking into it."

The man Colin had introduced as Burl came out of the office, followed by Peter, a member of the local VCMO squad, who was holding an empty soda can. "We've picked up all the prints we can find, and we discovered this in the trash." He held out the can.

Colin grinned. "DNA."

"Yep." Peter said. "Plenty of saliva."

"Did you clean up the powder?"

"As best we could, without a vacuum."

"Just wanted to make sure. We need to keep this under wraps as best we can."

"Fabron doesn't know you're doing this?" Kaitlyn eyed Colin warily.

"Not yet. And I'd like to keep it that way until we have the results from AFIS and match his prints to those taken at the crime scene. On the bowl, the *poteau-mitan*, and the girl's body, once we find it. We'll probably find his DNA in the database, too."

She tilted her head. "What does AFIS mean?"

"AFIS Is the Automated Fingerprint Information System. Fabron should be in that and CODIS after being arrested by two of our agents. We'll know soon enough if we have a definite match."

"You will." Kaitlyn was sure of it.

Colin's intense gaze pinned her to the floor. "We know he's Fabron, but do you really believe he's connected with these crimes?"

She nodded. "I do."

"Maybe that explains his odd behavior."

"It might. But I have another theory, one you probably won't believe." She turned away.

He edged closer to her. "Try me."

"No. Not now." She flicked her gaze at the crime scene technicians lurking nearby. No thanks. When she voiced her new theory out loud, she didn't want an audience.

Colin frowned. "All right. But after they leave, I want to hear it." He turned to Burl and Peter. "Run the prints through Interpol too, just in case."

"Will do," Burl said.

"Thanks for your help," Colin said. "I appreciate your coming out here so quickly."

"No problem. I'll call you as soon as I have something." The crime scene tech pressed his mouth into a thin line. "What about the sheriff? Have you talked to him?"

"Haven't been able to reach him. He's not answering his phone. I'll call the U.S. Attorney in New Orleans later today, and see what she recommends. We need that body."

Burl motioned to Peter. "Let's get out of here before he finds something else for us to do."

"Always trying to avoid work." Colin kept his face deadpan.

"You've got us pegged." Peter laughed and turned to Kaitlyn. "Nice to meet you, Ms. Chambers. Wish the circumstances were better."

"Me, too." She stood next to Colin as the two lab techs walked out the door. Once it shut behind them, she said, "I should cast a wishing spell over them, just for luck."

"To ensure the prints at the crime scene match Fabron's?"

"It couldn't hurt."

"Wouldn't help, either," Colin said with a sharp laugh. "It'd be about as helpful as saying 'cross my heart and hope to die'."

Kaitlyn knew he had said it in fun, but still it hurt. She narrowed her eyes. "Don't say that too loud. Wishes often come true."

With that barb flung between them, she spun on her heel and left him standing there, gaping at her like a landed fish. She hurried up the stairs and through the parlor to her room. Beads of perspiration dotted her lip as she unlocked her door. The room was too warm. She adjusted the thermostat on the wall.

Leave Lyle alone. Do you hear me?

Breathless, Kaitlyn spun around.

A woman with skin the creamy shade of creamy café au lait stood in front of the window. She took a step forward. *"Please. I can't bear it if you send him away."*

"Camille?" Kaitlyn blinked. The woman looked like she was made of flesh and blood, yet her face had a pale, ghostly aura. "Is that you?"

"Yes. Lyle lives on inside this house, as do I. Please do not disturb him. With his wife gone, I have another chance at love. I must either take it, or lose what little existence I have left."

"Lyle is evil. Greed rules his life. He killed you because you wouldn't give him the Midnight Star. Don't you remember?"

Camille's hands flew to her neck. *"The sapphire."*

"Yes," Kaitlyn said. Her body trembled with excitement as she realized she was conversing with another ghost. It was incredible. She met the murdered woman's pleading gaze. "Your life meant nothing to him. All he could think about was that blue stone."

The woman's dark eyes filled with sorrow. *"He regrets that now."*

"You're wrong." Kaitlyn edged closer to her ethereal visitor. "He's still searching for the sapphire. He told me so himself."

"He wouldn't do that."

"That's why he's still here. He wants to take it with him into the afterlife. He believes it will help him live forever."

"No!"

"You took it back, though. And you hid it. Didn't you?" Kaitlyn watched the other woman's face carefully. "After you killed the Forrester children."

"Susannah killed her own little ones."

"That's not true." Kaitlyn laughed nervously. "But that's what you want everyone to believe. You took over Susannah's body that night. *You* killed those children."

"Liar!" Camille screeched, her face contorting with rage.

She flew at Kaitlyn, who fended her off with a searing stare.

"No!" Camille cried. And before Kaitlyn could finish, the ghost disappeared in a thick white cloud. The curtains moved, but there was no other sign she had ever been there.

Kaitlyn blinked in dismay.

"You'll never banish me." Camille's bitter words swirled through the air, even though she was nowhere to be seen. *"No matter how hard you try. I'm not leaving this house without Lyle."*

"We'll just see about that," Kaitlyn muttered as an icy shiver rolled through her. She stalked over to her suitcase and drew out her book of spells. These recalcitrant ghosts were testing her patience. She needed to learn a few new tricks if she was going to get all of them out of the house. They were a challenge, yet she had every confidence she would succeed.

She was a witch, after all.

CHAPTER SIX

Etienne Fabron wiped the sweat from his burning eyes and limped out of the Keep. He wanted to sneak in through the kitchen and wind his way back to his office via the dining room, but the place was crawling with the staff preparing dinner. He would have to go around.

Thunder rumbled in the distance as he stepped through the tall grass. Darkness was falling, and deep shadows lurked beneath the trees. As he trudged past them, the wind stirred the leaves above his head. He cursed. He was bone tired and sick to death of digging.

The ever-elusive Midnight Star was still out of his reach, even though he'd turned up every brick in the Keep and dug for hours. His pocket jingled with the handful of shiny coins he'd unearthed. His joints ached, and he knew he'd be smelling dirt for days. Yet he was still empty handed. No sapphire.

The entity in his head stirred to life as he let himself into the house. Etienne gritted his teeth and halted just inside the door. Solidifying his thoughts, he squashed the being's weak attempt to scold him. Both of them were too tired to fight right now.

The odor of fried fish hung in the air, and he suddenly realized he was famished. He went to his room and cleaned up, and then made his way to the kitchen and

asked the chef subbing for Gillian for an early plate. The
man was clearly perturbed. Yet he did as Etienne asked.

Etienne took the plate and headed into the foyer. To
his relief, both it and the library were empty. He ducked
into his office and shut the door. One look around, and
he knew his space had been violated. The odor of cologne
hung in the air and he felt an odd heaviness. A spirit of
anger and subterfuge. He put down the plate and eyed
the light sheen of white powder the offenders had tried to
clean up. Luckily for him, they'd done a sloppy job.
Anger rushed in to replace his fatigue. *Winter was
responsible for this.*

Etienne gritted his teeth as the entity roared past his
defenses.

*I told you to kill him and the witch. Your delaying tactics
may cost you your life.*

"You gave me two days." Etienne's temples
throbbed. "I've already tried for the witch once—"

And you failed.

"I know I did." He tried to swallow around the
lump in his throat. "I'll try again tonight."

*Don't fail me this time, or you'll pay the price. Do you
hear me?*

A sharp pain lanced through Etienne's scarred neck.
He cried out and clutched at it with both hands. "Stop it!
Ow!"

The stabbing pain was immediately replaced by a
burning sensation. The entity purred. *You have until
tomorrow at midnight to take care of both of them.
Understand?*

"Y-yes," Etienne rasped, desperate for the stinging to
cease. He'd promise anything—

Don't make this an idle promise, my friend. Do it!

"I will." He went rigid and squeezed his eyes shut as the stinging intensified. Sweat rolled down his back. "Please! I can't take any more."

The entity laughed, the sound like teeth tearing at Etienne's raw flesh. *You can, and you will — when and if the time is right. Do what I say, and you'll enter eternity sated and happy. It's what we all want, now, isn't it?*

Etienne's eyes flew open. He wasn't ready to enter eternity. He had to find that damned sapphire and finish living the life Garner Reboulet had tried to end. A knot of apprehension lodged in his gut. With effort, he broke the entity's tight grip on his psyche. Yet he couldn't get the damned thing out of his head, and he wasn't sure he wanted to. He found the being's taunts extremely motivational.

He wiped his face with the hem of his shirt and dropped heavily into his desk chair as the stinging in his neck slowly eased. His breathing grew more regular, but his head swam with images of Kaitlyn fleeing the Keep. The white powder coating the desk mocked him. And for that, Colin Winter and that damned witch would pay.

Etienne dragged the plate of cold food across the desk and forced himself to choke it down. He had to move before the FBI ran those prints and Winter went into action, so he would need his strength. No more playing tug of war with the entity in his skull. He would complete his task, find the sapphire, and finally be free.

"*Lyle?*"

The silky female voice startled him. He looked up to see a beautiful mocha-skinned woman in a classic dark green gown standing in front of the desk. Her face had a ghostly aura. Still, he knew her immediately.

"Camille," he said with a smile. He put down his fork.

Her lips curved in a brittle smile. *"I know you remember me, Lyle."*

"My name is Etienne. We are related."

"No, you're Lyle Forrester. You did this to me." She lowered her collar to reveal a series of dark bruises ringing her delicate neck. *"You murdered me – and stole my necklace."*

"I did not!" Anger flooded Etienne. He surged to his feet. "I'm trying to get the sapphire back. Lyle Forrester took it from our family—"

"You took it from me." She stared deep into Etienne's eyes. *"Didn't you, Lyle?"*

The entity inside Etienne's skull stirred back to life and began to shriek like a madman. Etienne's eyes watered. His head rang with the awful noise, and he lost his breath. Desperate to make the being shut up, he slapped his hands to his temples and squeezed. A red haze blinded him.

"Well, well, well." The woman's bitter laugh cut deep into his soul. *"You do know me. I'm Camille, the woman you killed so you could get your greedy hands on the Midnight Star. My legacy."*

"I want that damned stone," Etienne snapped, spittle dripping off his lips. His knees wobbled. He was desperate to regain control of his traitorous body. "Give it to me."

"I don't have it. You do."

"No, I don't."

"You stole it from around my neck," she snapped. *"Don't you remember?"*

"No. Give it to me!" he screamed, determined to get the sapphire. To keep it, he'd have to oust the entity from his head. Maybe if he shouted loud enough, it would leave. He squeezed his skull between his hands until pain radiated down his neck and the thought his spine might crack.

Camille laughed at him. *"Not in this lifetime. Oh, wait — you're already past this life. Aren't you?"*

Etienne ground his teeth.

"Why did you do it, Lyle?" Her voice softened. *"Why did you kill me? I would have done anything for you."*

"You wouldn't give me the necklace," the entity snapped. The words came from Etienne's mouth, yet he hadn't said them. He stared at Camille in dismay.

Her haunted eyes filled with tears. *"You told me you would leave your wife."*

"I asked you to give me the sapphire," the entity repeated. "You wouldn't. Not even after we became lovers."

"I would have, if you hadn't stayed married to Susannah."

"I couldn't just leave her."

"That's right. Without her, you were nothing. It was her money that kept you in high cotton."

"She was my wife."

"Yet you made love to me."

"You were…convenient." Stunned to hear more of Lyle's cruel words coming from his mouth, Etienne covered it with his hand and backed toward the wall.

Camille pulled out a white lace handkerchief and dabbed at her cheeks. *"I wanted you to love me. But all you loved was that jewel. You still value it over your very soul."*

The entity in Etienne's head began to shriek. He gritted his teeth and pressed himself against the wall. His whole body quaked with fear. Sweat rolled down his brow.

"Stop it!" he shouted, rubbing his temples with shaking hands. He opened his eyes. Camille was gone. Thank God. He ground his teeth and said sharply, "She's not here any more. Shut up!"

With one last shriek, the entity finally quieted.

Etienne's heart hammered like an overworked engine. Still shaking, he slid down the wall until his butt met the floor. His clothing clung to his damp skin. He could smell himself, and the odor wasn't pretty. He raked both hands through his disheveled hair.

Voices from the foyer startled him.

He jerked his frantic gaze to the door. He had to get out of here and find a hiding place; at least until he could find the sapphire and get the damned entity out of his head. Someplace Colin Winter would never look—and where Etienne could bring the witch once he grabbed her. Killing her inside the house wasn't a good idea.

A door slammed.

Fear skittered over Etienne's clammy skin. He rose on unsteady legs and staggered into the library and to the window overlooking the side yard. His hands slipped as he unlocked it, but he finally made the latch move and pried the window open. Clammy, fish-scented air rolled over his skin.

His stomach bucked. Taking one last look around, he slithered over the windowsill and slinked out into the darkness.

*****

Kaitlyn shook off a bout of uneasiness as she tucked the small leather pouch of herbs into her pocket and scurried through the parlor to Colin's room. She hated asking him for help, but she didn't want to venture outside alone. Not in this terrifying place.

She took a deep breath and knocked on his door.

He pulled it open. A startled smile creased his handsome face. "Kaitlyn, I didn't expect to see you again so soon. Hello."

"Hi," she said, her heart jumping at the sight of him. She peered past him into the room. "Am I interrupting anything?"

"Not unless you count interfering with my curiosity." He laughed. "I was about to go outside and check the property. But it can wait."

"No." She gnawed her lip. "I need to go outside myself, but I don't want to go alone after what happened with Mr. Fabron. I was hoping you'd go with me."

"I see." He eyed her warily. "More witch business?"

"Yes. I need to return to the Keep, but I don't want the kitchen help to know what I'm doing. So I need to go around the house and enter from the other door." She swallowed. "I'm hoping to run into Lyle and Camille. Now that it appears Susannah is gone, they may be together."

"And you don't want to meet up with Fabron again by mistake."

"Exactly." She shivered as she remembered the concierge's attack inside the Keep. Her eyes locked with Colin's. "So you'll go with me?"

"On one condition," he said softly, his warm gaze dropping to her mouth.

Moisture pooled low in her belly, and she went still. "What's that?"

"That you don't perform your hocus pocus in front of me."

His words were like a slap. Her desire fled. "I wouldn't think of making you uncomfortable. Just get me there. You can wait outside while I contact the spirits."

"That should work. Give me a second."

She waited while he pulled on his shoulder holster and shrugged into a dark gray jacket. With him, even that small movement was sexy. Her passion for him returned, and suddenly it didn't seem to matter that he had just insulted her. She couldn't take her eyes off him.

"Isn't it a little warm for a coat?"

"Yeah, but I don't want to advertise the fact that I'm armed." He stepped out into the parlor and shut the door. "Ready?"

"Yes." She jerked her gaze off his handsome face and turned away.

The house was eerily silent as they walked onto the shadowy landing and descended the stairs. Colin paused when they entered the foyer.

Kaitlyn halted beside him. Her nerve endings prickled. "What's the matter?"

"When was the last time you saw Fabron?"

"In the Keep, when he tried to grab me." She folded her arms as another chill passed through her. The concierge wasn't behind the desk, thank goodness. And she hadn't seen him lurking in the library. "I haven't seen him since. And believe me, I don't want to."

"That's totally understandable." Colin pressed his lips together and stepped into the library.

Kaitlyn reluctantly followed him as he angled across the rug toward the office door.

"He's got problems," Colin said. "And if he discovered we dusted for prints—"

Kaitlyn's nerves thrummed as he opened the office door and peeked inside.

"Damn it," he said, shoving the door all the way open. "He's been in here, all right. But he's long gone now."

"How can you tell he was here?" She stepped up to the door.

Colin pointed out the empty plate on the desk. "That wasn't there before."

"Oh, my." A warm gust of bayou-scented air slid over Kaitlyn's skin. She turned and eyed the open library window. Her stomach turned over. She pointed. "Look, Colin—he went out that way."

"Son of a bitch." Colin walked over to it. "Wonder where he went?"

"Probably either back to the Keep or to visit his favorite killing ground." Remembering the blood soaking into the sandy soil, she swallowed.

Colin shut the window and flipped the lock. Then he grabbed her hand. "Come on. Let's see if we can find him."

The sudden contact startled Kaitlyn. His hot callused palm sent a delicious tingle up her arm. She went along with him readily, her heart pounding like she'd just run a mile.

He led her past the stairs and back into the ballroom. "We can see the Keep door from here."

Kaitlyn struggled to regain her composure.

He let go of her hand and pulled back the thick draperies.

She swallowed. "Do you see a light on inside the Keep?"

Colin leaned against the window frame and peered out into the darkness. "Can't tell. Looks like the door is closed."

"He may be inside."

"I'm sure he is." Colin pushed away from the window. "But if he tries to get back inside the way he went out, he's out of luck."

"Why would he go out the window when he has the run of the house?"

"Probably because he spotted the fingerprint powder." Colin bobbed of his head toward the library. "That told him we're hot on his trail."

"So he ran. That means he really is a murderer." A knot formed in the center of her chest.

Colin nodded. "I'd bet my life on it."

"Please don't say that." She grabbed his hand. "He's dangerous and well versed in Vodun. He could hurt you."

"Would that bother you?" He laced his fingers with hers and held on tight.

Another warm tingle spread up her arm as she peered up into his intense chocolate eyes. "Yes. It would bother me very much."

"Good," he murmured, his searing gaze dropping to her lips.

The moisture in her belly began to sizzle. He had the ability to melt her into a smoldering mass with just one long, heated look. The coarse feel of his hand in hers only made it worse. Drawn by a power much stronger than her good sense, she leaned toward him and closed her eyes. The expectation of his kiss made her quiver from head to toe.

"We need to go." His brusque voice startled her.

Her eyes flew open. He abruptly released her hand and turned toward the door.

Shock filtered through her. Pressing her hand fingers to her mouth, she stumbled after him. How stupid was she to think he wanted to kiss her again? He'd made it clear last night and again this morning that he didn't like her claim of being a witch. So he wouldn't get involved.

Cursing herself over and over for being a fool, she lifted her chin and got a grip on her emotions. No way was she letting him know how much his rejection had hurt. She made a fist and trailed him into the empty foyer.

To her surprise, he opened the front door and paused on the threshold. "I'm going to try to talk to Fabron."

"By yourself?"

"Yes, unless you want to come along." He eyed her warily. "I didn't figure you'd want to venture out in the dark since you checked out the keep from the window."

"I'm game if you are," she said. He wasn't going to scare her with his talk of Fabron. She slipped past him onto the veranda, making sure he got another good whiff of the delicious lavender scent she'd spritzed on her neck before leaving her room.

He shot her a dangerous glare.

She fielded it calmly and marched down the steps. "Coming?"

Colin caught her not-so-subtle innuendo, and it sent his libido racing into overdrive. He gritted his teeth so hard it hurt. It had taken every ounce of his willpower not to kiss her, and now he felt the urge to wrap his arms around her and spirit her off into the darkness. A hot tryst out in the open was just what the doctor ordered.

On the other hand—she believed she was a witch. He shook his head. Supernatural beings casting spells simply did not fit into his neat, orderly world. He needed a normal woman, one with Kaitlyn's warm, ripe curves. With a sweet, delicious mouth, and skin as smooth as alabaster.

His eyes remained riveted on her perfectly proportioned backside as she preceded him through the night. He could tell himself over and over that he wasn't interested in wooing her, but his body had other ideas. Just being close to her these last few minutes had made him hard as stone.

Damn it. He halted in the shadows and quickly adjusted himself. Just as he started off again, a shrill scream echoed through the darkness. Colin jerked his hand off his fly and grabbed Kaitlyn's arm, pulling her against him for protection.

Her warm breath bathed his neck. "Wh-what was that?"

"A bobcat, probably." Starkly aware of her soft, quivering body next to his, he stared toward the bayou. "Or maybe some unfortunate little animal caught by a gator."

She shuddered.

"It's okay." Unable to help himself, he stroked his hands down her smooth back. She smelled so sweet. Was that lavender? He pressed a gentle kiss to the crown of her head.

The wind whispered through the trees. He looked up, and noticed a web of lightning lacing the horizon. A low rumble of thunder sent blood thundering through his veins.

Kaitlyn shifted away from him. He longed to draw her back into the circle of his arms, but he didn't dare. This was no doubt payback for his refusing to kiss her in the ballroom. So he let her go.

She stared out into the night. "I don't hear anything else. It must be safe to go on."

"Yeah." He adjusted his glasses. "Guess it is."

She turned and continued on the path around the house. Thunder rolled again as Colin fell in step behind her. Dark shadows loomed beneath a low-hanging oak at the corner. He edged closer to Kaitlyn as they rounded the Keep so she'd feel more at ease.

"It's so dark out here," she said, her voice carrying a quiver of uncertainly.

He glanced up as they walked. More clouds had moved in. "There's no moon."

"Yes. It's called a new moon."

He smiled, and zeroed in on a loud splash from the bayou.

"Oh my God." Kaitlyn suddenly halted, and he ran right into her. The hairs stood up on the back of his neck.

Her hand shook as she pointed dead ahead. "Look!"

He gripped her shoulders and peered past her into the thick darkness. A thin stream of light seeped from beneath the Keep's painted door.

"He's in there all right. Digging. He must have just started."

Colin gave her shoulders a light squeeze. "Go back to the house."

"No!" She shrugged free of his hold. "I want to see you catch him."

"I'm not going to arrest him tonight. I have no evidence."

"But you said—"

"If we get a hit on the prints and can match them to with those taken from the crime scene, we'll bring him in for questioning. Otherwise, we have no lawful reason to detain him."

"Oh." She gripped the pendant hanging from her neck.

Colin stepped around her. "Wait here. I'm going to see what he's doing."

"I thought you were going to talk to him."

"I might." He gave her arm a squeeze. "Depends on what he's up to. Be back in a minute."

The brick wall beside him offered some protection as he approached the door, but on the other side he had no cover. He clenched his jaw and tramped on through the tall grass, wondering why in hell Remy hadn't seen fit to hire someone to cut it.

Thunder grumbled again, closer this time. Colin scowled up at the pitch-dark night sky as he neared the door. All they needed was a hard, slashing rain right now.

He slowed his pace. Studying the closed door, he reached inside his coat and pulled out the Glock. His heart thumped. Fabron had never made a move against him. But after what the concierge had tried to do to Kaitlyn, Colin didn't want to take any chances with the man.

He halted beside the door. There were no places outside where Fabron could hide, so he felt safe going right in. He raised his hand and knocked on the whitewashed planks.

No answer.

He glanced in Kaitlyn's direction, but couldn't see her thanks to the dark shadows beneath the tree. He swallowed in an effort to dissolve the lump in his throat. It didn't work. He took a deep breath and knocked on the door again. Long seconds ticked by.

Still no sound or movement from within.

He gripped the Glock in one hand and twisted the doorknob with the other. The door opened with a soft creak just as a streak of lighting flashed overhead. Illuminated in its brilliance, Colin shoved the door open wide and entered the Keep pistol first.

The room was empty.

Odd shaped mounds of dirt littered the overturned bricks. Two bent spoons lay inside a foot deep crater in the middle of the floor, and Fabron's black coat was draped over a single wooden crate beside the wall. A brand new lantern sat atop the largest pile of dirt, reminding Colin of a lighthouse on a point overlooking a chaotic sea.

He lowered the pistol. *Shit.* Where in hell had Fabron gone?

A muffled scream carried through the night, hitting his heart like a surge of electricity. *Kaitlyn.* He'd left her unprotected.

*****

Kaitlyn squirmed hard against Etienne Fabron's tight hold. "Let go of me, you filthy bastard!"

"Shut up, witch," he growled into her ear.

The feel of his wiry, earth-scented body against hers sickened her. He had her arms pinned to her sides, making her unable to call up a circle. She should have already done it and not relied on Colin for protection. If she had, Fabron wouldn't have been able to sneak up on her from behind.

Damn it. She needed to see his eyes. They were the windows into his vacant soul, and the only way to reach the entity guiding him. She wriggled harder. His arms tightened around her with lung-bursting strength, and he shoved her along the path.

"Stop fighting, or I'll hurt you."

"You're making a big mistake," she snapped, trying desperately to turn so she could look into his face. "You are powerless against me."

Fabron cut her off with a sharp laugh. "Oh really? Not even your silly witchcraft or Mr. FBI can help you now."

Kaitlyn snapped out another curse and eyed the cemetery fence. They were skirting it on the way to the edge of the bayou.

Fabron's killing ground.

She went cold inside. He wanted to use her as a pawn in his sick little Vodun game. If he could subdue her, he would kill her and her death would act as nothing more than an end to an odd ritualistic dance offered up to a mythic god. Then he would die himself.

Anger crawled over her skin as he dragged her deeper into the trees. Leaves rustled overhead and a damp burst of wind wafted over her, bringing with it the ripe odor of the bayou. Her heartbeat mimicked the rhythmic chorus of the bullfrogs nestled in the thick mud along the bank.

The closer they came to the clearing where she'd seen the puddle of blood, the harder she fought. She would defeat him, if only she could free her hands and stare into his eyes. She elbowed him in the gut.

Fabron screamed. "Stop fighting me!"

Kaitlyn ignored his order and twisted hard to her left. He made a shrill, unworldly sound, and his grip on her body loosened. She punched him in the ribs.

"Oomph!" Air rushed from his throat, and he let her go.

She spun away from him and raised her right hand. A glowing blue circle sprang from her fingertips and quickly engulfed her in a neat bubble of protection. She sent Fabron a mocking look.

He roared his displeasure and lunged at her. The circle repelled his attack and he tumbled to the ground. She whirled and waited in the thick darkness beneath the trees. *Come on, Fabron. Get closer. Let me see your face.* Her heart hammered inside her chest as she willed him to look at her.

The entity inside his head must have known what she had planned for him, because Fabron kept his gaze averted as he scrambled to his feet. "Damn you, witch. Stop trying to trick me."

"Look at me, Etienne." She forced herself to keep her voice even. Her heart pounded as she began to circle around him, her arc of protection firmly in place. "I'm over here."

"Stop taunting me!" Rage showed on his face, but he still wouldn't look at her. He fisted his hands and stared into the trees instead. "You have to die. It's pre-ordained."

"By whom? The being keeping you alive?" A fallen log lay in her path. She stepped over it. "Has he told you that by killing me, you will regain your former life?"

"Shut up!" he shouted. His hands bunched into fists. He dodged a tree and flew at her, his solid weight slamming in the circle around her. His high-pitched shriek rent the air.

Kaitlyn laughed. "If he told you that, Etienne, he lied."

"No!" Fabron levered himself onto his knees and clawed at the surface of the bubble. No way could he penetrate it. He screeched like a banshee.

She stared at him. *Look at me.*

"No! Stop playing mind games!" He grabbed his head and screeched. His sour breath, along with the thick odors of torn leaves and freshly turned earth, penetrated the circle.

She fought off a surge of nausea and willed him to raise his head. He was a disgusting creature. Back from the dead, and so easily turned by the spirit that had invaded his mind.

He put his trembling hand to his throat, and blood bubbled between his fingers. He jerked them down and peered at them. His face turned white as a sheet. "Look what you did! You made him angry."

"Look at me, Fabron," she said. "And let me help you."

"No. You want me dead," he growled. A gurgle spilled from his lips. "Stop it!"

"Kaitlyn!" Colin's frantic voice floated to her on the edge of the wind.

The wound gaping across Fabron's throat closed up, and his face morphed into a picture of death. She continued to stare at him, willing him to meet her eyes.

"Kaitlyn! Where in hell are you?" Colin's frantic voice drew closer.

Fabron raised his arms and roared like a man possessed.

"Damn you, Fabron!" Colin shouted, his footsteps pounding over the damp ground. "Get away from her!" A loud crack rang out.

The Zombie jerked, and a black stain rolled down his arm. He lifted his head and met Kaitlyn's eyes. *Yes!* She held his gaze and directed every ounce of energy she possessed into diminishing him, searing him with twin lasers and knocking him backwards on his ass.

"Hold it right there! Freeze!" Another jarring crack bounced off the trees just as lightning flared overhead, illuminating Colin, who stood about ten feet from the Zombie, his pistol drawn. The lightning reflected eerily off his glasses.

Kaitlyn stepped between them. "He can't hurt you now."

"What did you do to him?"

"I diminished him."

"Is he dead?" Colin asked, his voice a stunned rasp. "Shit. I shot him."

"He's already dead, remember? What can a bullet hurt?"

Looking totally confused, Colin stared at her blankly.

She bit her lip. "Don't worry. The entity's keeping him alive—sort of. He's a Zombie, remember?"

"A Zombie. An entity." He circled around Kaitlyn, his eyes glued to the blue bubble surrounding her. "And my God—what in hell is that thing? Are you all right?"

"I'm fine." She put out her hand and absorbed the circle into it.

He blinked. "Sweet Jesus. This is straight out of science fiction."

"No. It's real. It saved me from Fabron."

He gaped at her.

"Do you believe me now?"

He swallowed.

"Colin?" She'd expected him to be stunned, but his sudden stillness unnerved her. She walked over to him. "I really am a witch. You just witnessed some of the ways I can protect myself."

"You lasered him with your eyes?" He stared at her.

She nodded.

He holstered his pistol and turned to look at Fabron, who lay curled in a fetal position on a bed of leaves. "Son of a bitch."

"I don't do it except in extreme circumstances. I could really hurt someone."

"No shit." He wiped his brow with his sleeve. "Remind me never to make you mad."

Thunder growled overhead, and fat raindrops began to patter down through the trees. A strong breeze rolled in from the bayou, chilling Kaitlyn to the bone. She folded her arms, and the bullfrogs and other night creatures stopped their throaty calls.

Colin met her eyes. "What in hell happened after I left you under the tree and went into the Keep?"

"Fabron sneaked up on me and dragged me out here before I could fight back."

"You did a helluva a job of that."

"After I broke free. He wanted to use me in a Vodun ritual."

Colin narrowed his gaze. "He said that?"

"He didn't have to." Kaitlyn swung her arm in a wide arc. "Look where we are. The clearing."

"Bastard." Colin shuddered visibly. "He could've killed you."

"Do you really think so?" She walked over to him.

A muscle jumped in his cheek. "No. Not after seeing that display."

"Are *you* afraid of me now?" she asked, not sure she wanted to know the answer to that question. But she had to know how her actions had affected him.

He lifted his hand and ran his knuckles along her jaw. "Should I be?"

"Of course not," she said softly. "I would never hurt you."

"Dear, sweet Kaitlyn." He drew her close and wrapped his arms around her. A splatter of rain hit his glasses. "I still find it all so fucking hard to believe."

"Just so you do."

"How can I not, after watching you laser him?" Colin peered down into her face. Seeing those bands of light emanating from her eyes had shocked the hell out of him and upended his nice, neat, orderly world. Yet he still wanted her. She was so beautiful and filled with such incredible energy. It was a powerful aphrodisiac. He brushed a lock of hair from her forehead.

She pressed herself against him and parted her lips. "Colin?"

"God, Kaitlyn—" Her name caught in his throat. He bent his head and took her mouth in a plundering kiss. She gasped into his mouth and gripped his shoulders.

Her delicious lavender scent tickled his nose. He deepened the kiss. She tasted like cloves and honey. Spicy and sweet, all at once. A raindrop trickled down his cheek and tickled their joined lips.

Beside them, on the ground, Fabron groaned.

That startled Colin, and he broke the kiss. What in hell was he doing? He set Kaitlyn away from him. She had just proven to him that she indeed *was* a witch, which went against everything he'd ever believed. So how could he still be attracted to her?

"What's wrong?" she asked. The forest around them had gone silent, except for the patter of the rain, the whisper of wind in the trees, and the grumble of thunder.

He wiped his mouth and scowled. "I can't do this."

"I've upset you." Kaitlyn's teeth chattered.

Colin abruptly realized they were both soaking wet and the weather was growing cold. He set his jaw. "We can talk later. Right now, we should go back to the house. Before we both get chilled."

"Yes," she said, rubbing her arms. "I have goose bumps."

"What about him?" Colin eyed Fabron.

"Leave him there. He'll be okay."

"Are you sure?"

"Yes. The entity will revive him after he rests a while."

"If you say so." Colin scowled and wiped his glasses as best he could. Then he took her hand and led her from the clearing. The rain peppered down harder as they plunged through the trees. Soon the cemetery loomed up ahead, and thanks to the magical acts he'd seen Kaitlyn perform, Colin swallowed back a deep sense of foreboding.

"There's no fog tonight." Kaitlyn's softly spoken words startled him.

He eyed the graveyard beyond the fence. She was right. He could see each headstone with no problem. His mind whirred. "Maybe the rain washed it away."

He led her around the cemetery. As they passed the gate, he heard the sharp caw of a raven. His blood curdled, and he halted. "Damn. It's back."

"It won't hurt us. I won't let it."

Colin glared down at her. "So now you're Superwoman?"

She met his disturbed gaze with an innocent one of her own.

Damn her. She really thought there was no problem with what she'd done. He scanned the cemetery, but he didn't see the bird lurking among the graves. "I'm surprised they fly in the rain."

"That's not really a bird."

"Excuse me?" He shot her a sideways glance.

Her mouth curved in a knowing smile. "It's Lyle Forrester. He's a ghost who can change his shape at will."

Colin bit back a sharp retort and gritted his teeth. "Let's go inside."

Dripping wet, they trudged through the yard and entered the house. To Colin's relief, no one was in the foyer. Kaitlyn shut the door behind them with a soft click. He halted and wiped moisture from his glasses, and then took her elbow and guided her toward the stairs.

He led her up to her room and waited while she took out her key and unlocked the door. She did so, and stepped inside. He stayed out in the hall.

She turned. "Aren't you coming in?"

"I don't think so." He started to back away, but his feet rooted themselves to the floor. Hell. Leaving her was much harder than he had imagined. He wanted her too damned much.

Her mouth curved in one of those brilliant smiles, and she mocked him. "I don't bite."

"No. You just laser men with your eyes."

"Give me a break, Colin." Kaitlyn's smiled faded. "I did that for my protection. I would never hurt you. You know that."

Deep down inside, he did. But he also knew that he shouldn't get involved with her. Her powers would always come between them.

She put her hand on the door. "Whatever you decide, I'll honor your decision. I just know that the kiss we shared—"

"Shouldn't have happened."

"Really?" She raised her eyebrows. "You kissed *me*, remember?"

He scowled. She had him there. *Damn it.* For just that one moment, he'd let himself believe—and it had been beyond his wildest dreams. Yet it hadn't been real. Life wasn't a fantasy.

She smiled. "And you liked it. I know that wasn't your pistol jabbing my hip."

He quirked his mouth. She had him there, too. He was attracted to her, and that scared the hell out of him. She was everything he'd sworn he would avoid in a woman. Strong-willed, flamboyant, and…well…*out there*. She was a witch.

Kaitlyn let go of the door and put out her hand.

Colin couldn't stop himself from imagining those long, eager fingers on his body. His cock stirred. And against his better judgment, he took her hand and went inside. Her room smelled faintly sweet, like fresh flowers with a musky undertone. He spotted a long wooden incense burner, a small wooden wand, and a pair of carved purple candles on the nightstand. A small bundle of green straw and several colored stones sat on the table, and an ancient, leather-bound book lay open on the bed.

Was that her book of spells? A wave of uneasiness skittered through him.

She faced him, and smiled. Her hair was wet and her blouse was plastered to her sexy curves, and for a moment he had trouble reconciling her vibrant beauty with that of the laser spraying, energy ball-forming witch who had neutralized Etienne Fabron. Yet Kaitlyn and that witch were one and the same. He shook his head.

She curved her mouth. "I know what you must be thinking."

"You can read minds, too?" He prepared himself to leave. "This is just too weird."

"No. I know you." She caught his arm. "You're a man — and an FBI agent. You've sworn to serve and protect — especially women and children. And you want to take care of me. My powers are a threat. Not only to your desire to protect me, but to your neat, orderly world. Am I right?"

"Am I that obvious?"

"Yes." She took his hand and entwined their fingers. "And it's really sweet. But totally unnecessary. I'm the one who can protect *you* in this house. You should let me."

"How are you gonna do that? With magic?"

"Let me show you." She released his hand and walked over to her suitcase. After fishing around for a while, she drew out a small box.

He watched her with trepidation. "What's in there?"

"An amulet." She set the box on the table and drew out a sleek black cord, from which dangled a round silver pendant about the size of a nickel. "This will keep you safe."

"Kaitlyn—" He shook his head, and caused water to drip down his neck. He shrugged it off. "I don't wear jewelry."

"Not even to keep you safe?" She raised her eyebrows and scoffed at him. "Of course you don't. You have your pistol."

"Yeah. And I carry a badge." He crossed his arms. "I have fifteen years in law enforcement to back it up."

"Do those things make you infallible?"

"Of course not. But they can sure—"

"Protect you from black magic?"

"I doubt it. But—"

"Trust me." Her lips curved in another dazzling smile. "They can't."

"And that amulet will." He bobbed his head toward the pendant.

She nodded. "Yes. Will you wear it?"

"I don't know. It's—" He broke off. He didn't need the damned thing, but Kaitlyn meant well. He met her probing gaze. "Maybe."

"No one has to see it. You can wear it underneath your shirt."

"Yeah?" That would be better. Still, he'd never been superstitious. This seemed extreme.

She held out the pendant. "Here. Just for you."

He took the piece of jewelry reluctantly and examined it. It reminded him of a coin, with a lightning bolt etched down its center. She'd taken the time to dig it out; he could at least wear it overnight. He looped the cord over his head and slipped it inside his collar. It felt cool against his damp skin.

He smiled. "Thank you."

"You're welcome." She turned away and tucked the box back into her suitcase.

Watching the gentle play of her shoulders, he felt a surge of protectiveness. No, she didn't need him. But that didn't quell his need for her. Despite the roaring in his head that said he should keep his hands to himself, he stepped up behind her and put his hands on her upper arms.

She went still.

He kissed the nape of her neck. Her silken skin was cool and clammy. They were both soaked to the skin. He turned her around. "We need to warm you up."

"That would be good," she said, a fine tremor riding her skin. She peered up at him with those beautiful green eyes.

He brushed the backs of his fingers across her cheek, and reveled in the sexy smoothness of her skin. "A hot shower would help."

"Yes, it would." She slipped her arms around his neck. "A shower together."

"Whoa," he said softly. He pictured her naked and wet, with those long, elegant fingers on his burning flesh.

His cock leapt to attention. "That wasn't exactly what I had in mind, but—"

"You'll consider it?" She kissed his cheek. "You and me, with hot water beating down. Soap suds. All slick and sopping and—"

"Jesus, Kaitlyn." He groaned and pulled her flush up against him.

Laughing, she kissed his mouth.

She tasted cool and sweet, like homemade vanilla ice cream. His body throbbed with desire. Witch or not, she turned him on. Reluctantly, he broke the kiss and tugged her toward the bathroom.

"You've convinced me. Let's go."

Kaitlyn loved the need she heard in his voice. She let him lead her inside, then pulled away and began unfastening her blouse. Her magical display outside had obviously unnerved him, but he still wanted her. Maybe even more than before. He didn't want to want her; and she didn't want to push him. Yet her body thrummed with unspent energy. It was always this way when she used her powers to their fullest extent. The only thing that helped her overcome the tension firing through her was a mind blowing, out of this world orgasm.

He turned on the hot water, set his glasses on the counter, and stripped down. His body was perfect. All hard planes and taut muscle and pulsing desire.

"Ooh. I like what I see," she said, unable to stop smiling. Moisture pooled between her legs. Aching for him, she shucked off her slacks and panties. She needed to feel his hands on her.

His nostrils flared. He stepped closer. Her eyes took in his tight pectorals with their delicious dusting of hair, his six-pack abs, and his lengthening cock. Her mouth watered. Steam rolled from the walk-in shower, misting their skin and making her even warmer. Finally, he was close enough to touch. She reveled in the silken hard feel of his chest.

He kissed her, and she melted in a pool of need.

"Let's go, or I'm gonna take you right here," he growled, grasping her around the waist. He opened the shower door and propelled her inside.

Warm water cascaded over her, making her flesh burn. She'd gone from ice cold to steaming hot in two seconds flat. He shut the door and all at once, her luscious breasts were in his hands. A moan slid from his lips as he cupped and shaped them. He bent his head and suckled first one, and then the other. She cried out his name.

He lifted his head, ran her hands over his body and shuddered.

She smiled seductively. He felt so good. But it wasn't enough. She kissed him and rubbed her hips against him. He gripped her buttocks and lifted her against his burning arousal. She wrapped her legs around his hips and grasped his shoulders. They fit together like two pieces of the same delicious puzzle.

"Fuck me," she begged. "Now."

"Not yet." Colin rubbed his fevered flesh along the damp niche between her thighs. Even with the rush of water, he could smell her. She was more than ready for him. Longing to sheathe himself inside her slick depths, he groaned. But first things first.

Her legs tightened around him, and she rocked up and down. Not wanting to break contact, he pressed her against the wet tiles.

She pressed a flurry of kisses along his neck, over his stubbled chin, and up to his hungry lips. "Are all lawmen this *hot*?"

"I don't know." He grinned against her mouth. "I've never slept with one."

She laughed and used her tongue to tell him just how hot she thought he was.

He nipped at her earlobe to distract her, and slipped his hand between her legs. Her satiny skin enthralled him. She spread her legs wider to give him entrance, and he used his fingers to massage her soft folds. She moaned with pleasure. "Colin—"

"Your body's absolutely perfect," he whispered. Fire shot through his groin.

Desperate to feel him inside her, she caressed his hard length. "I want you, Colin. *Now.*"

"Like this?" He rocked against her hand.

Pleasure shuddered through her in a compelling wave. Grasping his slick shoulders with her free hand, she gasped. "Oh, yes! I want you inside me. I need you there."

His body shivered with the effort not to slam her down on his pulsing erection. He wanted to taste her first, and to have her taste him. The very idea made his arousal leap. Priming his taste buds, he glided down her slick body, halting to feast again on her generous breasts. They were soft and supple except for her pebbled nipples, reminding him of tart strawberries and fresh cream.

She groaned as he suckled her. Her fingernails bit into his skin, and she writhed against him.

Enjoying her greedy response, he raised his head. Her eyes had rolled back and her shoulders pressed the tiles behind her. He grinned. "Feel good?"

"Oh, yes," she moaned, gripping his hair and curling her leg around his hip. She rubbed her mound against his leaping arousal. "Come inside me, Colin. Please!"

"Take it easy." He pulled back. "Anticipation's half the fun. Don't you agree?"

"Yes, but I'm about to explode."

"You need to relax. If you came now, your orgasm would be like a firecracker." He dropped to his knees and licked water from her belly. She gasped in surprise. His voice dropped to a raspy whisper. "Let me taste you, and you'll be a fucking volcano of passion. I guarantee it."

He kissed his way across her wet stomach and swirled his tongue inside her bellybutton. Her smooth skin made him burn. Trembling with his own harsh need, he moved lower and urged her legs apart. She smelled like all woman.

Quivering with eagerness, she tangled her fingers in his hair. He blew on her weeping flesh.

"Colin—oh my!" She sucked a sharp breath.

All at once, his mouth was on her, devouring her slick juices. She tasted musky and sweet, like overripe plums. He used his teeth, tongue, and lips to draw a frenzied cry from her mouth. His own flesh hardened in response.

Water beat down on them, warming them and sending their passion spiraling higher. Kaitlyn dissolved in a swirling flood of hunger. Her mewling cries echoed off the tile walls, making her wonder if anyone besides Colin could hear her passionate words.

He continued suckling her petal soft flesh, until she fisted her hands in his dark hair and pulled his head back. Her legs trembled. "Stop it! I...can't...take any more."

He grinned up at her, his lips glistening with water and her body's ripe juices.

"I mean it." Her breath hissed out. "Please quit before I can't...stop."

Never breaking contact, he rose, kissed her mouth, and swung her around until his buttocks met the wall. She tasted herself on his lips.

"Go down on me," he begged her. "Will you?"

"Oh, yes," she said with a throaty laugh. Her body teetered on the edge of a precipice. She sank to her knees and wrapped her hand around his hard, slick shaft. Steel encased in satin.

He groaned as she took him in her mouth and began to lave his sensitive flesh with her tongue. Pleasure rocketed through him. He braced his shoulders on the wall and threaded his hands into her wet hair. Water pounded down on them, but all he could feel was her mouth drawing on his throbbing cock. Reaching the edge of his control, he shuddered and pulled free.

"That's enough." He gasped for air. "I want to come inside you."

She rose on shaky legs.

He kissed her, then pushed her against the wall and gripped her hips. His arms shook with the effort to center her on his bobbing shaft. She helped to guide him, and smiled down at him.

"Show me what you've got, FBI man."

She didn't have to tell him twice. He kissed her hard, and slid part way inside her. She was slick and warm and fit him like a glove. He groaned.

Kaitlyn wrapped her legs around his waist and looked into his eyes. "Ummm...more."

He obliged her, but still didn't slip in all the way. He wanted to savor every second of being inside her satiny depths. She gripped his shoulders and pushed her hips against him.

"I need all of you, Colin. God. Please!"

"You asked for it," he murmured, her ravenous kisses making him drunk with passion. He gripped her thighs and with one powerful thrust, took himself in to the hilt.

She gasped at the sudden feeling of fullness. Yet before she could recover, he began lifting her up and down, moving her faster and faster along his hard length. She moaned against his wet neck and held on for the ride. And what a ride it was.

Surrounded by a billowing cloud of steam, Kaitlyn exploded in a pulsing shower of reds, yellows, and greens as water splashed down on her, the lights behind her eyes blinding her with their startling brilliance. Wave after wave of passion washed over her, and she dug her fingernails into Colin's slick skin.

He roared his pleasure and pushed her against the slick tiles. Pleasure blasted through him as he spilled his seed. His body bucked wildly, and his breath caught in his lungs. Water blinded him.

Afterward he began to calm, they clung together, rocking in that primordial rhythm as their passion slowly receded. Kaitlyn pressed his face to his neck and struggled for air. She'd never felt so wild and yet so free. Colin could be a stuffed shirt, but he made love like a dream. She closed her eyes and held him close. She could stay like this forever.

He grinned and kissed her neck. She'd matched him thrust for thrust. Witch or not, she was damned good at water-logged sex. He drew in her warm, wet scent, and swore he'd protect her with his life. And somehow, he knew she'd do the same for him.

They took their time with the rest of their shower, taking turns lathering each other up and washing every inch of exposed skin. Kaitlyn giggled as Colin washed her toes.

He rose and kissed her, and soon their passion re-ignited. Their moans of pleasure echoed inside the enclosed space until finally, the water turned cold. Spent and shivering, they laughed as they turned off the shower and took turns toweling each other dry.

Kaitlyn handed Colin the robe from the back of the door and wrapped a towel around her middle.

He took the robe, and frowned. "What are you doing?"

"You don't have any clothes here." She smiled. "I do."

He nodded at her practicality, and shrugged into the warm garment. She was right. Again. His body hummed as he watched her slip from the room. Raking a hand through his mussed wet hair, he looked in the mirror. A sated man stared back. Sated, and exhausted. His muscles quivered from their aquatic acrobatics. He craved sleep like a drug.

Kaitlyn returned wearing a pretty white cotton gown.

Whoa. She certainly didn't look like a witch in that outfit.

She bumped him with her hips. "What are you staring at?"

"You." He touched the gathered rows of lace covering her breasts

She made a face.

He slipped his arms around her and buried his nose in her hair. She smelled of flowers and herbs. A tantalizing, sexy fragrance.

She met his gaze in the mirror. "Do you want to stay?"

"With you? You mean, all night?"

"Yes," she said. "Are you up for round two?"

"We've already had round two," he said with a twist of his lips. "I can go for three, but it might take me a while."

"We have all night."

He laughed. "Okay. Just this once."

She pushed away from him and picked up a comb.

As Colin watched her, he couldn't help wondering if he was making a grave mistake. She was working her way under his skin, and he was powerless to stop her. Had she cast a spell on him? He couldn't tell. Yet he knew he was getting in way over his head.

CHAPTER SEVEN

A bone deep weariness settled over Kaitlyn as she combed and blew her damp hair dry. Colin had gone across the parlor to get his shaving kit, and to her delight, she had the bathroom to herself. Her body ached from their wild lovemaking, and she needed a few minutes to come down off her sexual high. Usually an orgasm took the edge off her nerves after a major display of her powers. But not tonight. She'd had two, and they had only served to key her up and make her hungry for more. No man had ever affected her like Colin.

She turned off the hair dryer, and heard a soft thump from her room. He had returned. Her body grew dewy in response.

"Kaitlyn?" he called out. "I'm back."

She put down her comb and opened the door. He stood by the bed dressed in a pair of gray sweat pants and a rumpled white T-shirt, his hand wrapped around the butt of his sleek black pistol.

Her stomach fluttered. "What are you doing?"

"Checking the magazine." He slapped the cartridge into the grip. "Just in case."

She watched his hands caress the gun. Damn, if that didn't turn her on. "Because of Fabron?"

"In case he turns up during the night, and your lasers are on the blink." He slipped the pistol back into its holster and set it on the nightstand next to the rune candles.

Then he turned his gaze on her. His mouth curved. "You don't look like any witch I've ever seen."

"You were expecting an old crone, perhaps?" She sauntered over to him. "Or maybe that the water in the shower would melt me?"

"I'm damned glad it didn't." His deep baritone flowed over her like warm chocolate syrup.

She inched forward. "Does that mean you're sleeping with me?"

"Well, I'm not sleeping on the floor," he said softly.

She laughed, and a tidal wave of desire ripped through her. "I'm damned glad of that."

"Come here." He reached for her and pulled her into his arms. He smelled like soap and sexy man. "You look beautiful."

"Thank you." She put her hands on his chest. "Does this mean you accept me?"

"I don't wanna talk about that tonight." He ran his finger down her cheek, the sensation so soft and fleeting Kaitlyn wondered if he'd touched her at all. He dropped his hand. "Let's just enjoy each other. Okay?"

She met his intense gaze with a searing one of her own. "Colin—"

"All right." His expression tightened. "Yes, I accept you. But I don't know if this thing between us will work. I just—" He shook his head. "I don't know if I can deal with this in the real world."

"Fair enough." Moisture pooled between her legs, and she was surprised she didn't spontaneously combust from the feel of his hard body. "Let's just enjoy each other while we're here, and then take it one step at a time. How's that?"

"It works for me," he said. "I can't stop thinking about you. Every time I breathe, I draw in your delicious scent. And tonight, watching you blast the hell out of Fabron—" His fevered gaze roamed down her thinly clad body.

She delighted in the sexual awareness embedded in his hungry eyes. He didn't want to be turned on by her powers, but he was. The realization of the control she held over him stunned her. It was more forceful than any spell she'd ever cast. She gripped his shoulders to keep her hands from trembling.

"You're so damned sexy," he whispered, his new arousal evident in the hard bulge meeting her belly. He backed her against the wall and reached out to curl a lock of her damp hair around his finger. Her name slipped from his lips. "You were awesome in the shower. Now—"

"We'll try it in the bed," she whispered. She reveled in his warm, masculine scent and the rub of his T-shirt clad chest against her cotton covered nipples. Her body melted into an oozing puddle of passion. Her breathing grew erratic. She rose up on her tiptoes and pressed a gentle kiss to his lips.

He growled a curse. "I don't want to want you. God knows I've tried to stop myself. But it's damned near impossible. You've cast some sort of magic over me." His eyes glittered with raw need.

She cupped his stubbled cheek, and enjoyed the rasp of his beard against her hand. "Kiss me."

"You don't have to ask me twice," he said, edging closer and lowering his head to her mouth. His lips curved. *"Witch."*

She smiled. He tasted like soap, mint and sexy man. Kaitlyn wrapped her arms around his neck and pressed herself to him from ankles to lips. Fire skittered over her skin.

He moaned softly, and lifted his head. His lips glistened from their fierce kiss. He caressed her bare arms with his fingertips, and murmured an oath about her beauty. Then he lowered his head and traced the edges of her lips with his tongue.

The feeling was exquisite. Kaitlyn shuddered and pressed herself to his hard body. All sinew and rippling muscle. She put her hands on his cheek and kissed his mouth. "I want you. Again."

"Three's the magic number," Colin whispered. The feel of her generous curves pressed to his aching flesh sent a rush of heat through him. Her sweet herbal scent mesmerized him. Just imagining the silken brush of her hair against his skin made his body turn to marble. He feasted on her lips, and then kissed her cheeks, her eyes, and her temple. Her skin was soft as satin and tasted as though it was coated with fresh honey. His cock throbbed against the soft cotton of his warm-ups.

Kaitlyn dragged his T-shirt off over his head and tossed it on the floor.

He grinned, turned out the light and together, they climbed into bed.

*****

An hour later, Colin kissed Kaitlyn and settled her against his chest. His breathing slowly returned to normal. He ran his fingers through her hair. "No more. I can't take it."

She laughed softly, the sound like musical notes bouncing off the darkness. "Me, either. We really should get some rest. I have to work tomorrow."

"Does that make you tired?"

"What? Witchcraft?"

"Yes."

"No." She put her hand on his stomach. "It energizes me."

"No wonder you didn't want to stop tonight."

"Yes—that, and you." She chuckled. "Go to sleep. You have to work tomorrow, too."

"Yeah, I do." He stroked his hands down her back and let his mind drift to the case. It grew more puzzling with each passing day and now, with Kaitlyn claiming that Fabron was a Zombie, it threatened to become embarrassing. Colin wasn't sure he knew exactly what a Zombie was, although he had some idea. Still, how would he ever explain it to his pals at Quantico? They'd never believe him. Hell, he'd be a laughingstock.

He tried to come up with a reasonable explanation, but his eyes kept drifting shut and he finally gave up. He'd worry about it in the morning. Right now, he needed to rest. Enjoying the feel of Kaitlyn curled against him, he gradually relaxed and a pleasant lassitude stole over him. Her rhythmic breathing soon lulled him into a deep sleep.

It lasted until he woke with a start several hours later. He picked up his glasses and glanced at the bedside clock. Four a.m. The room was dark, the curtains drawn. Kaitlyn slept soundly beside him. Her even breathing gave him comfort. Yet he eased her away from him and looked around. What had awakened him? He rolled onto his side, and a strong sense of foreboding stole over him.

"You've put my children in danger." The woman's shrill voice hovered in the darkness like an energized demon. *"I won't allow it."*

What in hell? Colin jerked into a sitting position.

A woman dressed in blue hovered at the end of the bed, her matching eyes flashing with angry lights. Her lips curled into a sneer. *"The witch convinced me to leave, but I want what's mine."*

"What? Who the fuck are you?" Colin's nerves jumped. He blinked. "Get out."

"No. She sent me away, and my husband turned to his mistress like before." The woman edged around the bed. *"Get up. You're coming with me."*

"Like hell I am." Colin snatched up his pistol and aimed it at her. "Freeze. FBI."

"Put that gun away. It won't do you any good." Susannah sneered at him. *"Bullets go right through me. I've seen to it that the witch won't wake up for a while. Now, get out of bed and come with me, or I'll make her sleep permanent. I mean it. Move! "*

Uncertainty cascaded through Colin as he stared at her. She had to be a ghost, a figment of his imagination. He shook his head. She didn't disappear. Wonderful. He rose on shaky legs, keeping the pistol trained on her. Her face took on an eerie white glow and she averted her eyes.

"Get dressed," she said. *"Please."*

"Who in hell are you?" he croaked. "What do you want?"

"I need your friend's help, and she won't cooperate unless I have leverage." The woman sniffed. *"Hurry up. Get your clothes on. I won't parade around the property with a naked man. It isn't proper."*

Colin looked down. Shit. He was nude. He grabbed his briefs and jeans off the floor and hurriedly dragged them on. Then he yanked his shirt on over his head and shrugged into his shoulder holster. Just in case.

The apparition floated toward the door and motioned for him to follow her. *"Come with me."*

"Wait just a damned minute," he snapped. He planted his feet. Yet he felt a strange pull.

She turned and flashed her eyes at him. Was she about to laser him like Kaitlyn had Fabron? Colin braced himself for it, but it never happened. He was suddenly no longer in charge of his own limbs. He tried to call out to Kaitlyn, but his mouth wouldn't work. His legs began to move and he found himself following the ghost.

In only moments, they were outside on the veranda. He didn't remember going outdoors, but the cold, damp night air washed over him and he drew in the musky odor of the bayou. Blinking red eyes watched him from the trees. He shivered.

"You must convince the witch to leave the property," the woman said. She prodded him off the veranda and out into the yard. *"She's interfering with our existence here."*

"I don't understand."

"I still love my husband, Lyle." Her eyes filled with tears. *"She wants us out of the house, but he won't leave without the sapphire. So therefore, I must stay. You two are the ones who must go."*

Colin started to speak, but the ghost held up her hand. She had to be Susannah Forrester. He gulped. A chill shimmied down his spine. He reached out to touch her, but only found air.

"You can't hurt me. So you might as well put away your weapon." Susannah paused before leading him around the corner of the house.

He stared at her a moment, and then stuffed the Glock in his waistband. He felt impotent and small. Unable to protect himself. He hated that feeling.

Her eyes gleamed. *"Thank you."*

"Where are we going?" he asked as she started moving. His pulse pounded in his ears.

Susannah lifted her chin. *"Why, to the Keep. Of course."*

"Sweet Jesus." Colin swallowed, hard, and suddenly he knew what she had in mind. "You plan to lure Kaitlyn out here using me as bait."

His mind raced as he tried to come up with an escape plan, but he had nothing. He was well and truly trapped.

*****

Kaitlyn woke up to find the sheets cool. The pink light of dawn seeped in around the curtains, and energy hummed throughout the room. She stretched. Her body felt deliciously sated, and just a bit sore. Last night, she'd used muscles she hadn't used in quite a while. She smiled a happy smile. Colin was quite a lover.

Colin. The thought of him made her heart pound. She rolled over and reached for him. Her hand met cold sheets. She opened her eyes wide and sat up. Where was he?

She eyed the open bathroom door. The light was off, and the room appeared empty. Her eyes roamed the floor beside the bed. His clothes were gone, as was his pistol.

Her insides twisted. He'd left in the night. Did he regret all they had done?

Damn.

She fell back against her pillow. If only he hadn't seen what she had done to Fabron—maybe then he could accept her powers. But, no. It was better this way. He needed to know about her craft up front. If he could accept her powers, he could accept her.

A deep-seated ache began in the center of her chest. She longed to go to him and ask what she had done wrong, but deep down she knew there was nothing she could say. Still—

She sat up. Maybe they could at least talk. Keeping a dialogue open between them might just help her cause. She stretched a little more, then rose and dressed quickly in jeans and a white cotton blouse. Next she washed her face, brushed her teeth, and dabbed on a little makeup.

Her hands were sure as she tucked her room key in her pocket and marched out the door. The muted darkness in the parlor made her blink. She gave her eyes a moment to adjust, and crossed the landing to Colin's room. Pausing at his door, she knocked.

Silence.

She rapped again. "Colin? Are you in there?"

Still no answer.

A sinking feeling filled the pit of her stomach. She stared down at the brass doorknob. Should she open it? A little voice inside her answered, "Yes." Yet she still had reservations. If he didn't want to see her, he had that right. He deserved his privacy. Yet that tiny voice kept niggling at her and the hairs stood up on the back of her neck.

She turned and eyed the parlor. It was eerily silent. The entire house seemed to be waiting. For what, she didn't know. She turned back to the door. She would just take a quick peek inside and make sure Colin was all right, then pop back out. Simple enough.

Her heart thumped as she examined the brass doorknob. It was just like the one on Fabron's door, so all she had to do was concentrate. She shifted her feet and trained her practiced gaze on the lock. After a moment, it gradually began to turn. So slowly she could hardly tell— but it *was* moving. After a few moments, the lock popped open. Relief slid through her.

She stood quietly, listening for sounds from within. She heard nothing. So she turned the knob and let herself in.

The bed was empty.

Kaitlyn clutched the pendant and stepped across the threshold. No one was in the room, or in the bathroom. There was no sign Colin had been back since last night. His suitcase wasn't disturbed, his toothbrush was dry, and his bed hadn't been turned down. She swallowed.

He could be taking a walk around the property to revisit last night's eerie scene, or maybe to make a call and check on the case. But she didn't think so. He was on the run from her, because of what he had seen her do to Etienne Fabron. A lump formed in her throat.

She turned to leave, and the curtains ruffled. She whirled to see an apparition take shape in front of them. A woman? No. *A man.*

Her pulse racing, Kaitlyn put out her hand and called up a circle. The energy flew from her fingertips to loop around her in a burst of shimmering blue light. She lifted her chin and peered through the protective ring as Lyle Forrester's haughty features took shape.

"I'm not here to hurt you, witch." He stared at her with eyes like a raven's. *"I wanted you to know that my crazy wife has your lover."*

Colin was with Susannah. Kaitlyn digested that. "Care to elaborate?"

"No. Lyle's mouth formed a sneer. *"That was quite a display you put on last night. Poor Etienne. Death hardly becomes him. Without me, he is nothing."*

"I chased you out of him," she snapped. "What have you and Susannah done with Colin?"

"I haven't done anything. Yet." Lyle took a menacing step toward her. *"Weren't you listening? I just told you that Susannah has him. What she has planned, I wouldn't know."*

"Damn her," Kaitlyn said to herself.

Lyle laughed. *"My sentiments, exactly."*

"She left Scarlet Oak on her own."

"At your suggestion," he said. *"Now, she's back. You must talk with her again. I can't have her interfering in my quest to find the Midnight Star."*

"You mean, you don't want her coming between you and Camille."

"Camille has nothing to do with it." He sucked in his cheeks. *"I won't have any woman getting in my way. Including you. Witch, or no witch."*

"You can't stay here. You must leave Scarlet Oak, too."

"Get me the sapphire, and I'll leave today."

"It doesn't belong to you."

"Yes, it does." He edged forward another step. *"I had it last."*

"It's not a matter of possession. Camille was the rightful owner." Kaitlyn fisted her hands. "You stole it from her. The stone belongs to her heirs."

"No. It belongs to me!" he bellowed. A white haze formed around his head. *"Damn you, witch."*

"Where did Susannah take Colin?"

"Find out on your own." The cloud of white thickened, and he began to vaporize.

She lunged toward him. "Wait!"

"Find my wife, and you'll find your lover," he snapped. Then he was gone.

Kaitlyn quickly drew in the circle and left the room. The empty parlor mocked her. She checked the entire upstairs, then descended the steps and peeked into the dining room and the kitchen. The only people she spotted were members of the kitchen staff, busy making breakfast. No one had seen Colin. She left them to their work and strode through the library to Fabron's tiny office.

Empty.

Kaitlyn cursed. Susannah must have taken him outside. They could be anywhere. Her stomach knotted and she rubbed her mother's pendant, hoping for insight. Its warm presence consoled her and helped grow her resolve as she re-entered the empty foyer. Her mind whirred. Gathering her courage, she opened the door and walked out onto the dark veranda. Icy air enveloped her, and she worried that Colin didn't have his coat.

A bird near the house welcomed the coming dawn with a shrill song. Bullfrogs added a bass beat, their deep croaks carrying through the cold air as if trying to warn her of danger ahead. She stepped off the porch and rounded the house. The muggy wind stirred the trees, slinging water droplets into her hair. She ran her fingers through it and squinted in the dim light.

Nothing moved, except the branches swaying above her head. Uneasiness skittered along her skin like ants.

"Kaitlyn!" She heard her name floating on the breeze like a breath of air. Colin was calling out to her. She spun around. No one was there.

Yet she knew she'd heard her name. A picture of Colin's handsome face rose in her mind. He was in trouble. Kaitlyn battled a surge of panic. Would she find him in time?

"I have to," she told herself, her focus falling on the rear of the house. Maybe Susannah had taken him to the Keep. *Yes. That had to be it.*

She crept around the house to the entrance to the storage room. Her heart pounded. No one was about, but out of concern for her safety she called up a circle. Its shiny protection cocooned her. She quickened her step.

Worry for Colin propelled her forward. Cold air chilled the sweat breaking on her face. She halted beside the Keep door and listened intently. Her efforts were rewarded by the sound of a female voice harping from behind the closed door. It wasn't Susannah.

She drew her brows together. It had to be Camille, Lyle Forrester's mistress, the Midnight Star's rightful owner. Anger filled Kaitlyn. If those two had Colin—

Without stopping to think, she gripped the knob and yanked the door open. Colin was nowhere in sight. Instead, Camille faced Susannah across the torn up brick floor in a ghostly showdown. A strange energy sang throughout the room. There was a burst of light, and the Midnight Star sapphire suddenly appeared around

Camille's neck, dangling against the generous cleavage visible just above her low-cut dress.

Kaitlyn's gaze locked on the stone. It looked genuine. How in the world had it manifested itself on a ghost, and so quickly? Her nerve endings tingled as the energy field passed through her circle of protection. She blinked. The light seemed to emanate from the sapphire. How strange.

Lyle had killed for the Midnight Star. Legend had it that it had to be gifted in love, or its owner would die a horrible death. Lyle had — and he still roamed the earth an unhappy man. An icy chill rose in the air, no doubt from the animosity between the two ghosts. Kaitlyn shivered.

"You must leave this place," Susannah snapped. *"You stole my husband and murdered my children."*

"No. Your husband murdered me." Camille lunged at Susannah, the sapphire bouncing off her bulging cleavage.

Susannah's eyes blazed with hatred as she dodged the other woman and countered with a vicious slap to Camille's bronze cheek. The woman's head snapped back.

Kaitlyn stepped between them. "Stop it!"

Camille's face turned dark. She screeched like a wild woman and swung her fist at Susannah. Her arm went right through Kaitlyn and the circle; she didn't feel a thing. The ghostly aura in the room dimmed as Etienne Fabron opened the door and stalked inside. Only, it wasn't Fabron. It was Lyle Forrester, decked out in his riding gear. Kaitlyn's eyes widened. Since when did ghosts change clothes?

"Susannah!" Lyle said sharply, his eyes locking on his angry wife. *"Leave her be."*

"Cheater!" she shouted. Claws out, she flailed at him.

He fended her off with ease. Catching her hands, he snapped, *"Be still, you stupid woman."*

Susannah shrieked her disapproval. *"Let me go!"*

Kaitlyn pressed herself against the wall. This was her chance. All three spirits were here together. She raised her hands and murmured the banishing spell she had used on occasion, praying it would send them all to hell. "What is gloomy, be filled with light. Send these spirits from my—"

Camille screeched at Kaitlyn, the sound so loud and otherworldly she broke off mid-sentence.

Lyle shoved Susannah aside and rounded on Kaitlyn, his dark eyes blazing with devilish lights. *"Don't tempt fate, witch. I won't allow you to hurt me again."*

"Oh, no?" Kaitlyn met his angry gaze. "You have no power over me." She raised her hand.

Lyle shook his fist at her, which told her he knew his powers were impotent against her tight circle of protection. She turned, and her gaze landed on the sapphire. That energized blue stone was the key to banishing him from Scarlet Oak forever. Better grab it first. She sidestepped him and tore the necklace from the woman's ghostly neck.

Camille screamed. *"No! Give it back!"*

"The Midnight Star belongs to me." Lyle blocked her exit. *"Hand it over."*

"No." Kaitlyn palmed the blue stone and backed away. It was warm in her hand.

Lyle swung at her, and his punch bounced off the glowing circle. She stalked around him and angled for the door. Lyle grabbed at the tail of her shirt, and was repelled again. He fell on his face in the dirt. Ignoring his angry shout, Kaitlyn halted at the door and raised her hand.

Lyle and Susannah vanished before she could send them away.

She turned on Camille

"No!" The woman disappeared in a cloud of smoke, her shrill cry echoing off the walls of the Keep. *"I want my necklace!"*

Her plan thwarted, Kaitlyn murmured a curse and stepped back outside. She saw no one. Thoroughly irritated, she paused and tried to get her bearings. Somehow, she had to find Colin. Maybe if she continued around the house, she would find him.

The rain the day before had left a chilly wind behind. Icy air washed over her face. Goose bumps broke out on her arms as she churned over the uneven round. The oak tree at the corner of the house rose up in front of her like an ogre. She entered the dark shadows beneath its low hanging limbs and tripped over something in the grass.

She went down on her hands and knees and dropped the sapphire. Her palms skidded through the whipping weeds. Twisting sideways, she gasped. *Oh God. It was Colin, lying still as death.* His glasses lay beside him. She picked them up, and her heart skipped a beat. Was he breathing?

"Colin!" Desperate for him to be alive, she shook him. Wake up!"

His eyes blinked open.

Her stomach clenched. *Thank God.* He stared up at her, but did he recognize her? "It's Kaitlyn. Are you okay?"

His throat jerked, and he briefly closed his eyes. "My…head. Hurts."

"How did you get out here?" Worry spiked Kaitlyn's nerves. "Did someone kidnap you? Where's your pistol?"

"Pistol?" He dragged his hand through the grass and pressed his fingers to the back of his head. "I don't remember. Damn. Somebody must've hit me. Right here. Ow."

She pushed his hand aside and found a lump rising on his scalp. "Oh, my. Who did that?"

"Beats me." He winced. "Don't play with it." He batted her hand away.

Kaitlyn grabbed his shirt and dragged him into a sitting position. "Sorry if it hurts, but you have to get up. I just had a run in with the ghosts in the Keep. We have to get out of here."

"Where are my glasses?" He looked around.

She handed them to him. "Here."

"Thanks." He put them on, and blinked again. "You saw the ghosts, too?"

"Yes. Susannah and Lyle Forrester, and his mistress, Camille." She dug through the grass until she found the blue stone, which had lost much of its energetic glow. She held it up. "I stole this from Camille. She and Lyle both want it, so they may come after me."

"The Midnight Star." Colin's gaze locked on the sapphire. "Jesus."

"They'll kill for it." She rose and reached for his hand. "We need to go back inside."

"Why don't you just laser them like you did Fabron?" Though he wore a deep scowl, he accepted her help and staggered to his feet. "Hell, they've been dead for over a hundred years."

"They're ghosts." Kaitlyn grabbed his hand. "Lasers don't work on them."

"That figures. Where's my pistol?" Colin looked down at the grass. His body swayed.

Kaitlyn slid an arm around his waist to steady him. "Don't move. I'll find it."

"Okay." He put his hand on the tree trunk.

She dropped to her knees and sifted her fingers through the grass until she spotted the dark gun lying on its side. "Here it is." She picked it up and handed it to him.

He clumsily tucked it into his holster. "Thanks. Now, can we go inside?"

"Yes. We need to talk." She gripped his hand. "I need to know what happened."

"I don't know what I can tell you." He reluctantly stumbled along beside her. "I don't remember much."

"I'm so glad you're wearing the amulet. Without it, they would have killed you." She cupped the sapphire in one hand and used her other hand to grip his hard bicep. Her heart pounded as she guided him to the house. He tripped on the veranda steps, but Kaitlyn caught him.

"Careful."

"What about you?" He halted in the shadows. "Are you okay?"

"Yes. I'm fine."

"She said she would hurt you."

"Who?"

"The woman in the blue dress."

"Susannah."

"Yeah."

She opened the door and led him inside. He seemed to grow a little stronger as they climbed the steps. She cut him a sidelong glance. "We'll talk more once we're upstairs. I'll make a circle around the room to keep us safe."

"Okay." He lifted a hand to his scalp. "Your room?"

"Yes." She squeezed the sapphire in her fist. "I'll need my wand."

She would do all she could to keep Colin safe. And she would be prepared when the ghosts returned. No more walking around the house unprotected.

Once they entered the room, she put the sapphire on the table and called up a circle just for it. Then she picked up her wand. Colin sat down on the bed and watched her light the rune candles and say a protection spell. As a second barrier, she called up a circle and reveled in its soft blue glow.

"As above, so below and all around," she said. "The circle is sealed."

"They can't get through that?" Colin asked,

She lowered her hand and shook her head. "No. We're safe as long as we don't leave it."

"If you say so." His shoulders lost some of their tension.

She turned on the lamp and knelt behind him on the bed. Careful not to hurt him, she slid her fingertips gently across his scalp. The lump had grown larger.

"Is it bleeding?" He turned.

"No. Be still."

He eased back around and didn't move. "Do you think I have a concussion?"

"I don't know." She held two fingers up in front of him. "How many do you see?"

"Ten."

Fear fluttered through her. She grabbed his shoulder. "How many?"

"Just kidding." He quirked his mouth. "I see two."

"Stop it," she said. "This is serious."

"Sorry." He grew solemn. "I was only trying to lighten the mood. That ghost scared the hell out of me."

"I was worried when I woke up to find you gone."

"Susannah told me she wanted to lure you to the Keep."

"Her ploy worked." Kaitlyn frowned. "I went looking for you, and heard voices."

"They were going to bury me alive, but they started fighting." He blew out a harsh breath. "I guess I should be thankful. "

"The amulet saved you. It, and their desperation to get their hands on the sapphire." Kaitlyn glanced at the Midnight Star in its own circle on the table. "They'll do anything for it. Lyle believes having the stone will bring him back to life, and that once it does he'll never die."

"I don't know which one of them hit me, but I think they were aiming for each other." Colin pressed a hand to his temple and winced. "I got in the way."

"I don't doubt it." She touched his cheek. Her empathy for him had grown since they'd slept together. And his grudging acceptance of her craft didn't hurt, either. Emotion rose in her chest. Not wanting to confront it, she dropped her hand. "You should rest. You've had a nasty blow."

"Later. I need to know why Lyle Forrester is parading around as himself. Isn't he the one you said was inside Fabron's head?"

"Yes." She couldn't help but smile. He was trying so hard to understand. "Fabron must still be recovering from last night."

"I'm not surprised." Colin ran a hand down his face. "You zapped the hell out of him. And for him to be dead—" He shook his head. "It's pretty damned amazing he can recover at all."

"He won't, really." She drew her brows together. "He'll be possessed, just like before. The being, Lyle Forrester, who in this case is called an *entity*, will go back into his body. If he so desires, that is. If not, Fabron will stay dead."

"You mean, he'll be possessed like in *The Exorcist*?"

"Not exactly. Lyle isn't a demon." Kaitlyn slid to the edge of the bed to perch beside him. "He's a spirit who refuses to cross over. There's a big difference."

"I see."

"I've destroyed your neat, orderly world, haven't I?"

"You could say that." Colin tucked a lock of her hair behind her ear. "And if you weren't so damned beautiful, I just might hold it against you."

"I'm so glad you don't," she said gravely. "Because Lyle wants that sapphire. He killed once to get it, and he won't hesitate to kill again. I need to be able to protect you from his evil spirit."

"And yet you brought the stone back with you."

"Yes, I did," she said. "We can't make it easy for Lyle to get his greedy hands on it. It belongs to Remy and Gillian."

"Wish we had a way to lock it up." Colin shrugged out of his shoulder holster and gripped the Glock. "I'm sure there's a safe downstairs, but with Fabron having access to the office—"

"The circle will keep it safe."

He looked at her. "You're certain of this?"

"Yes." Kaitlyn met his intense chocolate eyes. "And I also know that a bullet won't stop a ghost. So you can put that gun away."

Colin looked at her. Deep in his heart, he knew she was right. But he wanted the Glock with him just in case. He put it on the bed. "I'm a sworn FBI agent. I need my weapon."

"Suit yourself." She rose and crossed to her suitcase.

His cell phone rang. Still groggy, he pulled it out. "Winter."

"Colin, this is Burl."

"Yeah?" Colin widened his eyes. "I didn't expect to hear from you so soon."

"I'm not calling you about the prints."

"Didn't figure you'd have those back this fast."

"I have news, and it isn't good."

"Wonderful." Colin braced himself. Kaitlyn turned and looked at him, and he met her curious gaze with a perturbed one of his own. "Well, hell. You might as well spit it out."

"New Orleans Police found a woman's body floating in the Mississippi River."

Colin took a moment to absorb that information. They were a few miles north of New Orleans, and the Mississippi wasn't far away. His gut clenched. "Is she our girl?"

"Could be. Word has it that she resembles the other dead girls found at Scarlet Oak."

"Damn. Fabron put her in the river." He scowled. "How old do they think she is?"

"Young, about seventeen or eighteen. That's about right, isn't it?"

"Yes, unfortunately." Colin released a pent up breath. "Get me more information soon as you can."

"You've got it."

"I need something tying her to this place," Colin said. "I don't suppose cornmeal would survive the affects of submersion in river water."

"I doubt you'll find any trace evidence on her skin after this length of time, seeing as she's a floater."

"That figures." Colin cursed.

Burl grew silent. "I know you really wanna solve this case. But don't get your hopes up about those prints, either."

"I won't," Colin said. He knew better than to get excited about any aspect of this case, especially now. He'd hoped to nail Fabron with evidence from the latest dead girl. Now all his evidence had been washed away. "Just get back with me soon as you know something, okay?"

"You bet. Take it easy."

Colin ended the call and shoved the phone back into his pocket. His nerves skittered like a mouse on cold concrete.

"Trouble?" Kaitlyn walked over and put her hand on his shoulder.

He looked at her. "Yeah. The missing body may have been found floating in the river. Water washes away evidence."

"I'm sorry." She gave his shoulder a squeeze.

He tugged her onto his lap. "Thanks for caring."

"I know you want to finish the job you came here to do." She wrapped her arms around his neck. She kissed him softly. "I like a responsible man."

He laughed and kissed her back. "I like a responsible witch."

"Why don't you lie down and get some rest? It's barely dawn." She ruffled his hair. "You had a nasty knock on the head and you didn't get much sleep last night. I can't let you sleep too long, however. Because of that."

"Yeah, head injuries are a bitch. Will you lie down with me?"

"For a while."

"Well, in that case—" He kissed her again. "Let's do it."

*****

Etienne Fabron fought free of Camille's clammy hold and slipped from the Keep into the yard. Warm, moist air engulfed him as he bolted toward the bayou. Camille gave chase, calling for her lover.

"Lyle!" She floated over the grass. *"Lyle, come back! Please."*

The spirit in Fabron's head began to shriek. Fabron called on his *loa* to help him subdue it, but his *loa* rebelled. More afraid than he'd ever been in his life, Fabron suddenly realized he needed a fresh sacrifice in order to appease the god he'd been counting on to save him.

The witch. A powerful blood lust raced through his veins. She was inside the house with the FBI agent. He would have to lure her back outside and feed her to his hungry *loa*. Soon.

The entity banged its fists against Etienne's throbbing skull. *Kill the witch for* me, *not him!*

"Stop it!" Fabron shouted, squeezing his aching temples.

Camille caught up with him and grabbed his arm. *"Lyle, stay with me. Please."*

The entity shrieked again, the sound coming from Fabron's mouth.

The ghost shrank away.

"Go away from me, woman," Fabron said sharply. "Now is not the time. Trust me."

"As you say, but I will stay close by," Camille said. Fear glazed her glowing red eyes. *"I must be with Lyle. Forever."*

Keep her away from me, the entity cried. *Do you wish to die this day?*

Fabron's throat began to burn. He clawed at it. "No! Please don't—"

Bring me the witch and let me *decide her fate.*

Warm blood seeped through Fabron's trembling hands. Falling to the ground, he writhed in agony. "I-I'll do it. Please stop hurting me!"

To his relief, the bleeding slowed. He rolled onto his side and lay still. After a few minutes, it had stopped completely and the searing pain began to recede as well. Dawn's pearl pink light soon gave way to the sun, and Camille drifted away.

And still Fabron lay in the grass, unable to move. He was still weak from last night's encounter with the witch, and fighting with the being had sapped his strength. He desperately needed more sleep. He was so tired. He closed his eyes. Tonight, when he was rested, he would grab the witch.

But for now, he would succumb to the need to nourish his weary body with sleep. The entity stirred in an effort to keep him awake, but he managed to suppress it. The entity was weary as well.

Overhead, the raven circled.

*****

Colin woke up feeling groggy. He and Kaitlyn had made love, and then he'd fallen into a deep, dreamless sleep. His head felt like it was filled with cobwebs. He rubbed his eyes.

Kaitlyn sat down beside him and touched his cheek. "Hey, sleepyhead. Welcome back to the land of the living. You didn't sleep long, but you've been out cold."

"What time is it?" he asked. The shadows had disappeared. "Feels like a new day."

"A new afternoon, maybe," she said. "You just missed lunch."

"Damn." He sat up. "You should've waked me up."

"You needed to sleep. I called room service." She pointed at a tray on the table. "I saved a sandwich for you, if you want it."

"Thanks. I might take you up on that. But first, I need some more clothes." Colin sat up and put on his glasses, swung his legs off the bed, and pulled on the sweats he'd worn after his shower last night. "I'll go to my room and change, and I also need to make a couple of calls"

"Want me to come with you?" Kaitlyn rose.

"No." He shook his head. It still throbbed, but he did feel better.

Kaitlyn walked around the bed. "Why don't I go for you while you make your phone calls? You can tell me what you need."

"Forget it. I'll be fine." He put on his shoulder holster and headed for the door.

Kaitlyn caught his arm. "Wait."

He looked at her, and widened his eyes as she put out her hand and called up another one of those weird circles. This one was green, and in only seconds it surrounded him like a giant bubble. He tried to touch it, but felt nothing. "Is this really necessary?"

"Yes."

"Too weird." He frowned. Then he had a thought. "Can anyone else see it?"

"Not if I make it invisible."

"You can do that?"

"Yes." She snapped her fingers, and the circle disappeared. Or, at least it seemed to.

He curved his mouth. "That's better. As long as it's still there."

"Trust me," she assured him. "It is."

Amazingly, he did trust her. He opened the door and started for his room. Despite the circles, he was relieved when he heard Kaitlyn shut and lock her door behind him. One couldn't be too careful, especially in this house.

"Colin." Burl's voice made him turn. He spied the lab tech at the top of the stairs. "Burl? What the hell are you doing here?"

"I tried to call you back, but you didn't answer. I got a preliminary report on the prints. Thought you'd want to see it for yourself." He waved a piece of paper in Colin's face. "It's gonna blow your mind."

"I can't believe you got it so fast." Colin motioned for Burl to follow him. "Let's go to my room."

"I ran the prints three times to make sure I hadn't made a mistake. Came out the same every time." Burl trailed him down the hall, bringing with him a cloud of woodsy cologne.

They entered Colin's room. He shut the door and eyed the paper in Burl's hands. "Show me."

"You ain't gonna believe it."

"Yeah?" Colin's lips twitched. "You might be surprised what I've come to believe."

Burl handed him the paper. "Don't say I didn't warn you."

"Nothing from AFIS?" Colin's heart pounded as he peered down at the printed report. The top part was blank. He looked up in surprise.

"Nope. His information has been deleted from the system." Burl crossed his arms. "But that's not all. Keep reading."

"You got a hit in the Louisiana database," Colin said. "The prints are Fabron's. I knew that."

The tech's mouth tipped upward. "Read the next line."

"This says he's deceased." He raised his eyebrows. Hot damn. Kaitlyn was right. He'd hoped it wasn't true, but this convinced him she was right.

Burl nodded. "The man was murdered here on the grounds at Scarlet Oak two weeks ago."

"Holy shit." Colin looked back down at the paper. Seeing it in print made it all too real. He broke out in a cold sweat.

Burl scrunched his eyebrows together. "You okay?"

"Huh?" Colin raised his head and plastered a bland look on his face. "Oh, yeah. Thanks."

"All right. In that case, I'm outta here."

"I appreciate your coming out."

"No problem." Burl opened the door. "I'll keep you posted on that body."

"You do that," Colin said.

The lab tech whirled and was gone. The door clicked shut behind him, the sound ominous in the heavy silence. Colin stared down at the paper in his hand.

Fabron really was a Zombie, and Kaitlyn was a witch. Yet nobody would believe him, if he dared tell his friends at the Bureau. This case would be lost before he ever went public, even if he had the balls to do it. He'd lose his credibility, his friends, his job—

He cursed.

His neat, orderly world had gone to hell in a hand basket, and he had no way to get it back. Funny how he wasn't sure he wanted to.

CHAPTER EIGHT

Once Colin left, Kaitlyn picked up the book of spells. Frustration crept across her skin as she flipped to the chapter on banishment. Banishing sickness, banishing a troublesome person, banishing pain. None of them would do. She kept reading. Banishing bad memories, banishing unwanted guests. *Banishing evil spirits.*

Kaitlyn's spine tingled as she read the words. That was it. Lyle and Susannah Forrester were evil personified. And Camille was insane, if a ghost could be said to be nuts. The three of them together formed a daunting presence. One she had to override, once she found them together again.

She set her mouth. She could do this.

The room grew cold as ice as she cradled the book and sat down where Colin had slept. She could still smell him, and his scent gave her comfort as she studied the spell.

She would have to focus all her energy on banishing the wickedness from this awful house. It was haunted not only by the three ghosts, but also by the deplorable acts that had taken place here. So much agony, pain, and death.

"You don't know pain."

Kaitlyn turned and spotted Susannah Forrester hovering beside the window, just outside the circle she had drawn. Her eyes widened. The ghost's blue velvet dress was dirty, and tears dripped down her flushed cheeks. She mopped them away with a wrinkled lace handkerchief.

"Lyle doesn't want me anymore."

Kaitlyn's heart pounded. She closed the book and got up.

"He still pants after that bitch, Camille."

"I'm sure he still loves you, Susannah—"

"You know nothing!" The ghost squeezed the handkerchief in both trembling hands. *"He's obsessed with the Midnight Star."*

"That doesn't surprise me." Kaitlyn remembered the legend Remy had related. "He killed Camille for it all those years ago."

"Yes. Right before she murdered my children."

"I'm so sorry."

"I don't need your pity." Susannah lifted her chin. *"Give me the sapphire, and I'll go on my way."*

Kaitlyn shook her head. "I don't have it."

"Yes, you do. You took it when you fled the Keep."

"Look around all you want." Kaitlyn spread her hands. "You won't find it here."

Unable to enter the circle, Susannah searched the room with her eyes. They glowed red. *"Where is it? Tell me, or at least let me look for it."*

"No," Kaitlyn snapped. "I can't give you the sapphire."

"You've hidden it somewhere." The ghost's skirt billowed around her. *"I know you have."*

"Believe what you want." Kaitlyn crossed her arms. The woman appeared to be on the verge of a breakdown.

Susannah's gaze landed on the *grimoire* lying at Kaitlyn's feet, and her face turned angry.

Kaitlyn picked up the book.

"Give it to me," Susannah stretched out her hand. *"I must search everywhere."*

"No." Kaitlyn wrapped her arms around the *grimoire.*

"Damn you," Susanna snarled.

"Be gone!" Kaitlyn shouted. Power infused her. She picked up her wand and waved it at the ghost. All at once, a bright light flashed and Susannah disappeared in a puff of smoke.

Still clutching the book of spells, Kaitlyn stumbled to the table and put it down. Her legs wobbled. She yanked out a chair and sat down. Her heart pounded out a steady beat. Sweat drenched her skin and she suddenly realized she was shaking all over.

An odd burning electrical odor hung in the air. She gripped the jade pendant hanging around her neck and rubbed it between her thumb and forefinger for extra protection. The circle had held, but having Susannah so close had unnerved her.

At least Colin hadn't been here. He'd already had one run in with the ghost. He didn't need another.

*****

Still mulling over Burl's DNA report, Colin took a quick shower. The cool water felt like heaven to his aching head. As he toweled off, he glanced at his reflection in the mirror, and his eyes zeroed in on a small love bite on his neck.

Kaitlyn had done that. He ran his fingertips over the tiny bruise. Were all witches that hot? He grinned and shook his head. Try as he might, he couldn't get his first perception of her out of his head. She was a beautiful, vibrant, sexy woman. Who, he had learned, also happened to be a witch. But that was secondary to the woman part.

He finished his ablutions and dressed in a fresh pair of blue jeans and a blood-red collared shirt. His shoes were still damp from last night's rain, so he pulled on his socks and set his shoes on a chair by the window. They should finish drying soon thanks to the bright streak of sunlight now streaming through the pane.

He sat down on the bed, put on his glasses, and picked up the file on the murders. His eyes scanned the first entry, but he didn't comprehend a word of it. He couldn't keep his mind from drifting to the way Kaitlyn's gorgeous jade eyes had widened when he'd first entered her yesterday in the shower. She'd clawed at his shoulders and her body had tightened around him like a wet velvet glove. He winced and adjusted the fly of his jeans. He was getting hard. Just thinking about her made him ache with need.

He blinked down at the folder. *The case.* He had to focus, so he could learn who had killed those four young girls. He read and reread the information, and discovered he was more confused than ever. Finally, he blew out a frustrated sigh and snapped the file shut. He was getting nowhere. Then he again thought of the body NOPD had pulled from the river. It would take a major stroke of luck, but if they could find at least one grain of trace evidence on her, he might still be able to pin the murder on Fabron—even if he was a Zombie. All he needed was a piece of cornmeal to match that found stuck to the other girls' bodies and/or the grains scattered at the sinister Vodun killing ground. He really should examine that area again.

He rose and started for the door. As he walked down the hall, he pulled out his cell phone and called Burl. The tech answered on the second ring.

"Johnson."

"Burl, it's Colin Winter," he said. "I know it's only been a few hours, but do you have anything on that body yet?"

"Nope."

"Have you printed it?"

"Yeah, and it's your girl. But as for any real evidence—haven't found anything so far."

Colin blew out a frustrated breath. His eyes slid across the parlor to Kaitlyn's door. He thought about knocking on it, but—no. He couldn't let himself be distracted right now. The case was too important, even if it might very well go nowhere.

Burl's voice rang in his ear. "That water has so many contaminants—"

"That doesn't surprise me." Colin deliberately tore his gaze from Kaitlyn's room and started down the stairs. The foyer was empty.

Paper rustled over the phone. "I'll let you know the minute I find something."

"Thanks, although I don't know why I'm asking."

"Why do you say that?"

"Doesn't matter. Never mind."

"Whatever," Burl said. "Trust me. I'm on it. I'll have something for you soon."

Colin thanked him and ended the call. Pots clanged in the kitchen as he entered the library and angled for Fabron's small office.

"I need to find anything that might help tie those murders together," he muttered to himself. Even if the case was essentially over, he needed closure. "Cornmeal, dirt samples, pollen—"

The office door was ajar. His skin tingled. He halted next to the narrow opening and pulled out the Glock. His gaze swept the room to make sure no one was getting a drop on him. He didn't figure Fabron would show his face in the hotel, but some crooks—even Zombies—were notoriously stupid. To his relief, no one was about.

He gave the door a gentle push and watched it swing slowly inward. The office was empty. Fabron's plate from the day before was gone from the desk, and a light dusting of fingerprint powder still littered most exposed surfaces. Colin checked the closet. *Nothing.*

He re-holstered the Glock. Someone had been in the office, though. Probably one of the staff, who had taken the plate back to the kitchen. Not another damned thing had been touched that he could tell. He looked around a little more and then slipped back through the library and into the foyer.

Raised voices from the kitchen echoed through the dining room.

"I told you, I haven't seen him," a man growled. "Do your own damned job, and don't worry about doing his. Understand?"

"Well, someone has to do it," a woman snapped. "Remy and Gillian are due back soon. We can't let the place look neglected."

"If it does, it's not our fault. Fabron left the hotel on his own accord."

Colin's eyebrows shot up. He marched down the hall to the kitchen and peeked inside. A swarthy-skinned man and a slim brunette faced off in front of the stove. A platter piled with fried catfish sat on the counter beside it.

The woman turned, and her eyes widened in surprise. "Oh, my. Hello. May I help you?"

"I hope so. I'd like to ask you a few questions." Colin pulled out his identification. "FBI."

"Okay." The man lifted a shoulder in a slight shrug. "Sure."

"I guess it's all right," the woman said. Her cheeks turned a funny shade of pink.

Colin put away his ID. "It's about Etienne Fabron."

"Ah. You heard us fighting." The woman crossed her arms.

With a brisk nod, Colin pulled a pen and pad from his jacket pocket. "What's your name?"

"Jenny Daigle." She jerked her thumb at the man. "This is David Blanchard."

The man bobbed his head. "We're from New Orleans."

"Both of you?" Colin asked, looking from one to the other.

Jenny nodded.

"Yeah." David scowled. "That Fabron dude—man, he's one weird cat."

"How so?"

"He's always lurking around the place, watching us." She looked jittery. "Even when he stayed out in one of the cottages."

David set his mouth. "I've seen him wandering the grounds at night—like he was looking for something. It was real creepy."

"I saw him do that, too," Jenny added. "More than once. It gives me the chills. I usually get David to walk me to my cottage every night and keep watch while I lock up."

"Have you seen Fabron lately?" Colin asked.

She shrugged. "Not in a day or two. I'm not complaining, mind you. I was thrilled when he moved into the house. That got him that much farther away from my cottage."

"I see. Where did he stay?"

"In the third cottage down. I'm in the second."

Colin noted that on his pad. "Why did he move in here?"

"I believe he said there was some kind of electrical problem in his cottage. Don't know if that's true or not, but who cares?" David shoved his hands deep into his pockets. "He spends a lot of time in the Keep. Seems kind of crazy to me."

"You didn't look for him after he disappeared?"

"Hell, no."

"We're just glad he's gone," Jenny said, her relief evident in her eyes.

Colin pocketed his pad and pen. "Well, thank you for your help."

"Sure thing," David said. "We'll be around if you need anything else."

"Dinner?" Colin asked, indicating the fish. It smelled delicious.

Jenny smiled. "Yes. Have a filet."

He nabbed one and bit into it. It tasted as good as it smelled, doubly so because he'd never taken Kaitlyn up on that sandwich.

`"Don't forget. We eat at six o'clock, sharp," David reminded him.

He grinned. "I'll be here."

They went back to work, and he sneaked another catfish filet before heading out the door. He exited the house via the back door and eyed the cottages strung like pearls along the bayou. He'd never grasped the fact that Fabron had once lived in one of those. Jenny said the concierge had stayed in the third one down. Curious to know if he'd left anything inside, Colin struck out across the yard. He was glad to see the grass finally had dried from last night's heavy rain.

A piercing caw above him brought him to a halt. He looked up and spotted the raven, circling overhead like some sort of demon. Evil bird. A cold shiver snaked down Colin's spine as he remembered Kaitlyn telling him the damned thing wasn't really a bird, but was in fact Lyle Forrester's ghost in the shape of a raven. He shook off the chill and kept going.

The raven circled closer. Colin broke into a jog. A burst of icy wind cascaded over him, and moisture beaded on his brow. The bird screeched, signaling that it was right behind him. His nerve endings tingled. He yanked out the Glock and whirled around.

The raven dove at his head.

"Colin!" His name swirled through the air on another burst of wind. He recognized Kaitlyn's frantic shout. "Don't shoot it! Please."

He ducked sideways and the raven flew by him with a frightening squawk.

Kaitlyn bolted toward him across the lawn. "Leave it alone. You'll anger the spirit world."

"Bullshit," he said, tracking the bird with the pistol as it circled back through the trees. One clean shot would take care of it.

She skidded to a stop beside him and put her hand on his arm. "Put the gun away. The raven won't hurt you."

"The damned thing just tried to skewer me."

"It did not. You scared it."

"I don't believe you." Colin re-holstered the Glock. "You'd probably try to catch the damned thing and make it into a pet. Even if it is Lyle Forrester's ghost."

"You were listening." She rewarded his correct remark with a brilliant smile. "Where are you going?"

"To Fabron's cottage. I want to look around."

"I'd forgotten he lived there." Her expression softened. "Mind if I come along?"

Hell, yes. Colin dragged his gaze from her pretty face and eyed the circling raven with contempt. If it wasn't for that damned bird, she might have stayed in the house. He needed time alone to help him come to grips with his shredded case.

She touched his hand. "Colin?"

"Okay." He met her insistent green eyes. When she looked at him like that, he just couldn't say no. "But you have to remember that I'm working." What good it would do, he didn't know. But he had to do something.

"I will. I promise I won't bother you or get in the way."

Oh, please. Just being around her made him remember all that had gone wrong since he'd first arrived at Scarlet Oak. Yeah, they'd made love, and it had been unbelievable. But he'd also found out that she really was a witch, and that his main suspect was a Zombie. That meant he couldn't pursue his case and keep his credibility. Talk about frustration. He yanked his gaze from hers and stepped toward the cottage. "Let's get going, then."

"What are you looking for?"

"Anything that incriminates Fabron. For what good it will do." He eyed the small white frame house up ahead. "Burl said the concierge was killed here at Scarlet Oak two weeks ago."

"You need something linking him to those crimes."

"For my files, if for nothing else." He shot her a sideways glance. "So don't touch anything."

"I won't."

Colin was relieved that she remained silent as they neared the cottage. If he walked a step ahead, he could almost imagine he was alone.

"The raven's gone."

Her words startled him. He looked at her, then up the sky. She was right. The bird was gone. A frisson of tension left his taut shoulders. "Good. I hate that damned thing."

"I sent it away."

"Thank you." He gave her a grudging smile. Why hadn't she done that in the first place? He shook his head and reached for the doorknob.

The door wasn't latched.

Alarm spread through Colin. He ripped out the Glock and put out his arm to stop Kaitlyn. "Stay back."

"We're still protected," she said. Even so, she edged back a step. "Remember?"

"Yeah." He raised his pistol. "Force of habit. Indulge me, okay?"

"Sure," she said. "You're a lawman, through and through."

"True," he said. "I'm going in. Wait here."

"I'll wait a few minutes, but if you don't come back I'm coming in after you," she said softly.

He raised his brows, and eased the door open. "Just keep your eyes open if you do. I don't want anything to happen to you."

She grabbed his hand and gave it a squeeze.

Colin was strangely comforted. He released her fingers and stepped over the threshold. The interior of the cottage was as silent as a tomb. An eerie chill crawled over his skin. The place smelled of wood polish and mildew. It was old, with peeling paint, old-fashioned plaster walls and crumbling baseboards. It was also empty. Like no one had set foot inside it in years.

He knew better.

Two arched doorways led into the rest of the cottage. His heart thumped as he crossed the small living area and entered a tiny kitchen. Modern appliances had been shoehorned in around a scarred oak table and chairs. A squatty window over the sink looked out over the green front lawn.

He yanked open a narrow door past the stove, and found an ancient gas water heater. To his left was an opening that led into what looked like a mudroom containing a sink and an old ringer-type washing machine. There was no sign of Fabron or any of his belongings.

He reentered the living room and slipped through the other archway. Straight ahead was a miniscule bathroom, which had probably been carved from the bedroom next door when indoor plumbing was added to the cottage. He poked his head inside. A toilet, a sink and a small shower took up most of the space. He saw no towels or anything else to show it had been used recently.

Two small bedrooms flanked the bathroom. He pushed open the door to one and found a full-size bed, a handsome chest of drawers, and a beautiful antique table. He checked the drawers and the closet cut into the wall near the bathroom. All were empty. Ditto for the second room.

Disappointment funneled through him. If Fabron had, in fact, stayed here, he hadn't left a damned thing, except maybe some fingerprints and other trace evidence. Colin made a mental note to remind Burl to check the drain traps for hair and fibers. As if it mattered.

"Colin?" Kaitlyn's voice startled him.

He whirled with the Glock to see her standing right behind him. A feeling of relief stole over him. "I thought you were going to stay outside for a while."

"I did." She brought a hand to her throat. "But I didn't hear anything, and I was worried."

"I'm protected by the circle, remember?" He sent her a knowing look, jammed the Glock back into his shoulder holster and walked to the window. "If someone had jumped me, he would have been repelled, and I would have killed him."

A look of pride flashed over her face. She liked that he believed her, and that made him feel good. Yet he

realized that his new knowledge was in direct opposition
to everything he'd ever learned. It threatened to derail his
career, and could cause him an infinite amount of
heartache. Soon, he was going to have to make a choice.
He set his jaw. "Still, you're interfering with a crime
scene."

"What crime scene?" She lifted her arms and looked
around. "The cottage is empty."
"I need answers, and I'm grasping at straws. If we
disturb what little trace evidence may be in here, we
could jeopardize what's left of my case."

"Don't worry. I'm just looking around." She turned
and headed for the kitchen. "Surely that won't hurt
anything."

"I guess not. He followed her and drew in her sexy
herbal scent. He wanted to hate her for teaching him
about Zombies and ruining his case, but he just couldn't
bring himself to do it. She had him totally bewitched.

She halted just inside the kitchen and shook her
head. "If Fabron did live here, he certainly didn't leave
anything behind."

"I know." He wet his lips.

She turned. "I should have brought my sage wand.
This place could use a good cleansing."

"Maybe you can come back later."

"Will you come with me?" Her guileless green eyes
searched his face.

He couldn't tell her no, even though he longed to.
He needed to distance himself from her in order to save
his career. Sadness filled him, and he forced a smile he
didn't feel. "Sure I will."

"Good." She put her hand on his arm, came up on his tiptoes, and kissed him, the brush of her lips warming him from the inside out.

He smiled again, this time for real. Damn, but she made him feel good.

She moved away, and the air in the cottage dropped ten degrees. He felt a sharp tingle.

Kaitlyn's eyes flew open in surprise. She reached for his hand.

A loud thud from the window over the sink startled them both.

He turned to stare at it, and was startled to find it cracked. Something had hit it.

"It was the raven." Kaitlyn squeezed his hand. "Lyle is here."

Despite the circle she had put around him earlier, Colin grew apprehensive. His hair stood on end. He pulled out the Glock for extra insurance.

"Lyle?" She walked over to the window. "Where are you?"

"The damned thing hit the window," Colin said. "See that broken pane?"

"I know. Shhh." She held up her hand. "Lyle, where are you?"

A cool breeze sailed through the kitchen, rustling the curtains over the sink. The light dimmed. Colin froze when a heavy sense of evil descended upon him. He gripped the Glock so tightly his hands ached. What in hell was happening to him?

"Something's going on in here, Kaitlyn," Colin said, his confusion quickly morphing into knuckle-biting fear. "There's no one here but us. Still, I feel something. My God."

The rustling stopped. The air warmed. The weight on his shoulders lifted.

Kaitlyn swallowed and turned to him. "It was Lyle. I think you scared him away."

"Because I talked to you?"

"Maybe. I don't know. He was here, and now he's gone. It could have been a warning."

"That wouldn't surprise me much." He noted her flushed cheeks and the excitement gleaming in her sharp green eyes. The deliberate jut of her chin. Damn. She was beautiful when practicing her craft. He touched her cheek.

Her mouth curved. "Me, either. Lyle is afraid of me. He could very well try to reach me by hurting you. "

Colin opened his mouth to assure her he was ready to take on the ghost, when a muffled thud from the back of the cottage made him turn around.

Beside him, Kaitlyn went still. Her heart thudded. "What was that?"

"I don't know." He fisted both hands around the Glock and took a step toward the door.

An odd scraping sound crawled across Kaitlyn's nerves. "Someone's in here with us, and it's not Lyle. I felt him go."

"Me, too," Colin said. "It was like a weight was lifted off me."

He really did believe. Happiness spread through her, but it was tempered by the sound of another thud echoing though the small cottage. She bit her lip.

"Hope it's not Fabron." Colin looked at her. "Could it be?"

"Maybe, but I doubt he's strong enough. Unless Lyle has gone back into him—and if that's the case, anything goes." Kaitlyn stepped up beside him. He radiated strength and heat, and she needed both right now.

"Stay here," Colin said. "I'll go check it out."

"You don't have to go alone," she said, her body tingling with alarm. She caught his arm. "I'll be happy to go with you, if you want—"

"Not this time." He gripped his pistol and started for the living area. "This one's mine."

"Wait, Colin," she said, worry for him blossoming inside her chest. She gave him a quick kiss. "That circle won't last forever. I can call up another one for you—"

Another thud from the back cut her off.

He shook his head. "There's no time."

He turned on his heel, and he was gone.

Kaitlyn curled her hand around her jade pendant and rubbed it between her thumb and forefinger for an extra bit of protection. Colin wanted to be chivalrous, and that was fine with her. She just didn't want him to get hurt.

A startled shout echoed from the back of the house. Fear skittered through her, and she turned. "Colin? What's wrong?"

Something slammed hard into her back, knocking her down. A sharp pain speared her right shoulder blades. She cried out. Her vision blurred. Suddenly weak as a kitten, she sank to her knees and called for Colin. This wasn't supposed to happen. She was protected by her circle. Wasn't she?

"Shut up. You're *mine* now, witch. No more damned bubbles." The gruffly spoken words broke through the white haze fogging her brain. She recognized the voice, but her mind refused to focus. She mumbled a rebuttal, but it was cut off when a piece of

foul smelling tape was slapped over her mouth. She
ripped it off and tried to rise, but her assailant shoved her
down face first on the cold ceramic tile and sat on her.
She couldn't get any air.

Colin. Her lungs felt like they might burst. What had
happened to him? She tried to squirm free, and only
managed to get a gulp of air.

"No." Her arms were wrenched back and tied with a
strong cord. Now she couldn't make a circle. "Don't fight
me, and you'll have more time on this earth."

Pain encircled her wrists, so much so that tears filled
her eyes. More tape was slapped on her mouth. With an
agonized cry, she cursed her attacker, her words muffled
by the thick plastic.

He laughed.

She struggled to breathe through her nose. Tears
rolled down her face.

A blindfold was wrapped around her head and tied,
so tightly it made her head hurt. Moments later, she was
dragged to her feet. She stumbled, and her attacker drew
her to him. He smelled like earth, old blood, and rotting
leaves.

A spear of dread pierced her heart. She'd recognize
that smell anywhere. *Etienne Fabron.* Lyle Forrester's
ghost had revived him, and somehow overcome the
circles she had formed for her and Colin. She tried to
scream for help, but the tape blocked her air.

"What was that you said? I can't understand you."
Fabron squeezed her ribs. "Don't run from me this time.
You're about to help me solve a very big problem."

"I'll do anything. Just please—take me to Colin," she
said, but not a word was recognizable.

He ripped the tape free a little bit. "What was that?"

She gasped for air. Then she bit out, "Please—I need to see Colin."

He laughed. "You're really stuck on Mr. FBI now, aren't you?" His laughter died and he made a strange clucking sound low in his throat. His sour breath washed over her face. "Too fucking bad."

She gagged.

He slapped the tape back on her mouth before she could completely get her breath and ran his ice-cold fingers down her cheek. "Get a grip on yourself, honey. We have to go."

She protested more loudly, but the tape muffled her words. She tried to pull away from him, wishing she could rip off the blindfold and look into his eyes, but he fastened his claw-like hand around her upper arm and dragged her forward. She planted her feet on the floor. He whirled and slapped her, snapping her head back and drawing another cry from her lungs.

"Stop fighting me, witch! Your fate is sealed. So you can forget that stunt you pulled last time. I won't look at you. You can't hurt me."

Terror flooded Kaitlyn as Fabron renewed his hard grip on her arm and hauled her out the door. The cool, moist air curled around her, making her wish she was in a sauna—with Colin—and that both of them were happy and safe. Her heart ached for him. Breathing in air through her nose, she drew in the rich, ripe odor of the bayou mixed with Fabron's scummy smell.

An eerie chill rolled down her spine.

He dragged her through the thick grass toward the clearing beside the bayou. At least, Kaitlyn figured that's where they were heading. She couldn't tell with the blindfold blocking her vision. The wind slithered through the trees above them, reminding her of the last time she'd been kidnapped by this creepy man. She had saved herself then. But now — would she get the chance? And what about Colin? Had Fabron hurt him? She pictured him sprawled unconscious on the floor of that empty cottage, and a shell of ice formed around her heart.

"Keep your feet moving," Fabron ordered, giving her elbow another hard yank.

Pain shot up her arm and she was tempted to renew her struggle. If only she could see. She needed to focus on the object she wanted to move in order to use telekinesis. Maybe, if she concentrated hard enough, she could make it work without using her vision.

That proved impossible to do as they walked on. Tall weeds whipped at her calves. She imagined them skirting the cemetery on their way to Fabron's special killing field, as Colin had called it. Kaitlyn remembered the blood she'd seen there, and cold fear molded itself around her soul. She had to either escape, or rip off the blindfold and get him to look at her.

His hold loosened momentarily, and she wrenched her arm free. With a startled cry, she took off at a dead run through the high grass. Vision be damned. Fabron let loose a string of harsh curses which turned into a snort. "You won't get far with that blindfold on."

Kaitlyn kept running, putting one foot in front of the other. Seconds later, she stepped in a hole and almost went down. Each step jarred her throbbing head. It was hard to stay upright with her hands tied behind her. She smelled the thick gumbo mud of the bayou, sensed Lyle's strong presence.

Fabron's leering laughter rang out behind her.

Kaitlyn crashed into a metal wall and bounced off. The air sailed from her lungs as she flew backwards, slamming her shoulder blades and skull against the hard ground. Stars flashed behind her eyes. Her chest burned. She moaned, and the duct tape over her mouth swallowed the sound.

Fabron stood over her, his crazed snicker adding insult to the pain rocketing through her body. "Forgot about the fence, didn't you?"

Her chest felt like it might burst open. She gasped for air.

"Quit playing dead, witch." He nudged her with his boot. "Get up."

*****

Colin jerked awake and rubbed his eyes. His head hurt, and anxiety ripped through his heart. He couldn't see a damned thing. He blinked and massaged his eyes again. The world remained dark and silent. He swallowed back a surge of bile. What in hell had happened?

His head throbbed. He moved his hands to the back of his skull and discovered another huge knot there. He vaguely remembered being hit. Had the blow blinded him?

Panic seized him, and he struggled for air. *No.* He forced himself to calm down. *Take it easy. Assess the situation.* His fingers shook as he felt for the Glock. His holster was empty. Damn.

He reached out and touched painted wood and a metal knob. A door sat directly in front of him. He swallowed and put out his other hand. A wall. Ditto for the other side, and behind him. A shiver danced over his skin. He was in an enclosed space. He staggered to his feet, and found himself tangled in an earthy-smelling swath of material. A jacket. He was in a closet. Etienne's Fabron's closet. The jacket hadn't been hanging there earlier.

Kaitlyn. The fear cloaking Colin's movements turned into full-blown terror. Fabron had knocked him out, locked him up, and gone after her.

If he'd gotten his hands on her, Colin had to save her.

His heart pounding, he found the doorknob and twisted it. It moved, but the door wouldn't budge. He hit it with his shoulder, sending an arrow of pain through his throbbing head. No luck. Fabron must've jammed a chair or some other object beneath the knob.

Colin growled an oath. His cop instincts kicked in, and he felt around on a shelf above the clothes for some sort of tool. Anything flat.

Nothing. The place was still empty except for that damned jacket. He ran his hands over it. Something hard in one of the pockets caught his attention. He dug into Fabron's jacket and pulled out a small knife. What a stroke of luck.

His head pounded as he felt for the door's hinges. He used his fingers to guide the small blade beneath the top of the hinge and struggled to shove the pin free. It wouldn't move.

He spat an expletive. A wave of dizziness swept over him and he dropped his arms. The darkness made him disoriented. He leaned against the wall until he got his breathing under control.

"I have to get out of here," he said to no one. "I have to find Kaitlyn."

He shook his head and went back to work on the hinge.

*****

Kaitlyn smelled the odor of freshly turned earth. The soft lap of water tickled her ears and old leaves crunched beside her. They had to be in Fabron's frightening clearing. She lay still and pictured the tall pole adorned with ruffled black feathers, the scattering of cornmeal. And the blood. She drew in its strong, coppery scent. A shudder coursed through her.

"So, you're finally awake." Fabron touched her cheek.

She cringed away from him. The odor of dirt mixed with the blood smell. She sneezed.

"God bless you," Fabron said. Then he laughed, his hoarse cackle raising goose bumps on her skin. He grabbed her arms and pulled her into a sitting position. Then he walked away. She heard a series of noises she didn't recognize, followed by a loud bang.

Anger ripped through her. She had to escape. Running away wasn't the answer. She'd already proven that. And Fabron was physically stronger than she was. So she'd have to resort to casting a spell. If only she didn't have on the blindfold and could look into his eyes. Damn him.

She wriggled around, trying to work her wrists free of the cords, and Fabron shrieked, the high-pitched sound hurting her ears. His palm lashed across her face. She cried out and fell sideways, landing hard on her shoulder in a crisp bed of leaves. Her cheek stung from the blow.

"Don't try that again, witch," he said, his voice strangely calm. "I will *not* allow you to free yourself and hurt me again. Not ever." It was Lyle Forrester speaking, not Fabron.

Tears of fury filled Kaitlyn's eyes. Damn this stupid blindfold. She couldn't even wipe her face, much less diminish him.

"Where's the sapphire? What have you done with it?"

She blinked. "It's somewhere safe, where you can't get to it."

"Damn you." He grabbed her hair and yanked her head back. She felt the cold blade of a knife bite into her neck. "Tell me where it is."

"No." She didn't want him going into her room. What if Colin had made it back to the house? He could be hurt, and she didn't want that. She loved him. The realization startled her.

"Let me guess," he said. "Either Mr. FBI did something with the stone, or you've used your mighty powers to lock it up somewhere. Which is it? I doubt either of you would just leave it in one of your rooms."

Kaitlyn snapped her mouth shut.

"So that's how it is." Fabron snickered. "You *did* leave it in your room."

She jerked away from him.

"Don't you move from this spot," he growled. "Not until I'm ready for you."

She rolled onto her back and tried to get up, but pain radiated up her spine and she stayed on the ground.

"I said 'don't move!'" He kicked her hard in the ribs.

She yelped, and the sound was caught by the tape over her mouth. Her body trembled. She forced herself to lie still so he wouldn't kick her again.

He snickered. "Now, that's a good witch."

Moments later she heard an odd, repetitive sound, and the fecund odor of freshly turned earth grew stronger. He was digging. She longed to ask him why, but instinctively knew he'd only kick her again if she tried to talk. Shivers of anger cascaded through her. He was going to kill her, if she couldn't escape. She knew that with a certainly that took her breath away.

Colin wasn't here to save her. For all she knew, he was already dead.

Her hollow heart swelled with pain. How sad to finally find true love, only to have it snuffed out by a mad ghost in possession of a Vodun master's body. Refusing to give in to self-pity, she bowed herself up and vowed to fight. She wouldn't give Fabron the satisfaction of knowing just how much he had hurt her, and she wouldn't die quietly.

The sound of his shovel meeting dirt echoed in her ears. Then it hit her.

He was digging her grave.

CHAPTER NINE

Etienne Fabron didn't like to sweat. He hated manual labor, and he abhorred the painful red blisters stinging his palms. Yet he took off his suit jacket and kept digging. The entity in his head wouldn't let him stop.

Make it deep, like I did when I buried Susannah alive all those years ago. You know how to do it.

A frightening chill slid over Fabron. With shaking hands, he wiped his brow. He had no idea how deep was deep enough to smother a woman.

Deep enough so no one will dig her up. I don't want her found. Ever.

"I figured that," Fabron muttered. He had no intention of letting anyone find Kaitlyn's body. Ever. Least of all her new lover, Colin Winter. Mr. FBI would be dead right now if that damned pistol of his hadn't skittered into an air conditioning vent in the floor when Fabron had attacked him.

He gripped the shovel and stabbed it hard into the gummy earth. Perspiration trickled down his cheek. Beside him, the witch stirred again like she was trying to sit up.

"Be still," he warned her, his anger growing. He should kill her right now.

She mumbled something, but the tape on her mouth prevented him from understanding her words. Her legs jerked. She rolled over onto her stomach and clumsily pushed herself to her knees.

He spat an expletive and hurriedly scooped up another shovel-load of dirt. The pile beside the crude grave was growing. The witch said something else, a rhythmic flow of sounds that sounded eerily familiar. She swayed back and forth, and her rocking posture startled him. She was saying his name, over and over. Was she trying to charm him? Make him go mad?

The entity in Fabron's head began to scream.

Fabron threw down the shovel and marched over to her. "Shut up!"

Kaitlyn ignored him and kept saying his name. "Etienne Fabron, Etienne Fabron."

He backhanded her across the face again, sending her reeling. Her startled cry scratched across his frazzled nerves. With another muffled shout, she fell sideways. Her head landed in a pile of leaves.

The entity laughed as the witch thrashed about on the ground, trying to find her footing.

Fabron nudged her. "Stay down and keep quiet, or next time I'll use the shovel."

She went still.

He put his hands on his knees and watched her pale face for any sign of rebellion. "Understand?"

After a few tense moments her throat jerked, and she nodded.

"See that you obey me. You don't want me to lose my temper."

The entity began to pace back and forth inside Fabron's head, the motion making him nauseous.

Hurry up with that grave. You have to finish it, and then dig a larger one. Time is running out.

Fabron snatched up the shovel. Soon the wind began to blow, icing his skin and plastering his damp shirt to his aching back. His hands stung and his arm muscles burned from too much exertion. He decided right then and there he would never dig another hole, come hell or high water.

Mr. FBI was a strong man. He could dig his own damned grave.

*****

Colin pried up the pin on the first hinge a quarter inch, but he couldn't get it to budge after that. The air in the closet was cold—and getting colder. Yet he wiped a layer of perspiration off his face. Moving slowly, he dropped to his knees and slipped the edge of the knife beneath that pin.

It moved up a half inch before it got stuck.

Colin bit out a nasty curse. His head felt like it was twice its normal size. He sat back against the wall and took a deep breath, although it was hard to do so in this tight space. Good thing he wasn't claustrophobic.

Despite the chilly air and his growing frustration, his mind flew to Kaitlyn. Where was she right now? What had Fabron done with her?

Colin wished she was in the closet with him, so she could use her telekinetic powers to free that pin. Damn. He shook his head. Listen to him. His father had drummed the realities of science into his psyche since before he could walk, and he had never seen anything strong enough to make him refute that knowledge, until now. Hell, he'd gladly give up everything if Kaitlyn could just wiggle her nose like that woman on *Bewitched* and make Fabron and Lyle Forrester's greedy ghost go away.

He wiped his forehead and slid back over to the door. His hands found the hinge and he started back to work. In went the knife. He twisted it back and forth and pulled up on the pin. It moved another fraction of an inch. If only he had some type of lubricant.

His cheeks burned with cold. He leaned over and spat on the pin. Working the sticky moisture into the cracks with his fingers, he tried the knife again.

The damned pin still wouldn't move.

Leverage. He needed to get above the blasted hinge and pull up on it. His head spun as he pushed himself off the floor. He put his hand on the wall for balance.

He closed the knife and felt the knot on the back of his head one more time. It had swollen out a little more. No wonder he was so dizzy. Maybe he had a concussion, which was pretty likely since he'd been hit on the head twice in the past twenty-four hours.

His breathing sawed out as he shook off the unwelcome bout of vertigo and went back to work on the hinge. He centered the knife blade in the slot and, using both hands, put pressure on the pin. It finally gave with an odd squeal. He stumbled backwards and slammed against the wall.

He stood there, stunned, squeezing the metal pin in his hand. At least he hadn't hit his head again. Sweat rolled down his back as he stuffed the pin into his pocket and spit on his fingers. He spread that moisture on the top pin. He blinked and rubbed his eyes. If only he could see. His head hurt from trying to peer through the intense darkness.

He took a deep breath. He needed to get out of the closet and find Kaitlyn. If Fabron had captured her, he wouldn't give in easily. Not this time. Colin gripped the knife and pretended the hinge was Fabron's disgusting neck.

"I'll kill that crazy bastard Fabron if he hurts her," he muttered. Icy fear spurred him on as he slid the knife blade against the top hinge and pried up on it. It squealed like a rat in a trap. And all at once, with a little grit and elbow grease, that pin popped out too.

Relieved, Colin stuffed it in his pocket along with the knife and put both hands on the doorknob. After a couple of hard yanks, the door pulled free and almost hit him in the face. Weak gray light flooded in. The board that had been beneath the knob hit his foot.

He muttered a few choice words and kicked it aside. Then he removed the door and shoved it out of his way. His head throbbed as he stumbled from the closet and gulped in several mouthfuls of fresh air. It was cold, but tolerable.

Once he got his bearings, he searched the back room for his pistol. It was nowhere in sight. Fabron must have taken it with him.

Irritation ate a hole in Colin's gut as he cut through the living room and went out the door. He'd get his backup pistol from the house. He chewed himself ten ways from Sunday for not strapping it to his ankle before he headed for the cottage.

He stepped off the porch and halted in his tracks.

A dead raven lay beneath the window over the sink.

*****

Curled up in the pile of leaves, Kaitlyn plotted her escape. The moment Fabron took off her blindfold — provided that he did — she would find a way to look into his eyes. Then she would diminish him and drive Lyle Forrester from his body.

Her heart pounded as she listened to the slow, rhythmic scooping of the concierge's shovel. The odor of dirt grew stronger and rose up to blend with the musky scent of the bayou. A bug crawled across her hand. She held her breath and shook it off, despite a painful shoulder cramp.

"Get up, witch. It's time."

It took Kaitlyn a moment to realize the voice belonged to Fabron.

"Did you hear me?" he snapped. His boots crunched near her face. "I said, get up!"

She gingerly raised her head. Her aching muscles plagued her as she tried to sit up. "Give me a minute," she muttered, the sound muffled by the tape.

"Be quiet," Fabron said. He grabbed her blouse and hauled her to her feet.

She gasped at the sudden change in equilibrium. Her mouth was so dry she couldn't swallow.

He gripped her elbow and yanked her toward him. "The angel of death is waiting for you."

Anger streaked through her. She jerked away from him. "No!"

"Be still." His hand clamped down on her wrist. Her body stilled as she felt the bite of cold steel against her hand. Fabron's sour breath bathed her cheek. She focused her thoughts on the jade pendant around her neck. Her mother had given her that for protection, and she had to remember that. Fabron couldn't hurt her no matter how hard he tried.

The rope binding her wrists tightened briefly, and then it was gone. Burning blood pulsed through her hands and shoulders. She carefully pulled them forward, wincing at the pain.

"Don't try to get away, or I'll kill you right now," Fabron said.

Go ahead and try, she thought. *You'll never succeed.*

He untied the blindfold, and muted sunlight met her eyes. She turned, trying to see his face, but he avoided her eyes. They were in a clearing, but definitely not the same one where he'd made his sacrifices. Her heart rate slowed a bit as she searched for a way to escape if she couldn't disable him.

He reached out and ripped the tape from her mouth.

"Ow!" she cried, the motion stinging her lips. She pressed a hand over her mouth and glared at him with furious eyes. "Stop hurting me."

"Shut up."

"You won't succeed," she said. Her mouth was dry. She tried to wet her lips, but she had no saliva. She needed water. Damn him for putting her in this position.

His lips curled back to reveal even white teeth, yet he still wouldn't look her in the eye. "You'll see soon enough."

He handed her the shovel and pointed her toward a five-foot long trench in the ground. "Dig."

She looked down at the tool in her hands.

He shoved her toward the hole. "Do it now."

A dark cloud slid over the sun, and Kaitlyn reared back and swung the shovel at him. He raised his arm, fending off the blow, and the shovel thudded against his forearm. He screeched and leapt away. She advanced on him.

"No!" His eyes riveted on the shovel, and he backpedaled, cradling his injured arm in his other hand. "Bitch!"

"Stop hitting him!" The voice came from Fabron's mouth, but Kaitlyn knew it was Lyle. Susannah Forrester suddenly appeared beside him, a white lace handkerchief gripped in her right hand. Her glowing red eyes clashed with the vivid blue of her dress.

Kaitlyn gripped her pendant and said a quick spell of protection as Fabron's pain-stricken face morphed into Lyle's. An icy chill washed over her, although the air near the bayou was growing more humid by the minute. Mosquitoes buzzed near her ears.

Lyle's mouth curved into a sneer. He rubbed his thin mustache. *"Hello, Susannah."*

Susannah's eyes widened. She gasped softly.

Kaitlyn stepped between them and raised the shovel.

"Get out of my way, witch." Lyle tightened his hands into fists. *"That's my wife."*

"Forget it. I'm not moving."

Susannah nervously wrung her handkerchief. *"Leave her alone, Lyle. I know where you can find the Midnight Star."*

Anger tightened Kaitlyn's throat. "You'll never touch it. I'll see to that."

"You don't understand. I must have it, if I am to win back my husband." Susannah's features tightened. She peered past Kaitlyn. *"It's in her room."*

"I knew it." Lyle's stance loosened, and his eyes locked with Susannah's.

Kaitlyn grabbed his sleeve and tried to get him to look at her. "Stay away from my things. You'll never get the sapphire. It's protected."

"Protection can be broken. I'll do whatever I have to do to get the Midnight Star." Lyle's dark eyes gleamed as he smiled at his wife. *"It belongs to me."*

"And me," Susannah cried.

"It doesn't belong to either of you," Kaitlyn told them. "Lyle murdered for it."

"Which means, you're cursed, Lyle." Camille suddenly appeared on the other side of the open grave. *"Forever. I'll see to that."*

His opaque eyes took on a fiery orange glow. He looked demonic. Electricity sparked through the air. Kaitlyn looked from Lyle to Camille to Susannah. She raised her hand and called up a circle.

Susannah took a menacing step toward Camille. *"You broke up my family and killed my children. You deserve to rot in hell forever."*

"Always the lady," Camille said, her lips curling as she mocked the woman who'd once been her employer. *"No wonder Lyle turned to me. You may be proper, but your bed is cold as ice."*

"At least I'm not a whore *like you."*

Camille made a high-pitched shriek and lunged at Susannah.

Colin didn't believe what he was seeing. The ghost who'd roused him from sleep the night before and another woman, fighting beneath the trees. He shook his head to make sure he wasn't seeing things. He wasn't. *Damn.* These spirits were wild.

Kaitlyn stood to one side, watching the women claw and spit at each other like a couple of angry wildcats.

Thank God she was safe. The ice around Colin's heart began to thaw.

Then he looked at Fabron, who stood only inches from a gaping hole in the ground. A grave? The concierge's face was paper white, and he looked like he might keel over any minute.

Colin's gut tightened. He clutched his back up Glock and watched the scene unfold before him.

Fabron lunged at Kaitlyn, who held up her hands.

"No!" Colin's deep bellow carried through the trees. He surged forward.

Kaitlyn sidestepped Fabron and whipped around to face him. He screeched and covered his eyes with one hand. The other hung limp at his side.

Colin raced toward them, his pistol drawn. She should have a circle around her, but if not, he couldn't let the concierge kill her. Anger rocketed through him. His heart pounded as he slid to a stop about twenty feet away from them. "Back away from her, Fabron."

"He's not Etienne," Kaitlyn said sharply. "Remember? It's Lyle Forrester."

"I know." He looked like Fabron, but Colin knew he was walking around only because he was possessed by the ghost. Colin kept his weapon trained on the concierge. His nostrils flared. "Do it, Kaitlyn."

"He won't look at me."

"*Of course I won't.*" Lyle lowered his hands, but kept his eyes averted.

She eyed Colin. "Please move away from us. If I get the chance to diminish him—"

"*You cannot hurt me,*" Lyle roared, his coal black eyes glittering with rage.

"Don't ask me to leave your side. We'll do this together." He had to, damn it. He loved her. A lump the size of Texas rose in his throat. "You take care of him your way, and I'll do it mine."

"She may not ask, but I will. Leave us be," Susannah said, her haughty voice daring Colin to act. *"We've a score to settle and there is no more putting it off. Go away."*

"Relax, Susannah," Kaitlyn said, her voice oddly calm. A brilliant smile curved her lips. "Colin is only being protective of me."

"He's disturbing my only chance at Lyle."

"You have no chance at all with me, woman," Lyle spat. *"I tired of you long ago."*

"He chose me," Camille said, gloating over Susannah. *"We were lovers. We still are."*

Tears welled in Susannah's eyes.

Kaitlyn glared at the warring ghosts. "Stop it, all of you!"

Colin began to circle around behind Fabron.

"No!" Worry ripped through Kaitlyn. He was trying to lure Lyle away from her. If he killed Fabron before she could take care of Lyle, all would be lost.

"Move away from her, Fabron." Colin leveled his pistol at the Zombie's gaunt face, and the ghost inside him screeched like a banshee.

Colin ignored it and edged closer to him.

"Please don't shoot my husband," Susannah begged. She blotted her eyes with her wadded handkerchief. *"I'm trying to win him back."*

"You won't succeed," Camille snapped. *"He's mine."*

The warm breeze stirred and brought with it the odor of the bayou. Kaitlyn held her breath and stepped in front of Fabron.

"Kaitlyn!" Colin shouted. "Get out of the way."

"No. I know what I'm doing." She tried to catch the Zombie's flashing gaze. "You can back me up."

"Me back *you* up?" He laughed sharply. "Move away from Fabron and let me take him out."

"Listen to her, Assistant Deputy Director Winter." Lyle's mouth curved in a haughty sneer. *"Or you will have made a grave error."*

Kaitlyn halted and started back toward them. "Colin?"

"Keep going," Colin shouted. He kept one eye on Lyle, the other on her.

"Leave him be and come away with me, Lyle." Camille's sultry tone promised the ghost a world of pleasure. *"We'll start over in another time and place – with the sapphire, of course."*

"He murdered you, you stupid bitch." Susannah gaped at Camille in disbelief. *"How the hell could you ever go back to him?"*

"I love him. That's why."

"Shut up!" Fabron screamed and dashed toward Kaitlyn. *"I want that sapphire."*

She met his eyes and stopped him cold. He screeched, averted his gaze, and began to back away.

Colin watched, fascinated, as she crept closer to the terrified creature, trying her best to catch his eye. Apprehension gnawed at his gut, but he kept himself in tight control and made sure his law enforcement mask stayed in place. He raised his pistol and slowly circled the two of them. "Do what you have to do, Kaitlyn. I'll finish him off."

"He's no longer alive,"" she said. "Put your gun away."

"Stay away from me, witch!" Lyle said. He jerked his gaze toward the trees and snarled at her. *"Give me the stone."*

"Lyle, don't do this," Susannah wailed. *"Please! Stay with me."*

"Quit your whining." Camille rounded the grave. *"Don't distract him. He might get hurt."*

Susannah glowered at her.

Kaitlyn tried to recapture Lyle's evasive gaze, but he kept his eyes on the trees behind her and began to circle around to her left. She knew she was safe inside her ring of protection. Yet she needed to take care of the three ghosts once and for all. If only she had her wand. This was turning out to be much more difficult than she had anticipated.

She tried to use telepathy to order Lyle to cooperate, but it didn't work. He kept moving, stepping when she stepped, screeching and jerking his gaze free whenever their eyes met. He wouldn't allow her to diminish him like she had before.

"Susannah, Camille —" Lyle snapped. *"Go to the house. Get the sapphire."*

Camille floated past Colin.

"No!" Kaitlyn shouted.

"I'll get it!" Susannah shoved Camille out of the way, and her agonized scream carried through the humid air. *"Stay away from him, you bitch. That stone belongs to Lyle — and me."*

Kaitlyn ignored them and edged toward Lyle. He was the ringleader. If she could take charge of him, she would have them all under her thumb.

"Run, Kaitlyn!" Colin shouted. His voice was tight. "This time, don't stop. They're going to capture the stone."

"They can't," she assured him. "It's protected."

Camille whirled and went after Colin.

"Look out!" Kaitlyn grabbed her pendant and began to rub it between her thumb and forefinger.

"No!" Lyle dove for her. *"No more witchcraft!"*

Colin fired.

Kaitlyn watched in horror as the bullet ripped into the top of Fabron's head, spraying brains, blood and pieces of bone all over the dead leaves behind her. She screamed.

Camille leapt at Colin, who cried out in surprise and dropped his pistol; even the ghost was repelled by the circle around him. His hand caught the chain holding his amulet, and the chain snapped. The amulet flew into a mound of leaves at his feet.

Lyle floated free of Fabron's ruined body.

Kaitlyn watched the ghost hover, and then begin to spin through the clearing like a tornado. It approached Colin. Then all at once, it disappeared.

She turned to look at Camille, and a large, hard body slammed into the circle surrounding her. Crying out in surprise, she tumbled backwards into the leaves. The heavy body hit the ground in front of her. It wasn't Fabron. He was dead—and this body was too solid and too muscular for it to be his.

It was Colin.

Oh. My. God. Kaitlyn's eyes flew wide. She met his eerie red eyes and went totally still. He wasn't the Colin she knew. *He was possessed.*

She gulped back the urge to rail at him. "L-Lyle?"

His lips curled back over even white teeth. *"I want that sapphire."*

"Yes." She wet her lips. "I know."

"It's in your room, under your protection. You must give it to me."

"You know I can't do that."

"You have to. It's life or death. Your life. Your death." He snarled at her. *"But first, you must get up and finish digging that grave. Your grave."*

"What are you doing, Lyle?" Susannah's anxious words jolted Kaitlyn. *"Get away from her. You're my husband."*

Kaitlyn scrambled to her feet. Colin couldn't touch her, because of the circle. Still, she was apprehensive. He knew her, inside and out.

She put out her hand and tried to freeze him where he stood.

He reared up and screamed. "No! You don't have that power."

He was right. She couldn't stop time.

Susannah and Camille sailed over to them, their screams echoing off the trees. The two women clawed at each other, their arms flailing air. They floated toward Colin

Her heart rising into her throat, Kaitlyn ignored them and focused on him.

His eyes had rolled back in his head and he convulsed. His glasses slid from his nose and landed in a pile of leaves. Then all at once, he snapped out of it and sneered at her. He looked like a stranger. A wild man.

She bent down and scooped up his glasses, so he wouldn't step on them.

"You must die," he said, spittle falling from his lips.

"No, Colin. You won't hurt me. I know it." She straightened up and slipped the spectacles into the front pocket of her jeans. She longed to help him, but she didn't have the right tools. She needed to find a way to lure him back to her room.

He glared down at her hands.

She folded them together. "Lyle!" she shouted, hoping to distract him. "Look at me. Look into my face."

Colin sidestepped the two fighting ghosts. His red eyes pinned her.

She held out her hand. "You know I have the sapphire. To get it, you'll have to come with me."

With a wild screech, he lunged at her.

"No!" She jerked her hand back and glared at him. "You have to relax and go with me quietly. Otherwise, you can forget ever owning it."

He growled at her and kept coming.

Her heart in her throat, she locked eyes with him and stared him down. Two beams of heat emanated from her eyes and held him in place.

Camille and Susannah both screeched, and vanished in an enormous cloud of white smoke. Colin screamed. His body spasmed and he fell headlong into the pile of leaves at Kaitlyn's feet.

He didn't move. The clearing grew silent except for the rustle of wind in the trees and the faint tinkle of Fabron's strange Vodun wind chimes from down along the bayou.

Kaitlyn hoped she hadn't done Colin irreparable harm. She had been forced to diminish him, in order to gain control. Oh God. Her body soaked with sweat, she sank down beside him and gingerly felt for his pulse. Her hand quivered as she touched his chilled skin. Was he still alive?

Yes. A strong pulse throbbed beneath her trembling fingers. Tears of joy filled her eyes. Totally drained, she slid her hands under his arms and pulled him into a sitting position. He was like a heavy rag doll. She hugged him to her and pressed a soft kiss to his pale cheek.

"Wake up, love," she whispered, desperately needing to make contact with him. She hoped Lyle's brief possession hadn't damaged him in any way.

He remained still as death.

Kaitlyn kissed his forehead, his eyes, his lips, his nose and his chin. "I love you so much, Colin. I never would have believed I could fall in love with someone so fast, but I have. Please wake up."

He moaned.

She took his hand and entwined their fingers. His skin was ice cold. Drawing him closer, she wrapped one leg over his to give him more of her body heat.

His eyelids flickered.

"Colin, it's me." She kissed him again. "It's Kaitlyn. Are you okay?"

"Huh?" He blinked.

She raised her head and frowned down at his ashen face. "It's me. Kaitlyn."

He looked up at her, but still didn't focus his eyes.

She brushed her hand over his forehead and kissed the bridge of his nose. "You're safe now. Lyle, Susannah and Camille are gone."

"Are you sure?" He cocked his head. "You banished them?"

"I don't know if they're gone forever," she said gravely. "But you shouldn't worry about them. I'm here—and I love you. I know that now, with all my heart."

"You...love me?" He stared up at her with a dazed expression.

"Yes." She thought her heart might burst. "More than anything in this world, or the next." She couldn't resist the last part.

"Kaitlyn," he said softly, her name a symphony on his lips. "My God. I love you, too—so much. I have ever since I met you. Even after I learned that you are a witch. I never thought you'd feel that way, too. We're so different—"

You can't love her. Colin shook his head against the unwanted thought. It wasn't true. He did love her. Where had that thought come from?

"Colin?" Kaitlyn's worried gaze locked on his face. "What's the matter?"

A sharp buzz rattled Colin's brain. He pressed both hands to his temples. "I don't know. It's weird. Almost like—"

Oh, come on. You know me. You answer to me now.

"No!" he shouted. His head throbbed. He rubbed the two knots that had sprouted after he'd been hit hard twice. Those blows must have affected him more than he thought. "Please—"

"What is it?" Kaitlyn gripped his arm. "Please, tell me."

"Damn. My head—" White-hot pain knifed through his skull. He clenched his teeth. Hell. He'd never had a headache quite like this. Not ever.

It will only get worse until you acknowledge me.

"Who *are* you, damn it?" Colin asked, desperate to stop the devastating pain.

"I'm Kaitlyn," she said, her brows furrowing. "You're not making sense. I'm getting really worried about you. Did you hit your head again? Hurt yourself?"

"In the cottage. Fabron hit me." He winced. "Only now—this is different. This is something else. I don't know—"

You'd better believe this is different. You belong to me now. Bow to me and the pain will cease.

"What the hell for?"

"Colin, you're scaring me." Kaitlyn blinked at him. "You're not making sense."

"I'm scaring me, too. Shit." Desperate to feel like he was in control, he pushed himself to his feet. A wave of dizziness swept over him, so strong he grabbed a nearby sapling for support. The world spun in crazy circles. His stomach swirled. Sirens blared in his head.

He jerked and grimaced at the accompanying pain.

Even the mighty FBI can't help you now. You are mine, forever. Get me the sapphire.

"Shut up!" he snapped, hoping to quiet the strange voice invading his mind. He let go of the tree and squeezed his head between both trembling hands. The pain had to stop. He couldn't take it much longer.

Pay homage to me, and the agony will stop. You must obey.

"Give me your cell phone," Kaitlyn said. "I'll call for help."

"No." He shook his head. "They'll think I'm crazy. I can't tell anyone about this."

"Colin—"

"Forget it. We should just go inside," He bobbed his throbbing head toward the house, which was visible through the trees. "Maybe if I lie down, I'll feel better."

I'm not going away, no matter what you do.

He clutched his head and groaned.

"Okay, let's go." She caught his arm.

"Go slow, and I'll be fine."

"Promise you'll stay with me."

"I will." He took one stumbling step, and halted. "Damn. My head."

"Do you want me to get help?" Her eyes dark with concern, she steadied him.

"No. I'll be okay." He blinked and peered through the trees toward the house. It seemed to shimmer in the distance, like a mirage. The edge of the clearing was close, but they would have a long trek through an acre of brush and then cross the lawn to reach it. He didn't know if he could make it.

His chest felt tight. He needed to relax, and have time to get his head together. Whatever was happening to him was unnerving.

On your knees.

"Excuse me?" he asked. Dismay funneled through him. Where were these errant thoughts coming from? A stab of pain spread through his head from ear to ear. A strangled sound bubbled up his throat. Was he dying?

Bow to me and the pain will go away. I promise.

"I don't know who the hell you are," Colin growled. He swayed sideways, and Kaitlyn grabbed him. "But I refuse to be bullied by you or anyone else."

"I'm not bullying you," she said, her face a mask of confusion. "I'm trying to help."

"I know," he rasped. "I'm sorry. It's not me. I—" A searing needle of pain suddenly penetrated his left eye socket and drove deep into his skull. He dropped to his knees and cradled his head in both trembling hands. "Ow! Oh, God. Make it stop!"

Lie down and pay homage to me, and it will. Do it now!

Pay homage to whom? His mind reeled. He couldn't think, couldn't focus. Couldn't see. The pain was like an electric drill bit tunneling into his brain. He clutched his head and fell flat on his face in a pile of old leaves. Dirt shot up his nose. He writhed on the ground like an injured animal.

That's better. I'm in charge of you now. Admit it.

"N-No." Colin shook his stinging head. He refused to be controlled. He wouldn't let anyone rule him. He was with the FBI, damn it.

Ignorant man. Maybe this will change your mind.

A wider shaft of pain rocketed through him. He clenched his teeth so hard he feared they might crack. His vision blurred and his eyes felt like they might pop from his head. As he rolled around in the soft dirt trying to escape the incredible pain, Kaitlyn knelt beside him and put her hand on his forehead.

All at once, the pain let up, except for a dull throbbing behind his eyes.

Get up. Appease the witch. I will not let her cause me trouble.

He pushed himself into a sitting position and struggled to orient himself. He was sweating profusely. The chilly wind blew dirt off his shirt. He sneezed and brushed the rest of it away with shaky hands. What in hell had just happened to him?

"Colin?" Kaitlyn's worried voice finally penetrated his addled brain. She held him and rubbed his back. "What's happening? Are you all right?"

"I don't know," he mumbled. He grabbed the sapling's small trunk and hauled himself to his feet. Appease the witch, the thing had said. Colin snorted a laugh and wiped his face with a trembling hand. He couldn't fool Kaitlyn. She knew something was wrong. He needed to get back to the house so she could help him. She was a witch, after all.

Kaitlyn tugged on his arm. Her worried green eyes were wide as saucers. "Colin, talk to me. Please — concentrate and tell me exactly what's happening. Does your head still hurt?"

"Yeah. Right now, it's just a dull ache. But before—" He rubbed his temples. "It was like I took a spike to the head."

"Can you walk?"

"I think so, if we go slowly."

"Lean on me if you have to," she said.

He smiled wearily. "I'm glad you're here."

"Me, too."

They started off, and he turned. "Wait. What about Fabron?"

"You shot him." Kaitlyn's face darkened. "That released Lyle. He took you over, but I think he's gone now."

"Did he hurt you before I got here?" Colin frowned. He couldn't remember what had happened. The last hour or so was a blur. "Damn. Everything is all jumbled in my head."

"He hurt me, before I was able to call up a circle."
She touched her side and winced. "But I'll be okay. I'm
just sore."

Colin spotted a large bruise at the front of her neck
and reeled as anger chased away some of his confusion
and fatigue. He grabbed her elbow.

"Son of a bitch," he snapped. "He did that to you?"

"Before I could fight him off. He tied my hands
behind me, so I couldn't enact a spell."

"He knew about your powers." He wanted to kill
Fabron all over again. But instead, he pressed his lips
together and forced himself to take another step. And
another. "We're lucky he didn't hurt you any worse
before you could defend yourself."

"How will you explain this case to your superiors?"
Kaitlyn asked.

Colin shook his head. "I have no idea. If I tell them
the truth about Fabron being a Zombie, they'll think I'm a
nutcase."

"And you certainly don't want them to know that
I'm a witch," she said. "Do you?"

"I'm afraid not." He flattened his mouth. He didn't
want to hurt her, but it was imperative that she keeps her
powers under wraps if they were going to have a
relationship. He realized that was a big if. She might
have no interest in keeping company with him after they
left Scarlet Oak. But still—

Kaitlyn tightened her grip on his arm and guided
him around a large oak tree. "I certainly don't want to
cause you problems in your career. But I know this case
will affect it."

"I need to call Burl."

"Wait until you're feeling better."

"No." Colin pulled out his phone and stumbled. He grabbed Kaitlyn around the waist. "Sorry I'm so weak. Guess those blows I took did some damage. But I've got to call him."

"Okay. I only hope Lyle left you. If he's still inside your head, we've got real trouble."

Colin looked at her. Nah. Those weird thoughts and noises couldn't possibly have been caused by a ghost. They had come from his imagination. Hadn't they?

CHAPTER TEN

Kaitlyn's heart thumped as she led Colin back to the house. He was much too quiet, as if his thoughts had turned inward and he wanted to keep them to himself. She couldn't help wondering if her comments about how this case might affect his career had upset him. She hated to say anything else about it so soon, so she kept silent as well.

Her gaze lifted to the threatening sky. Gray clouds had floated in to block out the sun, giving the day a worn, sad look. The weather matched her sudden dark mood. Unsettled, restless and promising rain. She blotted her stinging eyes with the back of her hand.

The musky odor of the bayou surrounded the house. She wrinkled her nose as they plunged on through the high grass. Once they reached the veranda, Colin halted and pulled free. He gingerly rubbed the back of his neck.

She studied his face. "Are you feeling okay?"

"Not really." He shook his head. "But I don't want to talk about it here."

"Okay. Let's go up to my room." She opened the door and urged him through the foyer and up the curving stairs. With each step, he seemed to move slower.

"Have you seen my glasses?" he asked. He patted his pockets. "I seem to have lost them."

"Oh, yes." She had forgotten. She dug in her front pocket and pulled them out. "You dropped them. I picked them up and held on to them because you — seemed upset."

"Tell the truth. I was acting crazy." He took his glasses from her and put them on.

"Well — I wasn't going to say anything. But you were a little off the wall." She twisted her lips and led him onto the landing.

He halted to catch his breath.

"Can you make it?" She searched his face. He looked tired and bedraggled, like he'd gone ten rounds with a prize-fighter. Her gaze drifted lower, to the chain around his neck. The amulet was gone. Fresh terror slid through her. *Oh no.* With it gone, Lyle could have moved in and easily taken him over. She muttered an expletive.

He retrieved his key from his pocket and looked at it like he didn't know what it was. Worry lanced Kaitlyn. She pushed at his hand. "This is my room, remember?"

"Oh. Yeah." He shook his head as if to clear it, and then stood to one side as she unlocked her door. The enticing odor of sage engulfed them.

"I gotta sit down," he said, making a beeline for the bed. He sank down on the edge of the mattress and dropped his head into his hands. "Damn. I've never felt anything like this. The room is swimming."

Kaitlyn crawled onto the bed on her knees and slid her fingers into his hair. A fresh knot had popped up next to the one he'd gotten the day before. No wonder.

He winced. "Ouch. Take it easy. That hurts."

"Sorry." She pressed a gentle kiss to his temple. Seeing him in pain made her ache inside. "Would you like some water?"

"Yeah. That would be good. I'm parched."

She pulled a paper cup from the dispenser in the bathroom and filled it at the sink. He took it from her and gulped it down. She couldn't help noticing his dark stubble and the way his strong throat worked as he swallowed. A man this virile shouldn't be brought low by a mere ghost.

"Do you remember what happened to you after you shot Fabron?" Kaitlyn was afraid she knew, but wanted his perspective. What would it feel like to be taken over by Lyle Forrester?

Colin lowered the cup and sent her a haunted look. "My head started aching, and I started hearing this weird voice. I have no idea why or how. I only know that it hurt."

Excuse me? You know exactly what happened, and who took control of you. Don't you?

His eyes opened wide, and his cheeks flushed red.
I took over your body. Admit it.

Wild laughter echoed inside Colin's head. He dropped the cup and grabbed his temples.

"Colin?" Worry lanced through Kaitlyn. Not knowing exactly what was wrong, she hovered next to him with her heart pounding. "What is it? Does your head ache?"

"It's more than that," he managed, though it hurt like hell to talk.

She sat down beside him and put her hand in the middle of his back. "What do you mean? Colin, talk to me."

Nosy bitch. She has to die!

"No!" Colin shook his head and was promptly repaid with a jagged pain knifing into his brain. He moaned and clutched his ears. A ringing sound made his head spin.

Don't argue with me, or I'll make your life a living hell. Kill her!

The blood drained from his face. Kill Kaitlyn? The very thought made him sick to his stomach. He clenched his jaw. "No. I won't do it."

"You won't do what?" Kaitlyn's face went bone white. "Who are you talking to?"

"I can't explain it." Another razor-sharp pain knifed into his skull. He groaned and clutched his head. "Damn it. Make it stop."

It won't stop until you obey me.

Kaitlyn frowned. His actions were frightening. Understandably, they'd just witnessed some freakish events, but Colin was her rock of stability. Her pulse rate increased as the fear in her heart grew stronger. He thought he'd killed Fabron, but all he'd really done was disable the husk that was Fabron – the Zombie Lyle Forrester had created.

Kaitlyn took a step back. Lyle hadn't gone anywhere. He'd simply transferred from Fabron into an unwilling vessel. And that vessel was Colin.

"You have to give me tonight. Please." The being grew silent. Colin could feel its ominous presence hovering inside his head, but it didn't speak.

"Colin?" Kaitlyn eyed him with trepidation. "I need to go get something from the kitchen. I'll be right back."

"I'm begging you to stop the pain."

She had to keep him calm and in place while she was gone. She stroked his back. "I would if I could, but I can't. Not until I—"

"Not you!" he snapped. His eyes narrowed dangerously.

Kaitlyn jerked her hand off him and stood up. Her eyes flew over his face. "You need to calm down. Please. You're scaring me."

"Sorry. I'm under a lot of stress trying to solve this case. And now—" He smiled weakly. "I didn't mean to snap at you."

"I don't think it was you." She frowned and crossed her arms over her chest. "You have to tell me exactly what's happening. Everything."

Colin slapped his hands over his ears and bent his head. "Leave her alone. I won't hurt her."

Kaitlyn got up and headed for the table. She had to help him.

"Wait, Kaitlyn!" Colin sprang up off the bed. "Don't go."

She spun on her heel and raised both hands to ward him off. "I won't be long. I'm just going to the kitchen. I'm going to help you, but you've got to give me some time. Okay?"

"Yeah, I promise," he murmured. His face had gone from a dull, angry red to chalk white.

Kaitlyn frowned. Was he talking to her, or to Lyle? If only she knew what the entity in his head had said. Trying to read his body language was so frustrating, especially in his agitated state.

Colin sent her a pleading glance. "I'm really sorry about all this. I can't help it."

"It's all right. I just need you to relax."

"I'll try." He winced and massaged his temples. "Damn it. I have to call this in."

"Why?"

"The shooting. I have to tell them about Fabron." He pulled his cell phone from his jacket pocket. "It's my job."

"They're going to have questions."

"I know. But it can't be helped." Colin frowned and punched a series of numbers into the phone. "I can trust Burl to keep things quiet."

"I hope so." She hoped he wasn't making a big mistake.

He told his friend about the body in the clearing, instructing him to pick it up with minimal help and to tell no one until Colin talked to him again. Afterwards, he turned off the phone and put it on the nightstand. His head pounded.

She stared at him a moment longer, and then checked to make sure she had her key.

He came up behind her and slipped his arms around her waist. "I'll fill you in on what's been happening. But first I need to hold you for a minute. Please."

She turned in his arms and burrowed against his hard chest. He felt so good.

"Kiss me," he said, looking down at her. Desperation was written all over his face.

Against her better judgment, she looped her arms around his neck and rose up onto her tiptoes.

His mouth was wet and warm and helped to chase away the dismay flooding through her. She pulled back before she drowned in his delicious taste.

He met her eyes and said, "I hear voices."

"Voices? Or one voice?" Her eyes dove into his.

"One. A man."

"It's Lyle." She dropped her arms from his neck and stepped away. "He's in your head."

He fought the surge of dread rising inside him. She might as well have just pushed him off a cliff. "He left Fabron and went into me?"

"Yes." Her lips formed a tight line. Her heart fluttered. "With Fabron dead, he needed a vessel, willing or unwilling. He chose you."

"Son of a bitch." Colin's bitter words hung in the air. "But I'm alive."

"Yes, you are. And I'm so glad."

"You may not be when you hear what he wants me to do." Colin rubbed his hands together.

She met his tormented gaze. "I don't want to ask, but I have to. What is it?"

"He wants me to kill you."

Her eyes flew wide.

"I won't do it." He touched her cheek. "I'm alive, and Fabron wasn't. He was a puppet. I can exercise free will."

"You're also a lawman."

"Well, yeah. There is that." He crooked his mouth. "Which reminds me—"

He shrugged out of his coat and took off his shoulder holster, which held his backup pistol. He gave it to Kaitlyn. "Hide this, please. Before you go."

He disappeared into the bathroom and shut the door.

She stared down at the weapon for a moment, then hurried around to the other side of the bed and slid it under the mattress. Returning to where she'd been standing, she looked at the door. "Colin? You can come out now."

He did. "I don't want to give Lyle the chance to shoot you."

"I appreciate that. But I'm not going to give him the chance." She lifted her chin. "I'm going to perform an exorcism. We have to get him out of your head."

"I don't know exactly what that means, but I'm willing to do whatever it takes to get him out of my head." He drew in a deep breath. "Either that, or you'll have to leave Scarlet Oak. I could never live with myself if I hurt you."

"Don't worry. You won't." She smiled and touched the pendant around her neck. "I'm protected. And you can forget the idea of me running away—I won't leave you at the mercy of a ghost."

"Thank you," Colin said, caressing her silken cheek.

She caught his hand and squeezed his fingers. "I need to know when he starts talking to you again."

"So you can exorcise him?"

"Yes." Her warm gaze licked over his face. "Now—lie down while I'm gone."

He nodded.

She stared at him a moment longer, and then slipped out the door. Her heart beat out a rapid cadence as she descended the stairs and crept along the hotel's quiet corridors to the kitchen. She'd performed exorcisms before, but never one involving someone she loved. It was a challenge she didn't want. Yet she had no choice if she was going to save Colin's life. She couldn't bear to watch him die.

*****

Colin lay back on Kaitlyn's bed and closed his eyes. He imagined himself floating on a mythical, rolling sea, filled with danger and uncertainty. Pain arced through his skull. He tried to ignore it, but it simply wouldn't go away.

He felt his love for Kaitlyn blossom, yet deep inside he was afraid for her. He closed his eyes in weary resignation.

Moments later, he awoke to the sounds of her returning to the room. He sat up.

She paused at the door. "Are you all right?"

"Yeah," he said. He looked down at her hands, which were filled with several small spice bottles and another, larger bottle. "I think so. What's all that?"

"Crushed garlic, cloves, cumin and vinegar." She swished the vinegar bottle. There wasn't much in it. She put the items on the table, took out another, smaller bottle and a pad and pen, and wrote something down.

Colin came to his feet and peeked at the pad over her shoulder. It read, "Lyle Forrester."

He lifted his eyebrows. "I don't understand."

"It's all part of the exorcism."

"*No!*" Colin suddenly screamed involuntarily, and a spear of pain shot through his head.

You can't let her do this. Kill her!

"I can't." He wagged his head. His voice grew agitated. "I *won't*."

"Are you talking to Lyle?" Kaitlyn met his eyes.

He nodded. Then he winced and squeezed his head with both shaking hands.

"He won't win. I'm more powerful than he could ever be." She took out a pair of black candles and lit them. Next, she lit a stick of incense and took out three hand-sized crystals. Her lips moved as she waved her hand over them and murmured what had to be a spell.

Colin started to speak, but the searing pain in his head intensified and his ears rang with an echoing screech. He backed away from her, clutching his head. He couldn't through with this. He'd just discovered the supernatural world, and now he had to put himself in Kaitlyn's hands, knowing he could kill her in the process. He couldn't risk it.

Tell her what I want. Tell her!

Sweat formed a slick layer on his skin, and he spoke words he couldn't stop," Lyle wants the sapphire. Give it to him."

"The Midnight Star." Kaitlyn leveled him with a harsh glare. "That's why he fought me so hard and took over your body. He's greedy. Stand still."

She walked toward him and put out her hand. A pale blue circle rose from her palm to encircle Colin. She raised her chin and looked him square in the eye. "As above, so below and all around. The circle is sealed."

He froze.

Kill her now, before she takes this any further!

An odd, prickly warmth crept into his brain and evoked a strange stirring inside his subconscious that pushed aside his free will and covered him with a thick blanket of hate. He saw red. His teeth hurt and his skull felt like it might explode. His muscles tensed. He growled.

Acting like she didn't hear him, Kaitlyn calmly waved her hand over the three crystals a second time. Then she bent and placed them in a triangular shape around him on the floor.

He lunged for her.

She stood up straight and stopped him with a laser-like stare. "You must remain inside the triangle for this to succeed.

"I...can't," he rasped. Oh God. His limbs trembled. He tried to leave the triangle, but an unseen force kept him there. His head burned. He swept his hand at her.

She sidestepped his grasping fingers and all at once, the screams inside his head stopped. The pain left him. Colin teetered on his heels, unsure what had just happened. He blinked.

Kaitlyn narrowed her eyes. "Colin?"

"Come here," he said, suddenly aching to hold her. He put out his arms.

She shot him a wary glance. "Just a minute ago, you wanted to kill me."

"That wasn't me. That was Lyle," he said. Still, he knew the words he spoke were not his own. He continued on, unable to stop reeling her in. "I'm better now. Please, Kaitlyn. Hold me."

"Colin—" She hesitated, and then stepped inside the triangle and wrapped her arms around him. Her tight hold took away the hollow ache inside his chest.

He captured her mouth in a hungry, heated kiss.

A snicker in his head startled him.

Don't let me stop you. You've got her now. Kill her.

His eyes flew wide, and he jerked his head up.

Keep kissing her, Mr. FBI. I'm enjoying it. Another wicked snicker crawled across Colin's nerves. *Make sure you distract her long enough to get the sapphire. It's mine.*

Colin released Kaitlyn and pressed his hands to his temples. It was all a trick.

The snicker in his head grew into a cruel laugh. *I won't leave you alone until I have that stone. You're just a pawn in my little game*

"Colin?" Kaitlyn put her hands on his chest and went still. "Is Lyle back?"

He gritted his teeth. "Yes, damn it. He's here."

That's right. I'm back. Put your hands around her neck.

"You have to go," Colin snapped. He raised his hands to her shoulders. "I don't need this."

Too fucking bad.

"What's he saying?" Determination glittered in Kaitlyn's eyes. She fisted her hands and stared up at him. "Tell me."

"He's come for the sapphire." Colin's ears began to ring. He squeezed her shoulders. "Give it to him before you get hurt."

"I won't turn over the sapphire. We're going to get rid of that damned ghost."

Lyle screeched.

Colin's head rang. Unable to stop himself, he slid his hands up to her neck. *"Give me the stone!"*

Her eyes widened, and she tried to jerk free.

Lyle shrieked. *No blasted woman, not even a witch as beautiful as she, has ever gotten the best of me. And no woman ever will! Choke the life out of her.*

"Shut up," Colin snapped. He squeezed Kaitlyn's neck.

Lyle screeched again, this time so loud Colin's teeth throbbed.

"Stop it!" Kaitlyn ordered. She grabbed his wrists and looked up into his eyes. "Let go of me."

"Give him the stone," he said shakily.

"He's a ghost, Colin," she said. "He's not of the physical world. He can't take the sapphire."

"Camille had it," he said.

"She used Vodun."

Camille is dead.

The ringing in Colin's ears intensified. He grimaced and loosened his hold on her neck.

Kaitlyn broke free and stepped out of the triangle.

No! Get her! Bring me the sapphire. Now.

"No!" he shouted, the word echoing off the walls.

Kaitlyn backed away from the crystals and watched him intently. Her chest heaved. She struggled to catch her breath. Then she raised her arms. "Bear, hawk, shark, and dragon, be my guardians of the circle. Stand point around us."

Colin growled.

"Guardians of the circle cast, stay with me until this danger is past. Move me to do what must be done to rid this house of the evil one." Kaitlyn opened her eyes and lowered her arms.

Lyle shrieked inside Colin's head. Totally unnerved, he squeezed his throbbing temples.

The room was ripe with tension. Kaitlyn put out one hand, palm up, and said, "Come to me, my cherished friend, the panther. With claws of steel and teeth of fire, this night I need you to do my desire. You carry strength and truth and the flames of love. Rush forward now and defend what I ask. On this night, this is your only task."

Colin dropped to his knees. His face was on fire. "Hurry," he whispered, afraid to speak, afraid to feel. His mind spun with terrifying black images. Scenes of death. Sweat beaded on his brow. "Please. Ow. My head…hurts. I can't…move."

Go after her.

"I can't. That thing—" He spotted a large dark sparkly blur out of the corner of his eye. Circling, ever closer. What in hell was that? A sharp twinge shot through his head. Despite the pain, he jerked his gaze from the eerie sight edging closer and focused on the candles on the table. Their flickering flames ignited new pain within him. He doubled over.

Tell that witch to stay the hell away from me.

"No!" Colin gritted his teeth, raised his head, and focused on Kaitlyn's confident expression. "Do it now. Hurry."

"Do you believe?" she asked.

"Yes." He fisted his hands. "Dear God. I never thought I'd say that. But I can't help but believe. Help me!"

*****

Burl Johnson supervised the pickup of the body from Scarlet Oak after receiving Colin's cryptic phone call, and hurried it back to the morgue as Colin had instructed. He'd taken only one assistant with him, a graduate student he often used when his usual assistant was out. Kevin was an excellent scientist, but he hadn't been trained in law enforcement. That could help Burl keep things quiet until he heard more from Colin.

Kevin readied the body for autopsy, and made the Y incision. Then Burl took over, weighing each organ as he took it out, and then putting them back inside. He only had a few more to go before instructing Kevin to sew up the gaping hole.

He'd done the same procedure on at least a hundred bodies over the course of his career, but he'd never seen anything like this. The man had died two weeks ago from a cut to the neck. Yet somehow he'd lived on, his organs still intact.

The chemical odor of formaldehyde hung in the air, reminding Burl of the heart and lungs he'd just weighed. The heart was as healthy as a teenager's, and the lungs were pink and clear. Add to that the fact that the scar on the man's throat appeared to be at least a year old and hell, it was downright frightening. He picked up Fabron's lungs and spleen and put them back inside the cavity. That was the last of them. Except for the heart.

"Dr. Johnson." His borrowed assistant's voice grew shaky. "Oh my God."

Burl turned. "What's wrong?"

"The heart. Look at it." Kevin pointed into the metal basin holding the fist-sized organ. It was pumping like a piston engine.

Burl swallowed. *Shit.*

"Have you ever seen that before?"

"No." He wiped the shocked expression off his face. "I haven't."

Kevin edged toward the door. "I think I'll take my break now. Okay?"

"That's fine. But we have to keep this quiet." Burl stared at him. "I mean it."

"Okay." The young medical student swallowed, hard. "I won't tell anyone."

"You can't, if you value your scholarship." Burl lowered his voice. "Do you get my drift? You didn't see that heart beating."

"Yes, sir." Kevin stared at him for a long moment. Then he bolted for the door.

Burl hoped to hell the young man wouldn't say anything. He eyed the beating heart. Watching it pulsate, he made a snap decision. He wouldn't put it back into Fabron's chest. He'd leave it out of the body and incinerate it, just in case. No one had to know.

Sweat broke out across his brow as he sewed up the Y incision. It was standard procedure to tuck all organs back into the chest cavity of the deceased. He sighed. He would have some tall explaining to do later if someone learned he'd done away with the heart.

Once he finished, he pulled off his gloves and dug out his cell phone. He punched in Colin's number. It rang and rang. No answer.

"Damn it, Colin," Burl snapped. His nerves tingled. "This is too weird. Pick up."

His gaze drifted back to the metal table beside Fabron's lifeless body. The basin holding his heart trembled with each fragile beat.

Colin's voice mail picked up, and cold fear wrapped itself around Burl's soul as he waited impatiently for the beep. When it sounded, he jumped.

His pulse throbbed along with the heart in the bowl. He cleared his throat. "Colin, this is Burl. Call me as soon as possible. We have a situation here at the morgue. It's—it's important."

Not at all sure what he should do, he ended the call and stepped closer to the table. The heart still throbbed out a steady beat. But how? The scientist in him longed to pick it up and study it more closely, but he knew he shouldn't touch it. Not here.

If only Colin would call.

Burl frowned. Maybe he should telephone Quantico instead, and ask the FBI's experts what they thought. Burl peered down at the cell phone clutched in his sweaty paw.

If he placed the call, Colin would be in hot water. Damn. He didn't know what to do.

*****

Kaitlyn turned away from Colin, tore off and rolled up the piece of paper bearing Lyle's name, and dropped it into the smaller of the two bottles. Next she poured in a quarter cup of vinegar and added even amounts of garlic, cloves and cumin. Covering the top with her thumb, she shook it vigorously. A shiver coursed through her. Lyle Forrester was evil personified. It was time to do battle with him. She only hoped Colin could endure the anguish Lyle would put him through. He wanted that sapphire so much he would kill to get it.

With her back to Colin, Kaitlyn bent and picked up the Midnight Star. It was a beautifully cut sapphire that glistened in her hand like a giant blue teardrop. She slipped it into her pocket for safekeeping. The room hummed with electrical energy.

She turned, and watched Colin wince. She stepped closer, and he stared at her with flat, evil eyes. Her heart fluttered. His mouth curled into a sneer, and he pulled back his lips to reveal feral teeth.

She braced her feet apart. The panther, her totem beast, would protect her. She lifted one hand and said, "This night with help, I will stalk my prey. My will shall be done by the light of day.   You will not escape this time, Lyle. The evil you possess will leave this place, as I say."

Colin growled like a mad dog. His limbs twitched, and his dark gaze landed on Kaitlyn's face. White foam gathered on his lips. She cringed inwardly, but didn't back down. This was Colin, invaded by Lyle. Not the gentle man she'd grown to love. She tamped down the rioting emotions surging within her. It was time to call on the Dark Goddess for help. She opened her mouth.

Yet before she could get a word out, Colin rushed at her with a crazed shout. She sidestepped him, but he whipped around and dove for her.

The panther let out a roar and lunged between them.

Colin growled at the animal. His eyes glowed red. "I'll kill you, you beast."

"No," she said, struggling to keep her voice even. She put down the bottle. "You have to listen to me, Colin. You must fight Lyle. You have to get him out of your head. It's the only way you'll survive."

"You can't rid the world of me, witch." The words were Lyle's, but they came from Colin's mouth. *"Not with your guardians or your totem. I want that damned sapphire!"*

"You can't have it." Goose bumps rose on her flesh as she stared up into his fiery orange-red eyes. "The Midnight Star is cursed forever because you murdered your mistress, Camille."

"You're wrong, damn it," Colin bellowed. *"It's mine."*

She winced as his evil hiss echoed off the walls. And she said, "The stone must be given in love. You broke that rule, and that's why you're being punished. Love, and not the Midnight Star, is the key to your freedom in the afterlife."

"Hah! Love doesn't exist." He threw up his hands. *"It never has, and it never will."*

A wave of wickedness washed over Kaitlyn. She fended it off with the help of her guardians.

"Where's the damned necklace?" he snarled. *"I want it in my hand."*

"I've hidden it," she said, deliberately keeping her hands away from her pockets.

His face hardened into a vicious, twisted mask. *"Give it to me, witch, or you won't survive the night. I'll see to it you die a painful death just like Susannah did. Buried alive."*

"You've already tried to kill me twice." She raised her chin. "You failed."

He stalked her across the rug. *"I won't this time. Mr. FBI is on my side."*

"No, he's not." She stared hard into Colin's crazed eyes, trying desperately to push Lyle aside and reach her lover's true heart. "He's on my side. He loves *me*."

"You don't deserve his love," Lyle snarled.

His words hurt, but she sloughed them off just like she had her father's cruel taunts when he'd first learned she was a witch just like her mother. He'd never accepted their craft, and had left their home and divorced her mother soon after Kaitlyn started school. She'd never seen him again.

"I'm a good person." Kaitlyn had finally learned to like herself, and this ghost wasn't going to change that. "You can't hurt me with your hateful words."

"Maybe not." He halted right beside her. *"But I can kill you. All I have to do is get past those rabid beasts."*

The panther paced toward him and growled.

Kaitlyn stopped it with a wave of her hand and looked up into Colin's fearsome red eyes. "What purpose would it serve for you to kill me? I'll be dead, but you still won't have the sapphire."

He snarled his displeasure. His eyes wild, he tried to grab her—but he couldn't break free of the crystal triangle.

Kaitlyn recoiled at his fierce growl of rage. *He's not Colin,* she told herself. She said those words over and over inside her head. She was dealing with Lyle Forrester, the most dangerous ghost she'd ever met—yet she would not let him coerce her into hurting the man she loved.

His lips curled back and he released an evil, guttural sound.

She steeled herself for his next growl. "You don't want to hurt me," she said softly, hoping to reach the real Colin. "You love me too much."

"No, I don't," he snarled. Yet his body shook and his eyes lost some of their evil glow, belying his harsh words. Had she broken through Lyle's tight hold on him?

She struggled to regulate her breathing. "Colin? Are you all right?"

"I don't know." His brow furrowed. He stared at the floor, and then returned his anguished gaze to her face. "You've got the sapphire. Please—give it to him. I don't want you hurt."

"Oh, Colin." She couldn't help it; she touched his arm. "It *is* you."

"For now." He rubbed his forehead. "Damn. My head hurts."

"Lyle's a strong spirit." She wanted to appease Colin, to give him hope. So she took out the sapphire and held it up. It gleamed like a blue diamond.

He salivated.

"Colin," she said. "Look at me."

He tore his gaze from the sapphire and met her gaze. *He was Lyle again.* She swallowed and tightened her hand around the stone. She couldn't give it to him.

She picked up the vinegar concoction, closed her eyes, and shook it. "Dark Goddess, hear my plea—"

"No!" Colin's face aged before her eyes. Deep lines creased his brow and his lips narrowed. He shrank away from her. *"No!"*

She opened her mouth to continue, and his expression morphed back into a tight, dark mask. His eyes flamed red. The candles flickered, and he muttered a lengthy Vodun curse, his voice sounding eerily like Fabron's.

Kaitlyn planted her feet. "Stop it, Lyle. Dark Goddess—"

"No-o-o!" Colin spat another Vodun curse and kicked one of the crystals out of the circle. It bounced across the rug and hit the wall. He grabbed her wrist and twisted the sapphire away from her. *"It's mine. Mine!"*

Anger washed over Kaitlyn, and she ground her teeth. "Damn you, Lyle Forrester."

"Stupid witch." His cold-hearted snicker burned her ears. *"To think you thought you could outsmart me."*

Shaking with rage, she retrieved the crystal and put it back in place. Colin danced away from her. She fixed him with her eyes. "Get back into the triangle. I have to finish the exorcism."

He growled and edged toward her instead.

Her heart pounded. She called on the panther for help, and was rewarded with a loud roar. The animal circled around behind her and fixed its yellow gaze on

Colin. She didn't want the cat to hurt him; it was Lyle that was the problem.

She called the cat back, and anxiety gushed through her veins. She was leaving herself open for an attack, yet she couldn't help it. She loved Colin.

His crazed eyes burned with evil lights.

"Don't come any closer," she said. "I don't want to have to hurt you.

"You can't fight me," he snapped, taking two more short steps. *"I'm all powerful."*

She scoffed at him. "You're an impotent ghost."

A furious growl rose from within him and the cloud of white around him grew. He curled one hand around the sapphire and reached for her with the other.

Her circle of protection held, yet anger embedded itself in her skin. She had to get Lyle out of Colin's head. It was the only way either of them would survive. She raised her arms. "Dark Goddess, hear my plea. I need you this night to aid me."

Colin's face contorted. He dropped the sapphire, and it rolled under the bed. His face went paper white. He dropped to his knees and began searching frantically for it.

"Damn you, witch!" he shouted, his hands raking over the rug. Sweat poured off his face. His body shook with convulsions, and he had trouble keeping his balance. *"I have to get the sapphire!"*

An icy wave of air flowed over Kaitlyn, and she remembered the pistol under the mattress. She didn't want to shoot Colin. But what if she couldn't corral him in the triangle?

She would have to stop him.

He shoved his hand under the bed and came out with the jewel. His red eyes gleamed. Saliva dripped from his mouth as he held the sapphire aloft. *"I've got it. It's mine. Forever."*

He uttered another loud Vodun curse.

The circle around her diminished, leaving her unprotected.

Lyle threw up a barrier between them and Colin surged to his feet. Ignoring the spirit wall, she aimed a laser-like gaze at the Midnight Star and begged it to leave Colin's clenched fist.

He bellowed a curse as Lyle's warring spirit entered Kaitlyn's veins and roiled through her bloodstream like a lethal dose of poison. Heat enveloped her. She winced from the resulting pain, but kept her gaze trained on the sapphire, which began to glow with a strange inner light.

Come to me! She said in her mind. *Come to me. I've known love, which Lyle will never see.*

Colin shrieked and dropped the stone as if it had burned him

Kaitlyn stared at it intently. *Come to me, Midnight Star. Leave the evil one.*

The sapphire rose off the floor and floated toward the bed. Colin growled his disapproval and lunged for it, but it flew higher and avoided his angry grasp.

"Give it back to me, you vicious witch!" Lyle snarled, his cruel gaze emanating from Colin's dead eyes. *"That's my necklace!"*

She kept her gaze focused and held out her hand. *Come to me. That's it.*

Colin staggered to his feet. His shirt was plastered to his skin and his disheveled hair stuck up in crazy spikes. *"I'll kill you if you don't give it back."*

The sapphire landed in Kaitlyn's hand with a soft plop. Thrilled that she had willed it across the bed, she wrapped her fingers around it and squeezed it. Heat radiated from the dark blue stone and she immediately felt a startling kinship with Colin, the man she loved. Her heart slammed against her ribs. This was no trick. She was actually getting through to him this time.

She held up the sapphire. "Dark Goddess, bring your warrior spirit to defend. Protect those who are unable to fight, rid us of this evil tonight."

Colin screamed and covered his ears, yet it wasn't really him screaming. It was Lyle.

"You can't banish me!" Colin's face twisted into a dark, evil mask. His red eyes gleamed with fury. *"Not without the stone. Give it back!"*

"No," she said calmly. Trying to be inconspicuous, she edged along the bed to where she'd hidden the pistol. She didn't want to hurt Colin. But if Lyle forced him to physically attack her, she would be ready. Maybe she could wing him in the arm or the leg. Not a serious wound, just enough of an injury to keep him from murdering her.

He pulled at his hair. Perspiration dotted his brow. *"You have to help me."*

"I'm trying to help you find freedom."

"I won't leave without the Midnight Star."

"You don't have a choice."

Colin screamed a string of curses and advanced on her. Keeping her gaze trained on him, Kaitlyn called on the panther. It crept closer, and she snatched Colin's shoulder holster from beneath the mattress and extracted the pistol. It was heavier than she expected. Her nerve

endings tingled as she backed away and threw down the
holster. She leveled the gun at him using both hands.

The bottle with the vinegar concoction was on the
table. She had to somehow get Colin back into the
triangle so she could get Lyle out of his head and into the
bottle. Then she had to seal it.

The panther put its lithe body between them.

Colin's eyes immediately changed from red to warm
mocha brown. "What in hell do you think you're doing?"

"Saving your life and mine."

"I'm not gonna hurt you."

"You might not, but Lyle will." The pistol wavered
in her hand. "He's tried it before. He also buried
Susannah alive."

"That was over a hundred years ago."

"He's evil, Colin." She pressed her back to the wall
and edged around him. "He wants you to hurt me."

"You think I'm trying to trick you?"

"Not you. Lyle."

"That's crap."

"Is it?"

"You'll find out soon enough." Colin held up a
hand. "Don't shoot me. I'm just going to sit down on the
bed."

She studied him carefully. "As long as you don't
make a move toward me."

He swung his legs over the edge of the mattress and
perched on its rim. A pained look crossed his face. He
rubbed his temples. "My head hurts like hell."

"It's because you're still possessed." Kaitlyn eased
backward until her hip brushed the table. *Almost there.*
Her palms grew sweaty on the pistol's thick grip.
"Please—just stay calm."

"I'm trying."

She clutched the pistol tightly in one hand and snatched up the bottle with the other. "Dark Goddess, protect me and mine tonight, cause Lyle Forrester to turn away in fright. Away from us, evil! Leave Colin—"

"*No!*" He jerked his head up. His eyes turned to twin pinpoints of red flame. He lunged for the vinegar. "*Give it to me!*"

The panther blocked him.

Kaitlyn aimed the pistol at his face.

"*Don't wave that damned gun at me.*" He spoke, but the voice was Lyle's. It was like conversing with Dr. Jekyll and Mr. Hyde. He staggered away from the cat. "*Come on, Kaitlyn. Help me.*"

"I'm trying to." She waved the pistol. "Step inside the triangle."

"*I can't do that. Lyle wants the sapphire. I can't let you keep it from him.*"

She pressed herself to the wall. Perspiration slid down her spine in an icy river. *Stay focused,* she told herself. *Don't let him trick you.* She called on the guardians for help.

"*Oh, Kaitlyn,*" he said a sing-song voice. "*Don't be a bitch like Camille. Give me what's due me.*"

She clenched her teeth and stared into his piercing red eyes. Her heart ached for what she was about to do, but she knew she had no choice.

"Dark Goddess," she said. "Protect me and mine tonight. Cause Lyle Forrester to turn away in fright. Away from us, evil! Leave Colin without a sound. Your nightmarish existence is over. We will have peace here unbound."

Colin shrieked and his eyes rolled back in his head. A deep red flush stole up his neck. He stumbled and went down on one knee. *"Stop the damned exorcism!"*

"No." Suddenly empowered, Kaitlyn lowered the gun. She held it high in one trembling hand, raised the bottle, and said the spell over and over again.

Colin collapsed on the floor and began to writhe in agony. Her soul ached for him. She longed to wrap him in her arms and comfort him, yet she didn't dare. Not while he was still possessed.

"Let him go, Lyle," she whispered. "Please."

His moans coalesced into a terrifying roar. She jerked up the pistol just as he surged off the floor and went for her neck. Her finger squeezed the trigger and two shots rang out, the resultant blasts stunning her ears. Shock registered on Colin's face. His eyes went from red to gold to brown in the millisecond it took Kaitlyn to realize what she'd done.

CHAPTER ELEVEN

Burl punched redial on his cell phone for the third time. Just like it had before, it just rang and rang. Worried that Colin didn't answer, Burl snapped the phone shut. He'd been trying to reach his colleague for over an hour. Something must be wrong, especially since Colin didn't meet him when he picked up the body.

He slipped the telephone back into his pocket and glanced once more at the heart pounding out a steady cadence in the metal pan. He'd called the experts in Virginia and gave them a hypothetical question, for research purposes. They'd tried to tell him the heart's movement was either nerve or muscle related. A spontaneous death reflex. He didn't think so. Especially after learning that Fabron had died two weeks ago—and after seeing the healed scar on the man's neck. He had a bullet wound in his arm, but that had proved to be only superficial. A cold chill slid over Burl.

He exited the cutting room and told Kevin he was heading out to Scarlet Oak.

"You mean, you're leaving me alone with that—that heart?" The young man's eyes rounded.

Burl scowled. "I don't have a choice. I have to go out on a case."

"What should I do with it?"

"Put it in the cooler with the body."

"Why don't you just open him back up and put it inside his chest?"

"Not with it still beating." Burl frowned. "Gives me an eerie feeling."

"Afraid he'll come back to life?" Kevin cracked his knuckles.

Goose bumps popped up on Burl's arms. "Yeah, maybe. Something like that."

"Okay." Kevin picked up the basin and tucked it beneath the sheet covering Fabron's lifeless body. "Just so I don't have to touch the heart itself."

"You know I wouldn't ask you to do that."

Kevin grinned. "I hope to hell not."

A strange uneasiness stole over Burl as he watched Kevin roll the gurney into the cooler. The young man set the brake, then backed out from the cold compartment and shut the door.

"I'd like it if you'd stay, though. Just until I get back." Burl took out his cell phone and tried Colin's number a second time. Still no answer. Worry skittered over his battered nerves.

Kevin stuck his hands in his pockets. "Sure, if you think it's necessary."

"I do."

Burl pocketed his phone and shrugged out of his lab coat. His collared shirt rubbed his throat. He preferred crew necks, but wanted to look at least a little bit professional when on the job. He adjusted his collar. Colin wouldn't give a shit what he had on. If he was okay.

Another uneasy chill rolled over Burl's damp skin. He put on his sport coat and yanked out his keys. It would take him almost an hour to get to Scarlet Oak.

A helluva lot could happen in that amount of time.

*****

The pistol felt like burning lead in Kaitlyn's hand. Horror filled her. She'd just shot Colin, the only man she'd ever truly loved.

His face turned paper white as he peered down at the blood blooming on his side. He began to shake. "Son of a bitch." He crumpled to the floor.

Kaitlyn braced herself as Lyle hit her full force. Her head snapped back against the glass. Desperate to retain control and get him into the bottle, she increased her grip around it and gritted her teeth.

She tossed down the gun.

Lyle screamed. White fog surrounded Kaitlyn. She let her powers overflow as she called on the guardians. The panther sprang into view.

"You won't possess me, Lyle Forrester," she vowed, more determined than ever to save Colin. She pulled out the Midnight Star and raised it high in the air next to the bottle. "You must cross over."

Lyle's spirit engulfed her. She began to twitch. Hot needles bombarded her brain. She closed her eyes and kept up the chant, hoping to thwart the ghost's evil plan. She faltered when pain rocketed through her chest. Her head snapped back.

Kaitlyn fought off the being's attempt to choke off her air. The panther roared. She braced herself against the wall as Lyle raced over her skin, stealing the strength in her muscles and sending her thoughts into turmoil. She tried to focus on Colin, but her vision swam and a thick haze slid over her eyes.

No more spells. Lyle's sharp words hung in the air.

She felt his nimble fingers tug at her hand, trying to force her to give up the sapphire. She tightened her fist around the stone. Then all of the sudden she was falling, with her hand wrapped around the bottle. She heard Colin calling her name, shouting for her to get up and continue.

"Let her go, damn it!" His desperate shout rang in her ears. She felt his hands on her, shaking her as he tried to get Lyle to leave her alone. Colin's warm blood dripped onto her hand.

She wanted to reach out to him. Only, she couldn't move. Lyle covered her like a blanket, his ghostly body pinning her to the cool floor as they grappled for the Midnight Star.

"Give it to me," a male voice said.

"No!" She fought hard to hang on to the piece of treasure.

Colin caught her hands and pried the stone free.

Kaitlyn cried out. Lyle screamed and jumped on Colin.

Suddenly free, Kaitlyn leapt to her feet and ordered Lyle off Colin and into the bottle. Her eyes widened as she saw the huge splotch of blood on Colin's shirt.

"Help me," he said, catching her eye. "He's...trying to get back into me."

Colin was talking about the ghost. Kaitlyn said the spell again. Her voice rang off the walls as the guardians closed in and wrestled Lyle away from them both.

Lyle screamed as they stuffed him in the bottle. Louder and louder, until the ghost's horrified screeches finally ceased and a startling silence filled the room. Kaitlyn's limbs twitched. She leaned against the wall so she wouldn't fall down.

The guardians shrank away, leaving the room empty.

"Hey." Colin's pained rasp stirred her.

She struggled to regain control of her body. Her eyes flickered open. She tried to speak, yet nothing came out of her mouth.

His hand gripped hers. "I need to sit down."

She forced herself to focus on his slumped form. Blood saturated the side of his shirt. Oh, God. *She had shot him.* Remorse washed over her in a chilling wave. "Colin—"

"It looks worse than it is."

She pushed away from the wall and stumbled with him over to the bed. She helped him sit down. Her breath slid out in a pained whoosh. "I'm so sorry."

"You put Lyle in the bottle."

"I'm not finished. I have to seal it."

"Don't let him out again, whatever you do."

"I won't." She left Colin and fished a circle of black wax from her bag. Using a candle, she melted it and used it to seal the bottle. Her hand was sure as she inscribed her personal sigil in the wax. Now Lyle was trapped inside…forever.

She doused the bottle with vinegar for an extra measure of protection, and made plans to bury it off the property, so he could never come back to haunt Scarlet Oak again. With him gone, Susannah and Camille should follow. The house would finally be free of ghosts.

A relieved smile broke out across her lips. She turned to Colin. "Thank you. Without your help there at the end, he might have escaped my grasp."

"I don't think so. You're too powerful a witch."

He did believe. Her heart fluttered, and she squeezed his hand.

"I need to call Burl."

"Did he pick up Fabron's body?"

"He said he would, but whether he did or not—"Colin shook his head. "I need my phone."

"Where's is it?"

"I don't remember. It could be anywhere." He pressed a hand to his bloody side, and winced. "Better find it, and my glasses. I don't know what happened to them."

"They're right here."

Kaitlyn rose on wobbly legs and dug his glasses from her pocket. They appeared to be okay. She handed them to Colin and then scanned the room, which was in wild disarray. Her pulse thrummed. She edged around the bed and checked the bed, the nightstand, and the table. The sight of the burning black candles comforted her.

Turning back to Colin, she spotted his jacket slung over a chair. She checked its pockets, and pulled out the telephone.

"I found it." She held it up. "You have four missed calls."

"Give it here."

She did so.

He pressed a button and squinted down at the display. "It was Burl."

"Shouldn't you lie down?" Kaitlyn asked, suddenly worried about his loss of blood. He was awfully pale. "It can't be good for you to be moving around."

"Probably." He wiped a hand over his eyes. "Let me call him first."

She started to argue, but a loud knock at the door made her snap her mouth shut.

Colin moaned softly.

Kaitlyn looked at him. "Who could that be?"

"I don't know."

"Colin?" A man's voice echoed through the door.

Kaitlyn staggered to her feet.

Colin grabbed her arm. "Take it easy. It sounds like Burl."

"Should I answer it?"

"Yes. Take the pistol, though, in case it's not." He motioned to where it lay on the floor.

A wave of anxiety roiled her stomach. She didn't want to pick it up.

He took her hand. "I know you didn't want to shoot me. It's okay."

"I had to do it, because of Lyle. He was making you crazy."

"I know." Colin lifted her hand to his mouth and kissed her palm. "Go on. Pick it up and answer the door before Burl knocks it down."

"You in there, Colin?" The lab tech's booming voice rattled the walls. "Damn it, answer me! You weren't in your room. You've gotta be somewhere."

"I'm here," Colin rasped. With a grimace, he leaned against the headboard. "Hang on."

Kaitlyn doubted the man could hear him. His voice was too weak. She snatched up the pistol and hurried to the door. Another sharp knock made her jump. Irritated, she yanked the door open and glared at Colin's friend. "You don't have to tear it down."

"I'm not. Where's Colin?" The tech peered past her to see him sitting on the bed. His eyes widened. "Oh my God. What the hell did you do to him?" Burl shoved past her. "He's bleeding."

"I know. Colin and I —" She found herself talking to his back

"Surprise attack," Colin rasped. "Bastard got my pistol and shot me. Kaitlyn was just about to call for help."

Burl looked at her. She was too stunned by Colin's lie to say anything.

"Who did it?" Burl asked, yanking his startled gaze from Kaitlyn to Colin. "Fabron's lying in my morgue."

Colin shrugged. "Might've been one of his Voodoo pals."

"Vodun." Kaitlyn's nerves were taut as piano strings. "But you know that's not what happened."

Colin sent her a warning look, and Burl frowned.

She wanted to support Colin's lie, yet deep inside she knew it wasn't right. She held herself rigid. "He's not telling you the truth, Burl. *I* shot Colin. With his pistol."

"Kaitlyn, don't," Colin said sharply.

"*You* pulled the trigger?" Burl's mouth fell open. "Why?"

"It was an accident." Colin pressed a hand to his side and aimed an aggravated glare at Burl. "And why are we having this conversation? Did you call 911?"

"Hell." He ripped out his cell phone and placed the call. Once he hung up he turned to Kaitlyn, who dodged him and hurried into the bathroom.

She gathered up a towel, dampened a washcloth and returned to Colin's side. "Lift your shirt."

"Now you're talking," he said, a weary smile curving his lips. He did as she asked and winced when she dabbed at the wound with the wet washcloth.

Once some of the blood was out of the way, Kaitlyn realized the bullet had taken out a chunk of flesh from Colin's side. Nothing more. The edges of the wound were black and it was still bleeding. Yet it really wasn't even that deep. She began to breathe easier.

"Doesn't look too bad," Burl said. "But you're still bleeding like a stuck pig."

"Thanks a lot." Colin peered down dubiously at the washcloth. "Take it easy, Kaitlyn. That hurts."

"Don't be a baby." Burl jostled his shoulder. "An ambulance is on its way."

"I don't need an ambulance. Call them back."

"It might be a good idea," Kaitlyn said with a frown. "You've lost a lot of blood."

"I'll be fine. If it's just a flesh wound, Burl can patch me up." He glanced up at his friend. "Can't you?"

"I suppose." Burl scowled. But he pulled out his phone and cancelled the ambulance.

Kaitlyn tugged Colin's shirt over his head. Without so much blood caking his side, he looked almost well.

"I need to get in the shower."

"Are you sure you're strong enough?"

"I don't think it's a good idea," Burl said. "You're still bleeding. Let me bandage the wound tonight, and you can shower tomorrow. Okay?"

"Colin?" Kaitlyn put her hand on his leg. The heat of his skin startled her. "You feel feverish."

"Another reason not to shower." Burl started around the bed. "I've got some first aid supplies in the van. I'll go get 'em."

"Thank you," Kaitlyn said.

"No problem," he said. He opened the door, and he was gone.

"Get up." Kaitlyn tugged on Colin's arm. "I need to pull back the covers so you can lie down."

Colin didn't want to move, but he knew Burl would need him to be prone when he patched up the hole in his side. Grimacing against the pain, he swung his legs off the bed. "Are you sure this is just a flesh wound?"

"Yes. It's deep, but the bullet went straight through."

"Guess I should be happy for small favors."

She slipped her hands beneath his arms. "Let me help you."

She smelled so good. He longed to drag her down onto his lap and kiss her, but he knew Burl might pop back in at any moment. He winced. Hell. He'd do it anyway if his side didn't hurt so damned much. He gingerly came to his feet and allowed Kaitlyn to brush against him as she leaned over the bed.

She yanked the covers out of the way and looked at him expectantly.

He cupped her elbow. "Kiss me."

Her eyes widened. "You've been shot."

"Yeah, thanks to you," He said softly. "Kiss me and make it feel better, witch."

Her eyes darkened and a pretty blush stole over her cheeks. "Only if you promise to get in bed before Burl gets back."

"You bet, although it'd be a lot more fun if you'd join me under the sheets." He bent his head and took her mouth. She tasted so sweet. Heat rose in his body despite his wound, and he found himself growing hard. With great reluctance, he pulled away. "Kaitlyn—I love you."

She swallowed. "Even after I shot you?"

"What do you think?"

Her blush deepened. "That you believe."

"Damned right I do." He remained very still, his gaze locked with hers. She seemed wary and more than a little antsy. That and her skittish body language told him his answer could mean the difference between his living like a monk the rest of his days or spending them sleeping every night with the woman he loved.

He feathered his fingers down her cheek. "Kaitlyn I—"

Burl burst back into the room with his med kit and slammed the door. He took one look at them and stopped short. "Oops. I'm interrupting."

Colin dropped his hand and sent Kaitlyn a rueful smile. "It's okay."

She bit her lip.

"Good." Burl strode over to the bed and knelt beside Colin. "You must be feeling better." Kaitlyn moved to the end of the mattress and folded her arms.

"Yeah, I'm okay." Colin shifted over on the bed.

Burl pulled out a bottle of antiseptic and a square of sterile gauze and began to clean Colin's wound. "I'm glad you're still kicking ass, because I need your help."

"With what? The case?" He cried out when Burl hit a tender spot. "Damn, watch out."

"Sorry." Burl furrowed his brow. "Guess you could say it has to do with the case. It happened during the autopsy."

"What did?" Kaitlyn asked, her face becoming animated as she looked at Burl.

Colin made a mental note to apologize to her as soon as the tech left. Then he refocused the case. "Was there something unusual about Fabron's body?"

"You could say that. For one thing, that big scar on his neck was fully healed—which was odd, considering the injury happened only two weeks ago."

"His body was possessed." Kaitlyn's steady gaze never wavered.

Burl turned to look at her. "Say what?"

Colin shook his head.

She wet her lips. "You heard me. What else did you find?"

"Um—uh—" The tech seemed confused. He tossed aside the used gauze and pulled out a pair of steri-strips. He used them to pull the wound together, and then put a clean square of gauze on top of it. "His heart beat on its own."

"Excuse me?" Colin lifted his eyebrows.

"You heard me right." Burl covered Colin's wound with clean gauze and began to tape it down. "I put that sucker in a basin for weighing, and the damned thing starting beating like it was still inside Fabron's chest. I almost peed my pants."

"Holy crap."

"What time was it?" Kaitlyn's eyes danced with curiosity.

"Huh?"

"When the heart started beating—I need to know what time it was."

Burl peered down at his watch. "Um—guess it was about an hour ago."

Kaitlyn looked at Colin. "That was about the time Lyle attacked."

Colin gave her a tiny nod. *Please don't say another word.* He gritted his teeth as Burl pressed a second piece of tape to the gauze over his wound.

Burl put the tape back in his bag. "Who's Lyle?"

"Nobody," Colin said. He met Kaitlyn's eyes and dared her to say anything else about the ghost.

She raised her eyebrows.

Burl put up the rest of his supplies and came to his feet. "Don't move around very much for a day or two. Eat right, and get some rest. You should be good as new."

"Thanks for your help, pal." Colin put out his hand.

Burl gave it a shake. "You're welcome. You know, if you don't want a scar, you might wanna contact a plastic surgeon. I didn't have what I need to sew you up properly."

"Okay."

"And about the heart—" Burl's cell phone shrilled. He muttered an expletive and yanked out the device. "Sorry."

"Johnson." He turned away. His face changed. "Hell. Are you sure?"

Colin looked at Kaitlyn.

"All right. Thanks, Kevin." Burl ended the call. "So much for that."

"The heart?" Kaitlyn sat down on the end of the bed.

He nodded. "It stopped beating exactly thirty minutes ago."

"That was the same time Lyle—" Kaitlyn halted mid-sentence. "Never mind."

"Who the heck is Lyle?" Burl eyed them both suspiciously. "You keep mentioning him."

"It's not important," Colin said. He was determined to change the subject. "Have you talked with anyone at Quantico?"

"As a matter of fact, I did. I said my questions were for research purposes, but they're sending a team."

"Good. You've saved me some time." Colin sat up gingerly. An arrow of pain shot through his side. He grimaced. "Ouch."

Kaitlyn was on her feet in a flash. "What are you doing?"

"Going to the bathroom. Do you have a problem with that?"

"Of course not." Her face reddened. She hurried around the bed. "Let me help you up."

"I can do it." He swung his legs over the edge and planted his feet on the floor. He tried to stand, but couldn't lever himself off the bed. Damn. He was much weaker than he thought.

Kaitlyn grabbed his arm and dragged him to his feet. "Don't be so obstinate."

"I could say the same thing to you."

Her eyes narrowed.

He turned to Burl. "Be right back."

"Take your time. I need to shove off. Kevin's alone at the morgue."

Colin frowned. "Where's the medical examiner?"

"At a conference in Baton Rouge."

"You'd better get back then," Colin said. "We don't need any more bodies going missing."

Kaitlyn watched both of them leave the room. She wanted to strangle Colin. How dare he deny his belief in the paranormal after all they'd just been through? He'd not only just refuted the fact that ghosts exist, but also he'd rejected their relationship.

She straightened the covers on the bed with a jerk and marched over to where the book of spells lay face down on the floor. Her heart fluttered as she picked it up. The ancient book had saved her life—and Colin's—thanks to the brilliant spells printed on its faded pages.

Her gaze fell on the pool of blood near the window. She had nearly killed Colin because of Lyle Forrester and his unbelievable greed. If she hadn't been able to banish him—

The bathroom door opened and Colin met her eyes.

"I'm sorry," he said. "I know you wanted me to tell Burl everything that happened, but I'm glad you didn't say anything else. He likes to talk."

"And you don't want anything about ghosts getting out."

"Exactly."

She closed the *grimoire*.

"You've gotta know that all this scares the hell out of me." He halted in front of her and peered down at the book in her arms. "It's hard enough for me to grasp the fact that Lyle Forrester hung around Scarlet Oak for over a hundred years because he wanted that damned sapphire. Add witchcraft and Voodoo to the mix and my head wants to explode."

"Vodun."

"What?" He creased his brow.

"You keep saying Voodoo for *Vodun*."

"Whatever." His frown deepened. "Do you have the Midnight Star?"

She patted her pockets. *Empty.* Startled, she jerked her gaze to his. "No. It's gone."

He stepped away from her and studied the area around the bed. Kaitlyn put the book on the table, dropped to her knees and lifted the bed skirt. Nothing.

"I don't see it under here." She dropped the piece of fabric and came to her feet. The air in the room grew icy. The curtains fluttered. And all at once, she *knew*. Her heart thudded. She took a deep breath and faced Colin. "Lyle must have taken it."

"No way."

"He did."

"How could that have happened? You had it."

"I put it in my pocket so I could hold the pistol."

"Maybe it fell out." Colin walked over to her and felt her pockets. "We have to keep looking."

"It won't do any good." She eyed the floor. "He carried it over to the other side."

"How is that possible?"

"I don't know." A chill slid over her. She crossed her arms. "I'm not sure I want to find out."

"Me, either. But still—"

"What about your case? Is it solved?"

"In a manner of speaking." He winced and put a hand to his side. "I need to sit down."

"Oh, I'm sorry." Regret sliced through her. She took his arm and helped him over to the bed.

His sigh was audible. "Thanks."

"I forgot you were shot." She perched next to him on the mattress. "Even though I'm responsible."

"It's all right. I told you that." He took her hand. "My question is how to write up the paperwork on this mind-boggling case."

She bit her lip. "You could lie."

"I don't want to do that. I never have before, and I don't believe in being untruthful. But no one will believe a ghost is responsible for murdering those girls, or that Fabron was a Zombie. I could lose my job."

"I'll help you think of something."

"Maybe you can wiggle your nose and put words to paper." He laughed and squeezed her hand. "Either that, or make my boss believe whatever I write."

"Maybe so." Kaitlyn smiled, and her whole face lit up.

Colin swallowed. "You're absolutely beautiful."

"Flattery will get you anywhere—as long as you accept me as I am. Spells and all."

"I do. You know that."

"That makes me happy."

"I believe, but you have to remember that I work in a concrete world," Colin said, hoping she would understand. He didn't want to lose her before he got the chance to show her just how much he loved her. And yet, he couldn't compromise his principles. Not even for love. He scowled. "The FBI deals in hard facts. Forensics, witness testimony, pictures—anything to prove a particular crime took place. The supernatural blows all that out of the water."

"I've heard of psychics being used to help solve cases."

"In some instances. Still, they're met with plenty of derision. Not many people believe."

"You could be the first."

"And be the laughing stock of the Bureau?" He shook his head. "No, thanks."

"I can't love someone who won't accept me without any caveats."

"Can't we compromise?" Anxiety prickled Colin's skin. He tightened his hold on her fingers. "When we're alone, I'll acknowledge all your powers — once you teach me what they are. But when we're with my friends and coworkers—"

"We keep the witchcraft under wraps."

"That's right." Worry burrowed under his skin. He swirled his thumb over the back of her hand, hoping that would in some way mark her as his. "Can you live with that?"

"Do I have a choice?"

"You can stop loving me." The words caught in his throat as he met her startled gaze. With that one look, he tried to telegraph just how much that would hurt.

She lifted her hand to his cheek. Her fingers were cool against his fevered flesh. "That's not going to happen. I don't know how you did it, but you've bewitched me."

He crooked his mouth. "Talk about irony."

"I've never met a man like you before." She bit her lip. He was so sexy, and yet so good.

His eyes locked with hers, he leaned into her warm fingers. "You mean a guy so unwilling to change?"

"No." She dropped her hand and jostled him with her shoulder. "I mean a man who swept me off my feet. A good, strong man. With integrity."

"You don't act like I'm so special."

"I've tried to." She sent him a sideways glance. "But maybe I'm scared."

"You? Scared?" He laughed sharply. "I didn't think you were scared of anything."

"I am of one thing." Her face turned pink. "I'm afraid of having a real relationship. I've never had one really work before. Not for the long term."

"I see. Well. I think we can do it. Don't you?"

"I hope so." She moved her thigh so that it touched his. "We both have free will, you know."

"Yeah. We do." Heat pooled low in his belly and he shifted to accommodate the sudden tumescence behind his fly. "Of course, that means I'll be having a relationship with a witch."

"Yes, you will." Her jade eyes searched his face. "The witch and the FBI's Assistant Deputy Director of Criminal Investigations. Long odds, don't you think?"

"I've seen worse." His body hummed with need. He grinned. "Enough talk. I'm gonna kiss you — unless you turn me into a frog first."

She giggled, and he caught her laughter with his lips. His heart swelled with love. Witch or not, he couldn't let her go. He wrapped his arms around her and pulled her against him. Her sweet herbal scent enveloped him. *Heaven.*

"Colin—" Her warm breath washed over his ear. "I love you."

He moaned and kissed her again, this time sliding his tongue deep into her mouth. She cupped his hard flesh. Unable to stop himself, he moved against her hand.

Her breathing quickened. She pulled back. "Should you be doing this after you've been shot?"

"I don't know." He grinned. "But it'll hurt a helluva lot worse if I don't."

Kaitlyn found herself melting. Her body ached for his touch. She rose up on her tiptoes and deepened the kiss. Colin moaned into her mouth.

Her pulse raced as he backed her toward the bed. She smiled and looped her arms around his neck. "Guess we should make love."

"Damned right. I'd say that's the best medicine I could have right now." He released her long enough to move her bag and the book of spells out of the way. Then he was kissing her again.

His lips tasted like cool rain and sexy man. She shuddered as his hands stroked up her back and over her shoulders. Then they slid lower, and he gripped her buttocks. Her whole body quivered with need as he pressed himself against her.

She reached for the hem of his shirt and seconds later, they were both naked. Colin drew back the covers and tumbled her down on the crisp white sheets. She reveled in the mouth -watering contrast between their cool softness and the fiery hardness of Colin's strapping body. His chest hair abraded her sensitive nipples, sending her hormones into overdrive.

"Love me," she whispered, clutching at his broad shoulders. "Just don't hurt your wound."

"Like this, witch?" He pressed his throbbing erection to the juncture of her thighs.

"Oh, yes!" She smiled and squirmed against him.

Colin lifted himself on his elbows and with one powerful thrust, joined their heated bodies. Kaitlyn gasped at the sudden intrusion. He caught her startled breath in his mouth and matched the slick movement of his tongue with his body's quickening rhythm. He wanted to take his time with her. This was the beginning of the rest of their lives together.

With a low moan, he rubbed himself against her from shoulders to toes. His skin tingled like he'd been hit with a taser. "Kaitlyn," he murmured, unable to control the emotion welling up inside him. "I love you so damned much."

"Oh, Colin, I love you, too." Hot tears of joy rolled down her cheeks. Cherishing the feel of him inside her, she arched her hips to meet his strong thrusts. She committed them to memory, along with his unique scent and the dark longing swimming in his warm mocha eyes.

She never wanted to let him go.

She continued to feed her hope for the future as they rocked together, locked in their own private world free of ghosts and evil, darkness and pain. Until the sky crashed around her in a brilliant flash of light and together they tumbled head over heels into wild oblivion.

His chest still heaving from his magnificent release, Colin pulled her against his quivering body and buried his nose in her hair. She was so sweet, so beautiful. And she was all his.

A full-fledged witch.

He had marked her with his passion. He closed his eyes and let himself drift.

Kaitlyn's body purred with contentment as she burrowed against Colin's heated skin. His strong heartbeat throbbed beneath her ear. She raised her head and kissed him.

He was fast asleep.

"Rest well, my love," she murmured, pressing a soft kiss to his cheek. Her heart swelled as she draped her arm protectively across his chest. They were together now, and she never intended to let him go. "We're going to have a good life."

Still, although she tried hard, she couldn't go to sleep. Her mind whirred with plans for their life after Scarlet Oak. She bit her lip and thought about what would happen when they left this place.

She snuggled closer to him. A witch and an FBI agent. She smiled. It could work.